Doublecrossed

Other Books by Laury A. Egan

FICTION

Jenny Kidd

Fog and Other Stories

The Outcast Oracle

Fabulous! An Opera Buffa

A Bittersweet Tale

The Ungodly Hour

The Swimmer

Turnabout

Wave in D Minor

POETRY

Snow, Shadows, a Stranger

Beneath the Lion's Paw

The Sea & Beyond

Presence & Absence

Doublecrossed

Laury A. Egan

Doublecrossed

By Laury A. Egan

ISBN (book) 9781954213227
ISBN (epub) 9781954213234

Desert Palm Press
1961 Main Street, Suite 220
Watsonville, California 95076
www.desertpalmpress.com

Editor: Kaycee Hawn
Cover photograph: Angela Previte
Cover design (ebook): Laury A. Egan
PhotoShop assistance by Vicki DeVico
Cover design (paperback) Laury A. Egan and Michelle Brodeur

Printed in the United States of America
First Edition April 2022

Chapter One

MARNIE HARDWICK and I met in the dark heart of February. Despite my emotional reticence, I was instantly bewitched by this sexy, funny, bright woman with fiery red hair and flashing green eyes. I believed luck had finally kissed me on the forehead. Everything about us seemed fated, as if we were floating down a river to happiness.

Our first date was hot, so passionate that the night migrated into a weekend. And we talked—really talked—about our careers, our many shared interests, and the years spent alone, searching for the perfect woman. I tried to keep my balance, to be logical, careful, and prudent, but I was smitten, besotted, infatuated, and hopelessly in love. Before I knew it, Marnie was spending more time at my tiny apartment than hers, neither of which was sufficiently large for two people. Then she began joking about buying a house. Today—a sunny Saturday in April—Marnie poured coffee into two travel mugs and suggested we go for a drive in her convertible with the top down, though the air was still cool.

"That's what the coffee is for, dear," she told me. "To keep us warm." She accompanied this comment with a sultry glance that implied she would do this better than the coffee.

We wandered south through curving country roads that were strangers to the orderly concept of north, south, east, west. A route marked north went east, for example, and another sign that said east actually pointed west. I decided its byways had been charted long ago by a man who had ventured out on his task fortified with whiskey and a perverse desire to mislead the public. Within no time at all, I was lost, but Marnie was at the wheel and seemed to know this area of New Jersey, an area I regarded as a backwater populated by horses and farms and deficient in theaters, bookstores, galleries, and concert halls—in other words, the necessities. After an hour of meandering and laughing at my directional confusion, we rounded a bend in the road and saw a "For Sale" sign in front of a house encircled by acres of dense pines, with a sprinkling of oaks, maples, chestnuts, and hickories. Marnie slowed the car and turned into the long driveway.

"Oh, Alexandra!" she cried. "Look at this place."

The two-story house was a hodge-podge, predominantly Tudor in style with a stout turret at left, its conical roof rising above the main building, and a few modern touches.

"It's unusual," I replied, examining the gray and brown stone façade frizzed with ivy.

"Unusual? It's wonderful!" Marnie switched off the ignition, rushed from the car, and walked toward the house as if she were already its proprietor.

Although I was worried about trespassing, I followed her down a path and around the back, where we discovered an expansive deck hemmed in by the thick forest.

Marnie turned to me, her green eyes bright with excitement. "Oh, isn't this romantic! Let's call the realtor."

"What?" I shook my head. "I don't know…"

She grabbed my arm and tugged like a small child. "Oh, come on! It won't hurt to see the house." She gave me the sweetest smile, an irresistible confection. "We've been talking about living together."

My reservations were my usual ones, sandblasted by a life of solitude and years of listening to my mother pontificate on the merits of financial separation and privacy. And there was the worrisome fact that Marnie and I had known each other only nine weeks, although the time together had been absolute bliss, without one cross word spoken. In all my thirty-three years, I'd never felt this way about a woman before, though I'd had several intense affairs. I asked myself what was the worst thing that could happen if Marnie and I bought a house and our relationship failed? With a legal agreement to protect our separate investments, the most I could lose was a few thousand dollars, which I could afford. At least I would have attempted commitment, something I'd never had the courage to do.

"Are you sure? It isn't too far from your work?"

"Just a different direction." Marnie grinned at me and removed her cell phone to call the realtor. Fifteen minutes later, the woman arrived—Sarah Carston-Smith—and greeted us in the driveway. She carried listing sheets and a survey.

"Hi. I'm Alex Wyatt." I shook the agent's hand. "And this is Marnie Hardwick."

"Nice to meet you both," she said as she unlocked the front door. "This is a very good buy. The house was renovated by a builder who died six months ago. His nephew is eager to sell. And I'm sure you know this is an up-and-coming area. Prices will skyrocket over the next few years. Taxes are modest. In short, the place is a shrewd investment." Sarah looked at me and then at Marnie, as if trying to ascertain who was the potential buyer or whether we were a couple.

Marnie raised her eyebrow, indicating that I should attend to these financial considerations. I listened politely as the realtor enthused, but a second tape was scrolling in my head, warning me to be sensible. As we stepped inside the house, I was determined to find fault, but the living room was stunning, with its high-beamed ceiling and skylights, a stone fireplace browed by an oak slab, and four tall windows framing views of the green woods. The quality throughout was first rate, down to the plush beige carpet. I liked the open floor plan too. The dining room flowed from the living room, both connecting to the large kitchen through an open pocket door. Although the kitchen needed new paint, its saving grace was an attractive dining nook that faced the deck, which was accessible through a sliding glass door.

Marnie walked from room to room, her mouth agape. She was falling in love with the place with the same speed she had fallen in love with me.

"If you two would like to venture upstairs, I'll wait in the kitchen," the realtor suggested.

We thanked her and proceeded to the second floor. It consisted of a bath and two average bedrooms—rooms for guests. Because we were on our own recognizance, Marnie and I then descended into the basement, which was a little damp but salvageable if we installed a dehumidifier. After returning to the foyer, we entered a short hall, walked past a bathroom and into the master bedroom, a large and airy room featuring an enormous walk-in closet that excited Marnie. Unlike me, who tended toward a modest wardrobe, Marnie was a clothes freak, especially about shoes. Her footwear collection would fill the floor on her side and mine in double-tiered racks, though since we wore the same size, I often teased I could wear her castoffs for the rest of my life and never buy another pair of shoes.

"I think this will *just* do," she remarked, tapping a finger against her chin and staring into the closet. "If you're willing to share the space a little." Her voice was changeable, sometimes strongly reflecting her Virginia upbringing, sometimes only faintly so. Husky, too, with a catch from years of smoking, a habit she had recently kicked.

I didn't know how she could make a discussion about a closet so provocative. I shook my head and steered her into the kitchen, nodded to the agent, and continued through to a study, then the laundry room to a circular staircase in the turret. After climbing to the top, I gazed from the peaked ceiling to the windows on two-thirds of its girth, including one facing north, the perfect angle of light for artists. The room was small but exactly right for a studio. Looking out, I had the sensation of standing in a lighthouse over a dark green sea of pines.

Marnie, sensing my enthusiasm, took my hand. "Isn't this fantastic, honey?"

"It is," I agreed, returning her hug and feeling her full breasts against me. Although I usually preferred slimmer, more athletic physiques like my own, I was helpless to resist Marnie's rounded full hips and encompassing softness.

"Now, now," she chided, her eyes merry with flirtation. "That's for later!" But her hand strayed lower on my back, pressing me forward as a tease.

Feeling the heat rise between us, I stepped away. "Marnie,

behave yourself!" I tempered this comment with a smile. "Yes…later."

Marnie tossed her sleek red hair, and her lips formed into a pout. "I will definitely, definitely hold you to that promise, Alex." She trailed her well-manicured, crimson fingernails down my neck, enjoying my reaction and then, with a hint of reluctance, turned toward the stairs. After a last glance at the enchanting room, I followed.

We asked Sarah if we could walk the property. She provided us with a site map that showed the location of the house on its three acres. Hand in hand, Marnie and I entered the forest, astonished at the mass of trees and vegetation. As we were threading through a nearly impenetrable thicket, Marnie tripped, catching herself on my arm.

"Oh, Alex, I am ever so clumsy! Dear me, all these branches and roots and things," she said. "I'm just not used to them. Not like you. You're a regular Davy Crockett. Oh, but I bet he didn't have your dazzling blue eyes, darling."

Marnie's outrageous flattery brought color to my face, an effect she loved to create.

"Now, let's find the end of this property." She grinned at me. "I swear, it does go on and on forever!"

With some difficulty, we located one of the pink ribbons marking the rear boundary. Marnie was impressed with the seclusion, made more so because the neighboring houses seemed to be set several acres past the border, creating an additional band of forest between. We followed the property line around to the road and sat on the split-rail fence by the mailbox, surveying the house, reading the listing sheet, and debating the house's pros and cons.

Marnie chewed her lip. "The price is a trifle steep. Not unreasonable, but I don't have much saved and couldn't put as much down as I'd like. Of course, I'm expecting some large commissions in July. It's a pity I don't have them yet. We could buy the place in a snap." She pondered this for a moment. "I'm sure the monthly mortgage would be no problem, however."

I hesitated, hearing my mother in that part of my head reserved for admonitions. "Maybe we should go home and talk about this—"

Marnie's eyes widened. "Oh, Alexandra! No! We absolutely must have this house. It is just right for us. I can see you sitting at your drawing table, working in your studio. Oh, how grand that would be! Just think, all this quiet."

I *was* captivated by the turret. Marnie saw this and gave me a deep kiss that made me dizzy. Next thing I knew, I was saying, "Don't worry about the down payment. I'll take care of most of it. We can work out the details." Stunned by my own capitulation, I had two seconds to be amazed before Marnie grabbed my hand and pulled me off the fence.

"Let's go find the realtor!" she cried.

We made an offer substantially less than the asking price, pointing out various problems. Sarah was pleased, accepted my one-percent check, and immediately called the nephew who had inherited the property. After three days of dithering, he agreed to our price. Closing was set for the last week in June.

*

Before we moved in, Marnie and I spent every possible minute together. Although I'd been with other women, I'd never encountered such a smooth and effortless fit. Our tastes were even similar when we shopped for our new home. Most of what we bought were accessories because the furniture I'd inherited from my mother—a jumble of styles and periods—seemed to suit the odd house. Marnie also provided beds, dressers, chairs, and tables.

After the mortgage was approved, I treated Marnie to dinner at our favorite restaurant. The party continued on the deck behind our future residence. It was a chilly night, but armed with two stadium blankets and stoked by a flask of Jack Daniel's Marnie provided, we snuggled in the corner, talking.

"I hope it's okay about the $5,000 I've contributed toward the ten-percent deposit," she said, her reddish eyebrows knitted together. "Our partnership should be equal, and yet you've paid $25,000 already and plan to spend more at closing. Truly, it's not what I want."

I pulled her close and smelled the Opium perfume she wore behind her ear, down her neck, and along the plunge of her breasts, a route I frequently took as I did now.

"I've always heard houses are good investments, so I'm sure my savings are safe. As we discussed, at closing we'll record what we each paid. When you're able, you can make up the difference." I was hardly paying attention to the conversation, intent as I was on unbuttoning her low-cut blouse.

Marnie shivered. "You are such a devil, Alex! And here we were talking business and all." She squirmed in my arms but raised her lips to mine.

Chapter Two

A HAPPY DATE, one I will remember forever: June 28, 1999. We were moving! As all such transformative days are, it was chaotic. My movers balked at the size of my library, particularly when they learned that most of the boxes had to be carried up the turret stairs. An extra fifty dollars sorted the matter, and finally all my things were in the correct rooms.

Marnie arrived with a rented truck and two men who gave the impression of being more inclined to steal her possessions than deliver them. In quick order, however, she managed to stuff clothes in all the closets and install a dining table set, an ugly, green-plaid, wing-back armchair, brass lamp, and end table in the living room, and twin beds in one of the guest rooms upstairs. After we were alone, Marnie surprised me with an array of aged cheeses, some pâté, grapes, and two bottles of pinot noir. She lit a candle on the kitchen table by the open slider, and we sat enjoying the breeze that carried the intoxicating smell of pine and sweet, summer night dampness.

During the next ten days, which we both took off, Marnie and I tackled the overgrown mess in the yard, piling debris on the roadside for pick-up and attending to a prodigious display of welts and scrapes from scrub trees and pricker bushes and—in Marnie's case—dealing with the miseries of poison ivy. We bought azaleas and rhododendrons and dug holes for them along the drive and planted impatiens, geraniums, and roses in the front yard, as well as rosemary, basil, and oregano in wooden flower boxes on the deck. Then we repainted the kitchen, stripped and re-applied new wallpaper in the bathroom, and I designed our walk-in closet to accommodate Marnie's enormous wardrobe, adding shelves, shoe racks, and hooks. Even after Marnie returned to work at NJ/Med-Tech Design, we made improvements as if each contributed to the solidarity of our bond. Afterward, we'd sit outside and watch the deer filter through the trees, and a large population of birds attack the feeders I'd hung near the kitchen and the living room windows.

I worked at home, appreciating my quiet studio. My primary job was creating intricate patterns for wallpaper and fabric designs, using natural subjects such as birds, flowers, vines, and leaves entwined, and employing grayed-down tonalities. Though others might think the work was tedious, I loved selecting combinations of colors for each pattern and engineering the various elements into a unit that repeated. The freelance business didn't require much interaction with the decorating firm run by Gregory Reynolds, my main client, and left time for my private projects, such as drawing a series of fantastical illustrations for my college friend, Copelia Bye, a well-known folk singer. She had selected my images for several CD covers, as backdrops for concert sets, and for general promotion—all credited to a pseudonym because I wanted to separate my whimsical and imaginative artwork from my commercial enterprises.

Much to my amazement, this sideline became very lucrative as other musicians requested my services. Since I deemed this to be extra money, it was saved in the special bank account opened with the inheritance from my father, an account that was growing substantially. Although I trusted Marnie, I had never revealed this inheritance, my ownership of his ocean-view property, or the secondary business with Cope because of a promise I'd made to my mother on my sixteenth birthday, a promise to keep my finances separate until a relationship had successfully survived several years. Now, I felt guilty about these deceptions and was tempted to confide in Marnie but decided to honor my mother's cautious approach—at least for a short while—even if I'd already veered from the promise by buying the house. I had also downplayed the inheritance received from my mother, implying my contribution to the house and the purchase of a new Jeep had nearly erased my savings. When an opportunity arose, I would confess the true state of my wealth.

Despite my financial dishonesty, which troubled me whenever

money concerns arose, I was thrilled with Marnie, the serene beauty of our house, and a new pattern I was creating, incorporating chrysanthemums, goldfinches, and asters. Everything was fine until this evening when Marnie and I were eating dinner and drinking wine. Suddenly, she set down her glass and blinked oddly.

"What's the matter?" I asked.

"Oh, dear," she sighed, "I hate to tell you, but I have a conference in Baltimore next Thursday."

This announcement wasn't surprising because Marnie was a sales rep and traveling was part of her job.

"Oh, really? Are you presenting a new product?"

Marnie blinked again behind her tortoiseshell glasses, which she sometimes wore instead of contact lenses. The candlelight refracted on them so I couldn't see her eyes clearly. "No, I'm not, nor am I a speaker," she replied. "It's just a conference."

"What's the subject?"

She sipped some wine. "Plastics and things like that."

Marnie was usually specific about her work, often providing scientific detail about advances in the manufacturing and design of medical equipment, so her vagueness was out of character. I ate some chicken, feeling disquieted.

"Is someone else going from your company?"

"No, just me." She concentrated on the food in front of her.

We were silent for a few minutes.

"I'd be happy to take you to the airport or the train station."

"No, thanks, Alex." Marnie brushed back a lock of red hair. "I've made other plans already."

She didn't say what they were. If I persisted with my questions, I'd sound like the Grand Inquisitor grilling a suspect. Yet, despite how straightforward her words sounded, her demeanor had altered perceptibly.

"Maybe I could take a few days off and join you?"

Marnie shook her head. "No, I don't think you should come. I don't want anyone to know about us."

She had been very tense about our lesbian relationship,

insisting that calls to work and attendance at corporate social events were not acceptable because her two bosses were both hyper-conservative Christians. In the flush of love, these restrictions seemed unimportant; at the moment, I wasn't happy about the enforced secrecy. After all, we were a committed couple and were living together.

"When will you be home?" I asked.

"I'll be back Sunday night, probably."

The "probably" rang another warning. Marnie had always been precise with dates and schedules. "Okay. I'll find something to do to stay out of trouble."

Marnie shot me a sharp glance. "Look, Alex, you know I have to travel. I'm in sales." Her voice, which was usually soft and southern, had developed an edge, a tone I'd never heard her use, perhaps because she had never been annoyed with me before.

"I know, I know. I guess I've become so used to having you around all the time. Kind of nice." I felt as if I were trying to appease her, though I had no idea why. It was a bit like talking to a stranger, someone I'd just met. Even though we were sitting in candlelight, the white china gleaming, the romantic mood had vanished. Marnie didn't seem to notice, but she didn't talk more about the conference and changed the subject to a renovation we were considering. Although her enthusiasm sounded forced, we slowly rekindled our romantic spirit.

*

The next day was Friday. After Marnie left for work, I went upstairs and tried to write invoices, but my thoughts kept drifting to her behavior. It was as if she had turned off her warm feelings and then mechanically switched them on again. I eventually convinced myself I was being too sensitive.

When I entered the kitchen to prepare my lunch, I noticed Marnie's calendar on the counter. I touched the red leather cover and removed my hand. Snooping was not called for. I made a tuna fish sandwich and immersed myself in an issue of *The New Yorker*. A few minutes later, the phone rang. I was tempted to let the machine take it, but then I decided to answer.

Marnie's voice came on amid static. "I'll be home late. Will you be okay eating alone?"

"I don't mind. I'll heat up some leftovers."

"Thanks…got to run." And with that, she was gone. No "I love you" or "see you later." The foreboding returned.

Shortly before midnight, as I was reading in bed, Marnie arrived wearing fresh lipstick, which seemed strange considering the hour. I kissed her hello and smelled wine on her breath, though she had attempted to disguise it with breath mints. I wanted to ask what project she had been working on—if she had been at work—and why she'd been drinking, but I assumed she would volunteer information. Marnie said nothing, walked into the bathroom fully clothed, and began to run the shower. Since she rarely took showers at night, this added to the sensation that something was amiss. Undressing in the bathroom was not usual, either. When Marnie emerged in a diaphanous, pale green nightgown, she jumped on the bed and burrowed in next to me as if nothing were wrong.

In the morning, we did some measuring for the living room extension to the deck. On Sunday, we painted two closets, and then Marnie studied me carefully.

"You're looking a wee bit shaggy, Alex. How about I trim your hair?"

My salon was closed for a two-week vacation, so I agreed, though with some hesitation. Marnie sat me on a stool in the bathroom, covered my shoulders with a towel, and snipped away, a little more exuberantly than I would have preferred, shortening the length over an inch so my hair now fell well above my collar.

I rose to study her handiwork in the mirror. "Looks nice, thanks. And you saved me sixty bucks," I said, smiling. "Another one of your hidden talents."

Marnie bowed and kissed my cheek. "My pleasure."

*

After Marnie returned to work on Monday, I went upstairs and completed a new wallpaper square and began selecting different palettes in which it could be printed.

It was 11:15 when I finished, so I decided to play hooky and go for a drive to my father's house by the sea. When he had died fourteen years ago, I was nineteen and had inherited the place. My mother had died after my graduation from Bard College, and I stayed at the house until I rented an apartment more convenient to Gregory Reynold's showroom. My plan had been to make a permanent move to my father's place in the spring, but when I met Marnie, her job was too far away, or perhaps this was the excuse I gave myself to avoid revealing the property and my additional assets. Luckily, the grounds were easy to maintain: no grass to cut, only a little weeding to do around the bushes, and leaf removal in the fall. Now that Marnie and I had our own home, it would be intelligent to sell the house, but I couldn't bear the thought of a stranger living there, even though it would have fetched a nice amount with its magnificent water view, big fireplace, and contemporary architecture. Maybe someday Marnie and I could use it as a second residence; someday when my promise to my mother could be broken.

*

It was five-thirty when I arrived at our house, fifteen minutes before Marnie usually came home, so seeing her red Toyota Solara in the garage was unexpected. She came out to greet me, waving from the side of the house, paintbrush in hand. Her denim shorts were rolled high on her thighs, and the tails of her yellow sleeveless blouse were tied around her midriff.

"Hi, Alex! I bought some paint to do some touch-ups."

She disappeared around the house where I found her a minute later, leaning over the deck stairs. She had hitched her blouse higher to reveal an expanse of creamy skin between shirt and shorts. The invitation clear, I obliged by pulling her against me.

Marnie giggled and turned around. "Now, where have you been, sugar? I got back hours ago. I took the afternoon off specially to surprise you."

"I had some errands to do." I felt annoyed with myself for being evasive, even more for missing time with her, though of course I hadn't known of her plans. "Let me run inside and change. Do you want some iced tea?"

"It's darned hot out here!" she said. "Make it a beer and we're in business!" Her face broke into a broad smile that crinkled the light dusting of pale freckles across her cheeks.

When I returned in cutoff shorts and a T-shirt and set my glass of iced tea and her bottle of beer on a low table, she laid her paintbrush across the top of the paint can and kissed me. As she did so, I noticed alcohol on her breath that wasn't from the beer. Since I had never known her to drink during the day, except for Sunday brunches, this was atypical behavior. I quickly forgot about it, however, as her kisses became more persuasive and urgent.

"Come on, Alex, help me," she teased in a voice reminiscent of good, rich earth.

There was no doubt my assistance was required but not for painting. She reached under my shirt and unhooked my bra.

"Well, I suppose you're no longer interested in working," I said.

Marnie nipped my ear, grabbed my hand, and began to strip off my clothes as we hurried into the bedroom. There, we stood naked in front of the big windows, secure in the knowledge that no one could see us.

"I want you," she crooned, running her tongue below my ear.

The hot room only made us hotter. Soon, perspiration streamed down our bodies, dampening the sheets and lubricating our skin so that we slid over each other, grasping at breasts and hips and legs until we were in a frenzy of excitement.

"Oh, yes!" Marnie moaned, as I righted myself above her. "You're so good, Alex. So tall and firm and strong and ever so slender." She ran her hands up my arms, along my shoulders, down the length of my back, kneading the muscles to emphasize each sinew.

I felt powerful and dominant, the role Marnie had encouraged at the start of our lovemaking. I leaned over to kiss her and she wriggled away, evading my lips and provoking me with her elusive behavior. I tried again, feeling her body undulate beneath mine, but she laughed flirtatiously. Placing my hands on either side of her head, I forced her to be still, then kissed her hard. She locked her arms around my neck as her submissive persona switched.

"So, you want me?" she demanded.

"Yes, I want you."

She shifted to the side and toppled me, mounting my body and pinning my wrists against the bed. "You like this, don't you?" she whispered in her husky voice.

And though I didn't understand why, something deep inside of me responded to the loss of control, to the vague fear glinting just beyond my conscious awareness. Only knowing I could reverse this role because I was physically stronger allowed me to be acquiescent.

"Yes," I replied.

Marnie thrust against my hips. "Give up, Alexandra," she murmured, her nails digging into my skin as her grasp tightened.

I struggled slightly. She gave me a triumphant smile and began her final seduction.

Chapter Three

ON THE WEDNESDAY NIGHT before she left for Baltimore, Marnie returned from work early. Since I was sketching ideas for a new illustration, I didn't venture downstairs until a short while later, at which point I made martinis, poured them into hand-painted floral glasses, and carried them into the bedroom, where Marnie was packing.

Seeing me, she flipped the suitcase closed. "Oh, you startled me!" Then she planted a quick kiss on my cheek and accepted the drink. "How lovely. You make the best martinis."

I agreed with her. Though dry martinis were fashionable, I mixed mine with more Vermouth, which we both preferred. I placed my glass on the side table and stretched out on the bed. "Will you be taking any harbor cruises?"

"Huh? Oh, no, I don't think so. It's a small conference. They're not going to offer much in the way of frills."

"Bet I can guess what you'll have for dinner. Let's see. Stuffed flounder or Chicken Kiev. Salad with iceberg lettuce, green beans almondine, cheap American wine."

Marnie laughed. "Maybe I'll go somewhere and buy some steamed crabs."

"Good idea," I said, sipping my martini. "In fact, we should go crabbing sometime."

"Yeah, that'd be fun." She smiled at me and walked into the bathroom for her hair dryer. "I may not need this, but sometimes hotels are not so well-stocked." Marnie was very particular about her hair, wearing it shoulder-length, with a spray of short bangs angled to the left.

I played with the olives at the bottom of my glass. "Where're you staying?"

"I'll write it down for you in a little while." She turned the suitcase around and opened it. After placing the hair dryer's nozzle inside a bedroom slipper, she clicked the suitcase shut. "Let's go and listen to some music, okay? I'm finished packing."

I agreed, went into the living room, and selected a CD featuring Mildred Bailey, an American jazz singer who became popular in the late twenties. Marnie joined me, and we kicked off our shoes and sat entwined on the sofa, looking at the forest through the large windows. A pair of cardinals were swinging on the birdfeeder—two frequent customers.

"This is a great house, Alex. We really made a good choice."

I was still new enough to the relationship to like the sound of "we." It made me feel warm inside. Together, we observed the sun wreathing the sky in orange and pink until the trees hid the final sunset from view. I made another round of drinks while Marnie slipped a pork loin in the oven. Mildred Bailey sang "Rockin' Chair," and everything was wonderful until I reminded Marnie about giving me the phone number and address of her hotel.

"I'll do it later," she replied, sounding impatient. "The information is in the car…in my briefcase."

"Okay, that's fine." It seemed wise to change the subject, though I had no idea why the topic was an issue. As I glanced at her, Marnie turned away and left to set the table.

*

In the morning, Marnie arose early, dressing before I was fully awake. She headed for the kitchen with her suitcase and seemed in such a rush that I quickly reached for my bathrobe and followed her. As I walked into the dining room, she emerged from her study with her briefcase. The next thing I knew, she kissed me goodbye and headed into the garage. I walked to the door and waved, but Marnie was already in the Solara.

I poured coffee, perplexed about her fast exit and the fact that she'd skipped breakfast. Replaying her behavior, I also realized her briefcase had been in the study, not in her car as she had told me. Then I remembered the hotel information and searched beside the phone, on top of her desk, and on the bulletin board by the refrigerator. Nothing. My rational side insisted I was being silly, that Marnie would telephone later after realizing her oversight. The other side made bets she wouldn't. I compromised by telling myself I would call her this evening.

I passed the day doing paperwork, answering e-mails, and wandering around the house like a lost dog. Though it was a relief to attend to some small procrastinations, I couldn't shake a loss of equilibrium. When Marnie didn't telephone, this feeling increased. At 10:20 p.m., I called her cell phone from our landline. She didn't answer. I left a message and tried twice more unsuccessfully. I considered researching hotels in Baltimore and phoning some by the harbor, but I decided that was ridiculous.

I went to bed unsettled. In the middle of the night, I awoke from a horrible, hazy dream, one I'd had before. It was set in an extremely hot, steamy grassland with an unspecified danger all around me. I wiped the sweat from my forehead and walked into the kitchen for a glass of milk, hoping it would restore my shaken nerves. Afterward, I wandered into Marnie's study. Except for a blue blotter, a container of pens and pencils, and a notepad, her desk was bare—not unusual since Marnie was meticulous about neatness. When I tried to pull out the first drawer, however, it was locked, as were the others. I couldn't think of any reason for this sudden security-consciousness. I often borrowed stamps and envelopes from her desk, and she had never minded as long as the stamps were replaced.

I picked up the phone in the kitchen and replaced the receiver. It was too late. I'd call in the morning, but sleep wouldn't come easily.

*

At nine the next day, after no luck contacting her, I tried Marnie's office—something I never did because she had asked me not to, explaining that she shared a cubicle with a nosy colleague who might discover she was gay. Up to now, I had never deviated from Marnie's wishes, even if her explanations seemed overwrought. When there was no answer, I telephoned the company's main line. The receptionist came on, and I asked for Marnie's hotel and its number. The woman placed me on hold for a few minutes and returned.

"Ms. Hardwick isn't in the office, but I don't have a number where you can reach her. And you are...?"

"I'm a friend of hers. She's at a conference in Baltimore."

"I'm sorry I can't be more helpful," the woman replied without much interest. "Perhaps she made arrangements through the company's agent. Would you like to speak to him?"

I told her I would.

After consulting a list, she gave me his extension. "Do you want to leave a message?"

I felt silly asking for Marnie to call me, so I said no. I checked with the agent but hit another dead end. He had made no reservations for a hotel, train, car, or anything else. I sat down to a cup of cold coffee and a whirl of thoughts. After finishing my cereal, I phoned Marnie again, but she still didn't answer. Puzzled, I meandered into our bedroom, soon finding myself in the closet, investigating what clothes Marnie might have packed. At first this task seemed nonsensical, but after a search, I saw that one suit was missing, two pairs of casual slacks, a turquoise linen overshirt, and a clingy, black satin evening dress she would never wear at a business conference. I knew about the dress only because she had recently modeled it for me, letting the spaghetti straps slide over her shoulders seductively, a prelude to several hours of lovemaking. Next, I searched for the black shoes with spike heels that she had worn with the dress. She kept them in a red shoe box. It was empty.

I turned this over in my mind. She wouldn't take evening clothes unless she knew she would need them. And why would she need them? At this point, my mood was hovering between concern and pique. I went upstairs and settled in to work.

*

Saturday passed with no communication from Marnie. That night, I went to the movies but found I couldn't concentrate and left because I was anxious to check for messages at home. As I drove toward the house, I decided to purchase a cell phone soon so I wasn't tethered to the landline. When I walked into the kitchen, I saw the "zero" flashing on the answering machine and was both disappointed and irritated.

About an hour after I had fallen asleep, the phone rang.

"Hi, Alex, how are you doing?"

"I'm fine." I sat up in bed and stared at the cable clock: 12:35 a.m. "Where are you?"

"In Baltimore, silly."

"Why haven't you called? You didn't leave a number or anything. I looked all over."

"I'm sorry. I guess it slipped my mind in the morning rush." Her voice sounded slurred. She'd been drinking.

"I was worried, Marnie."

"I'm sorry," she said with some heat. "I've been incredibly busy with clients and this conference…there wasn't time to call."

"I left messages on your cell phone."

"I forgot my charger. In fact, I'm calling from a pay phone right now." At which point, the recorded message came on asking for money. "Look, I'll be home tomorrow night. I love you." And she was gone.

This conversation left me with an excess of adrenaline from being awakened and a good dose of anger on top of that. I wrestled with the bedspread and pillows, trying to get comfortable, and couldn't. Most of the night I stared out the window.

Chapter Four

SUNDAY DAWNED with well-stoked summer heat untempered by a brief early morning shower. Everything felt sticky and tropical, airless, in the low 90s. My mood was as heavy as the dripping moisture running unhurriedly down the windows. I tried to convince myself that I should be happy Marnie was coming home, and to be truthful, I was eager to see her, but something wasn't right. Since no reasonable explanation for her behavior presented itself, I vowed to mend my suspicious ways.

I turned on the air conditioner, brewed coffee, and read the *New York Times*. After finishing it, I completed a two-mile run and then toyed briefly with the idea of cutting the grass. This had no appeal. Neither did staying at the house, waiting. After a shower, I drove thirty minutes to McEwan's Books, surveyed the classics and new titles, purchased a copy of Virginia Woolf's *To the Lighthouse*, and walked to a nearby restaurant, where I ordered eggs Benedict and settled down to read and eat. Friends and college roommates had always teased me about my concentration while reading—bombs could go off and I wouldn't notice. True as this usually was, today my mind wandered. I paid the check and succumbed to the pull of home. There, I went upstairs and fooled around with a landscape depicting white cranes and purple mountains.

It began to rain again, a soft, persistent drizzle. A few minutes later, Marnie's car entered the garage. Even though I had been thinking about this reunion all day, I was nervous. This was our longest separation since we'd met, so perhaps it was natural to feel apprehensive. I switched off the studio light and descended the stairs.

Marnie looked fresh despite the heat and dampness; her jeans and emerald-green polo shirt were crisp and well-ironed. In my clothes search, I had failed to notice they were missing from the closet. Suddenly, I felt aggravated with myself for rifling through her things.

"Hi, Alex!" She closed the car door and threw herself into my arms.

I kissed her. "I'm so glad you're home!" I kissed her again with more intensity. All my doubts quickly drained away.

She lifted her suitcase from the trunk and carried it into the bedroom, placing it at the end of the bed. I hung up her raincoat in the closet and followed her in.

"Oh, it's so nice to be back." She tossed her eyeglasses on the dresser and embraced me again.

I pulled Marnie onto the brown satin comforter, slipped beneath her, and stared up into her green eyes, which seemed larger and clearer than usual. She lowered herself a few inches and cupped my head between her hands. Her hair fell like a curtain around us.

"I missed you so much," she whispered in a honeyed drawl.

"Not as much as I missed you."

As if on cue, the phone rang.

"Leave it," she begged, but I was the type who had to answer the phone, whether due to politeness or curiosity.

"Hi, Alex. Sorry to bother you on a Sunday afternoon." It was Gregory Reynolds. He wanted to know if I could add a metallic version to one of my wallpaper designs. Since my attention was on Marnie, who had risen and was now sighing with annoyance, I had difficulty following the drift of his conversation, especially when she opened her suitcase to unpack.

Would Marnie remove the high heels and black dress? By the time I hung up the phone, she was in the bathroom, replacing her cosmetics in the drawers, and the two items hadn't appeared. I checked the nearly empty suitcase and confirmed they weren't inside. This was puzzling, but what could I say? That I'd been rooting around in her clothes and wanted to know where her slinky dress and heels were? Then I saw her cell phone charger tucked in a green slip-on flat she usually wore with her suit.

"How about a gin and tonic?" Marnie called to me.

"Coming right up." I tried to sound agreeable, though I itched to confront her with questions, to force her to explain about the charger. Had Marnie forgotten that she'd packed it? How could she fail to see it when she removed her shoe?

I walked into the kitchen and reached for two tall glasses, poured Tanqueray and lime juice in each, and topped off with tonic water. I placed a bag of potato chips and a bowl of peanuts on a tray and carried everything into the living room, where Marnie sat with me on the couch.

"I've been looking forward to one of your G&Ts for days!" Her smile was playful as she swallowed some of her drink, ripped open the bag, and placed a curly chip to my lips.

I fed her one in turn, determined to enjoy our reunion despite my uneasiness.

Marnie took another sip from her glass. "Ah, this tastes so good!"

I ate some peanuts. "So, how was the conference?"

"Oh, pretty boring. I only went to a few of the seminar lectures and one discussion group. And you were right. The first night dinner was flounder stuffed with crabmeat—canned crabmeat at that."

We laughed at the accuracy of my prediction. "And a salad with iceberg lettuce?"

"Fruit cocktail and *then* iceberg lettuce with glutinous blue cheese dressing," she corrected me, giggling.

"Dessert?"

"Blueberry pie with little American flags on toothpicks."

"How patriotic!" I leaned against the sofa. "And the meeting itself?"

"I already told you. I saw some clients and skipped most of the lectures. That's about it."

I didn't remind her that during the phone call she had complained of being frantically busy during the conference. "Did you wander around the Inner Harbor?"

Marnie frowned and reached for her eyeglasses. "No, Alex, there wasn't time…with one thing and another. I didn't get to do any sightseeing."

The "one thing and another" came out stiffly. The thought of the evening dress and heels bothered me. "Where did you stay?" I ate another potato chip, hoping the crunch would disguise the intensity of my question.

She glanced at me, her eyes narrowing as if she had just walked into a brightly lit room. "I stayed at the conference…at the Baltimore Grand Hotel." She stared through the window for a moment. "So, what did you do while I was away?"

Marnie was attempting to divert my reasonable questions, and her tone had become cool. I ignored this and described my weekend, exaggerating how lonely and bereft I had been without her and trying to achieve a faintly comic attitude. I noticed she wasn't listening closely, but at least the atmosphere had lightened. When I went into the kitchen to make another round of drinks, she tailed after me, asking about dinner.

"It's grill night. Lamb chops," I told her. "If you'll get the potatoes and onions ready, I'll light the charcoal."

Armed with the vegetables, Marnie joined me on the deck where I was standing under the roof's overhang, protected from the rain as was our grill. With tongs, she placed foil-covered red potatoes to the side of the gray-topped coals and lifted the dome on top.

"And we'll have some rosemary to go with the chops." Marnie snipped three green sprigs from one of our pots of herbs and waved the rosemary under my nose. "So, did you really miss me? Tell the truth."

"What do you think?" I kissed her.

The rest of the evening went perfectly. The rain stopped, but we ate inside looking at the deck and listening to the sounds of July mixing with the elegant strains of *Rhapsody in Blue*. We drank a bottle of French Burgundy and then retired to the bedroom, a bit high, but eager to get reacquainted.

*

Though I still had qualms, especially when there was no listing for the Baltimore Grand Hotel online, Marnie and I settled into life as it had been before the business trip. During the day, she called me once, sometimes twice. Each night we spent enjoying each other's company: gardening, trying new recipes, playing music, and, when the mood struck, dancing in the living room. Marnie, who was a natural dancer, was teaching me the tango and rumba.

On the Thursday after the Baltimore trip, Marnie returned from work. I finished a cover letter and addressed a Fed Ex package to Copelia Bye and placed it in the outside black box I used for pick-ups and deliveries. When I walked into the kitchen, Marnie wasn't there. I continued into the bedroom and was surprised to see her through the windows, standing behind a pin oak tree and talking on her cell phone. Why had she gone outside to make the call or to receive one? It seemed odd, but I didn't think more about it as I went into the closet to put on my old sneakers.

While tying the laces, my right foot resting on top of the hamper, I noticed the lid of the shoebox that contained the black heels was awry. I peered inside to find her shoes neatly packed toe to heel, covered with tissue paper. On the far right of the closet, hanging next to a navy jacket, was her black dress. And concealed in the back corner under a hat box was a white shopping bag, empty except for a dry cleaner's plastic cover. Had she used the shopping bag to bring in the shoes and dress from her car? I couldn't imagine wearing the dress at a technical conference, so why would Marnie have it cleaned when she had worn it only a few minutes during our evening together? And why would she hide its return from the cleaner's? Although I told myself to forget the whole thing, my suspicions were renewed.

*

On Sunday night, August 1, we attended a cocktail party given by Sarah, our realtor. I was delighted to attend and hoped to make some friends because Marnie and I knew no one in the area. Marnie complained about a headache, but I finally convinced her to join me.

Our hostess greeted us warmly and handed us margaritas in green Mexican goblets. Sarah pointed toward the margarita bowl and insisted we help ourselves. After one sip, I noted that the tequila had been generously proportioned in the mix. Contrary to her instructions, whenever my glass was empty, Sarah replenished it. I tried to keep pace with the growing alcoholic buzz, eating guacamole, shrimp, and stuffed mushroom caps. Finally, I switched to seltzer.

While I was mingling with the guests, Marnie parked herself next to the margarita bowl, indulging freely, and made no effort to talk with anyone. I brought her a deviled egg on a napkin, but she refused it. Then I struck up a conversation with a woman we'd met once at the local tennis courts, but Marnie stood there with a bored smile fixed on her face. Fearing her behavior was verging on the impolite, I asked Marnie if she wanted to leave. She took a long swallow of margarita and nodded.

Halfway down the driveway, I tried to take Marnie's arm because she was weaving unsteadily, but she jerked away and started walking faster toward my car, turning once to throw me a thunderous look. She staggered to the driver's side and demanded that I give her the keys to my Grand Cherokee. Since I was more sober and it was my car, I refused, opening the passenger door for her instead.

"I want to drive!" she shouted.

"Marnie, hey!" I walked over to her. "The house isn't far away. I'm fine."

"No, you aren't!" She swatted at my hand on her elbow.

"Come on. We're going home and I'm driving." I moved her aside and opened my door. She shoved my shoulder as I sat down. I turned on the ignition and ignored her.

Marnie stood there, fuming, hands on hips. "You always get your way," she hissed, as she circled around the car.

I was taken aback at this statement, believing that I was usually compliant with her wishes. Her unfair attack set me on the moral high road, always a disastrous place. "Marnie, we've had a bit too much to drink. This is no time to—"

"*You* have had too much to drink," she cut in. "I'm okay. Drive if you like." She slammed the door. "I don't care."

I raised my eyebrows, sighed, and backed carefully down the

driveway. Marnie didn't say anything until we were in the kitchen, where she threw her purse on the counter, ripped open the door to the liquor cabinet, and grabbed a bottle of vodka. After twisting off the cap and pouring half a glass and tossing in two ice cubes, she stared at me. "Do you want one?" Her tone was not inviting.

"No, I'll just have some water."

"Suit yourself, sweetie," Marnie replied sourly. She went into the living room and dropped onto the sofa.

She had never behaved like this before. I decided avoidance was the best plan, took some water into the bedroom, and switched on the television. About twenty minutes later, Marnie came in, her drink generously re-filled. She studiously made her way to stand by the window.

"Since when do you prefer watching *I Love Lucy* re-runs to being with me?" she asked, sarcasm and alcohol thickening her voice.

I had scarcely noticed what was on the screen because I was so upset. "Let's just go to sleep. It's late."

"Not late for me," she replied in a falsely perky voice.

I ignored her. Marnie was attempting to start an argument.

She kicked off her gold sandals, one of which banged against the wall, and took a large pull on her drink, sustenance for the fight she seemed intent on having. "The trouble with you is…is…the trouble with you is…oh, hell, you're…damn it…I hate you!"

"Marnie!" I protested, astonished.

"You heard me."

"What's the matter?"

"You're the matter." She was in no condition to make sense.

"Can't we call it a night?" I pleaded, holding out my hand. "Come to bed."

Marnie jutted her chin. "See? That's all you think about…that's all..." She drifted off, following the trail of an errant thought. Another sip renewed her concentration. "That's the trouble…we're always going to bed…having sex. Always, that's what you…that's one thing…" She shook her head, finished her vodka, turned to go into the kitchen, and fell onto the tan carpet. Her glass and the cubes of ice tumbled against the dresser.

I rushed to help her.

"Don't touch me!" she shouted, rising to her feet. "I don't want you to ever touch me again! Do you hear? I hate you!" And with this, she slapped my face.

I was so stunned that I didn't move until I saw she was going to take another swing, this time with her fist. I blocked her hand and encircled her tightly with my arms. "Marnie, hey, take it easy. Everything is fine. I'm sorry." I apologized, though there was no reason to do so.

She battled to get loose until, perhaps out of weariness, she stopped and allowed me to guide her to the bed. In seconds, Marnie was out cold.

I picked up her unbroken glass and set it on the table, then threw the ice into the bathroom sink. Unsure what else to do, I climbed upstairs to one of the guest rooms and fell into a fitful sleep.

Chapter Five

IN THE MORNING, Marnie was gone. No note, but she had probably left for work, which was fine with me. I could still hear the fury in her voice reverberating in my head.

I ate breakfast, and after a shower, I noticed a red welt along my jaw, testimony to her anger. Annoyed, I dressed, grabbed my car keys, and drove to the coast, to my father's house, a place where I felt safe.

The sea air was warm and salty. Boats dotted the bay, mostly fishing for fluke. I contemplated taking an afternoon charter, but the skirmish with Marnie had left me depleted and unnerved. Something very strange was going on with her, something of more concern than a flare of temper. Instead, it felt like the top had been knocked off of a volcano. Was she an alcoholic, and I was only just now witnessing evidence of a drinking problem?

I let myself in through the garage door and walked into the galley-style kitchen. Immediately, my tension dissolved as the effect of the cheerful room washed over me. The skylights allowed sun to pour white rectangles of light onto the floor, which was decorated with ornate blue, gold, and white tiles my father had bought in Spain. A year ago, during a visit to Toledo, I had purchased more and set them as a backsplash by the sink and on a section of countertop. I loved the effect, though it was sad my father hadn't lived to see the beautiful improvements.

Though I kept little food in the house, I mixed some canned chicken with a dollop of mayonnaise and spread it on a bagel defrosted in the microwave. Grabbing a cold ginger ale, I sat in my father's tan leather recliner and observed the ocean and bay, letting the restful view ease some of the turmoil, though much remained. After lunch, I fetched the mail under the drop slot in the front door. The house bills and payments from Cope's accountant and other clients from my sideline business came to this address. In the pile was such a check, which would be deposited in the separate account used for the house's upkeep and taxes.

I sat at my desk and paid the bills, and then, unwilling to leave, I removed a pad from the top drawer. Though I hadn't written any poetry in months, I knew when something was about to tumble out. After several scratched-out drafts, on a fresh piece of paper, I wrote:

THE PEACH

The peach lay halved, yellow, pink, brown-hearted,
in two porcelain cups pale with blue. Divided thus,
bathed in white milk, the separate parts nested between us
as chimes played sounds intermittent and light,
and the sun cast its last shadows on the low walls.

We could not eat the peach. It was too perfect,
a staunch reproach for the harsh words sticking
the silence.

After we watched the sea tuck the tide up
to the lapping shine of an early rising moon,
we stood and turned away, deaf to the scrape
of caned chairs on cobblestones. Untasted,
the milk soured in the warm breeze.

My lover read this and knew.

I recited the lines aloud. They seemed to catch my sad mood. For some reason—perhaps because of the concept of division and halving in the poem—Aristophanes' speech from *The Symposium* came to mind. Though the precise words eluded me, Aristophanes had been called upon to discuss the topic of love. He recounted the story of Zeus, who decided to split humanity in two so that they would be weaker and less troublesome to the gods. Because each half missed the other half, both were continually searching for the missing "twin." As I recalled my early feelings for Marnie, I had felt then like a raw wound was beginning to heal, as if our joining was a return to a previous state of wholeness, a state I had long ago lost.

I slumped against the chair, disturbed by the poem and its foreboding thoughts. Shaking my head, I decided this was a decent draft, but some time and distance were needed before additional refinements could be made. I placed the sheet of paper in a blue silk portfolio with my other poems, some of which I had sent to Cope, who had converted a few into song lyrics, and then inserted the box in my desk. After tucking the outgoing envelopes in the mail slot, I wondered whether I should remain in the house for a few days and let Marnie cool off. However, if I did, I would exacerbate the situation. Though disturbed by her hurtful behavior, I still loved her and had made a commitment.

I neatened the kitchen, locked the house, and reluctantly began the drive inland, visiting my nearby bank to deposit the check, and, when I noticed a two-for-one sale at a shoe store, I stopped to buy two pairs of Nike running shoes, both size 8B. One for myself and one as a present for Marnie. Footwear of any kind soothed her.

When I arrived home, it was nearly six and the house was empty. I poured some iced tea and went to my studio. An hour later, Marnie hadn't returned from work, so I fixed a steak and salad and watched a movie, all the while wondering why she had been so aggressive the night before and so mysterious about her Baltimore trip. After the eleven o'clock news, I went to bed.

Sometime after midnight, a door closed upstairs. Worried, I went into the foyer and noticed a light in the hall on the floor above. I walked to the garage. Marnie's car was parked next to mine. Now what was I supposed to do? She was clearly avoiding a confrontation. Should I ignore her arrival and return to sleep? Yet, if we didn't resolve our problems soon, the ill feelings would fester and might create an irredeemable split.

Although evasion wasn't the method I usually preferred, I was tired and returned to the bedroom.

*

It was late when I woke. Out of sorts and rubbing my eyes, I crossed the foyer by the front door and entered the kitchen. A note was propped on the counter.

Dear Alex,

I have to go to Harrisburg today on business and will spend the night there. I think it would be a good idea if we took a break. Let's talk tomorrow night at dinner.

Love, Marnie

This wasn't the abject apology I expected. It also presumed that getting tomorrow's dinner was my responsibility. I knew I was being petty, but it seemed like she should offer to cook. And then I wondered how she had removed a change of clothes from the closet while I had been sleeping. Marnie was sneakier than I thought.

Determined to divert my mood, I went upstairs and began working, though it was a struggle to focus. The day passed slowly. At three-thirty, my brain was fried, so I decided to go grocery shopping, though my resentment intensified as I threw items into the shopping cart.

When I returned home, I dumped barbecue sauce on country-style ribs and popped them in the oven. Marnie probably wouldn't call, but I caught myself listening for the house phone, half hoping and half dreading the first conversation with her. Irritated by my ambivalence, I walked up to my office and checked e-mail. A minute later, my studio phone rang. Thinking it was Marnie, I hesitated before answering but finally did. Copelia Bye.

We had known each other since our days at Bard College, where I'd studied fine arts and she'd majored in voice and classical guitar. Our paths crossed when I designed a stage set for a senior musical production, thus beginning years of exciting collaboration and friendship. Though we'd never had a sexual affair, our creative bond was exhilarating.

After updating our news, Cope asked how our home improvements were proceeding. I described what we had accomplished, and then she inquired about Marnie.

The need to share my concern, at least in part, overcame my

caution. "Well, Cope, to be honest, something is wrong. I almost don't want to talk about it because I don't understand what's going on."

"Alex, did something happen?"

I explained about the argument and the atypical behavior. "It's probably silly to be so suspicious, but I am."

"Hmm." Cope was silent. "Do you think she has an issue with drinking?"

"She doesn't come home drunk or drink during the day. Well, once or twice she might have had something."

"You know there are all kinds of alcoholics. In some, liquor triggers mood swings."

"Yeah, but why didn't she act this way before? Why all of a sudden?" I felt disloyal talking to Cope about Marnie. I also disliked complaining in general. "Maybe she'll settle down, and tomorrow we can talk it through." I didn't sound convincing.

Cope didn't sound convinced. "I hope so, but be careful, Alex." What she didn't say was loud and clear. Her sister had been in an abusive marriage, and Cope encountered musical people every day who were battling addictions.

"I will." I changed the subject to my new illustration.

She was curious to see the work. "Send some photos. Unless I can entice you to come for a visit?" Copelia lived in San Francisco.

"When the designs are finished, I'll mail copies. No trips for me. Not for a while."

"The invitation is open. And, in the meantime, I hope things will improve with Marnie."

*

I made a spinach salad, poured a glass of water, microwaved some leftover ribs, and carried everything into the living room and switched on the television. However, I soon realized my appetite was gone. Sighing, I returned to the kitchen, placed the ribs in the refrigerator, and cleaned the dishes, feeling on edge. With the television blaring in the other room, I walked into Marnie's study and turned on the light. Though the desk was still locked, it appeared that she had jotted something on the square notepad near her telephone and then scribbled over the writing in blue ink. On closer examination, I could see ten numbers underneath. A phone number?

I took the pad to my office and scrutinized the paper through a magnifying glass. Most of the writing was decipherable except for the last digit, which was either a "1" or a "7." Of special note was the 215 area code for Philadelphia, a code that also encompassed several outlying areas but not Harrisburg, where Marnie was supposed to be. I deliberated and then picked up the phone and tried the number ending in one. A movie theater. Then I called the number ending in seven. The Lumberville Hound and Hare Bed and Breakfast, according to the innkeeper who answered. Although tempted to ask after Marnie, I told the woman I'd dialed incorrectly and ended the call.

I turned on my computer and checked the inn's website. The listing was north of New Hope, in Bucks County. Definitely not Harrisburg and certainly not a conference center or a place to stay for any kind of business meeting from the look of the B&B's web page. It appeared to be a small inn with four rooms—three in the main house and one in a separate cottage. Could Marnie have written the number down for another purpose? Maybe she was planning to invite me for a romantic weekend at the Hound and Hare?

I went downstairs, set the notepad on Marnie's desk, turned off the television, and paced the living room, unable to concentrate on anything except this new mystery. At seven-thirty, I could stand it no longer and began the hour-and-a-half drive to New Hope, feeling ashamed and worried in equal measure.

Chapter Six

AS I CROSSED the narrow bridge to New Hope, the lights of town reflected in the Delaware River, doubling the festive appearance. The sidewalks were thick with pedestrians, shoppers, restaurant patrons, and bar-goers. I stopped at the traffic light at Bridge Street and almost turned around to leave. However, when the light changed, I made the right to go upriver and followed the twisting road for several miles until the small gathering of buildings at Lumberville came into view. After passing a Delaware rock quarry, I came to the Hare and Hound B&B. Three cars were in the drive. One of them, to my amazement, was Marnie's red Solara convertible. No matter how I tried, I could think of no reasonable justification for her presence. I needed to find out what was going on.

Curiosity now vying with anger, I hit the brakes, nearly scraping the car on the roadside guard rail. Since there was no place to park except at the inn, I turned around, drove to the quarry, left the Jeep behind a row of hemlocks, and walked a short way to a footbridge that crossed the canal. This led to a path running parallel to the Delaware River. The B&B's main house and cottage had been built on the land side of the canal, with rows of windows facing the water. I moved quietly along the trail, listening to the sounds of the river, the croaking of frogs, and the whine of mosquitoes. The moon was choked by clouds, and only a scattering of faint stars could be seen in the sky. On any other evening, I would have enjoyed the dark, moody river sliding along in the lazy summer heat. Tonight, I was too upset.

When I came abreast of the Hound and Hare, I saw that both buildings were nestled in thickets of mountain laurel. In the main inn, curtains were drawn across the windows in one room and three were dark. However, one of the two cottage windows was open, and the interior was faintly lit, perhaps by a candle. From my vantage point below, I noticed movement within: two black shadows dancing on the ceiling. I crossed the canal via a second pedestrian bridge and made my way to the safe cover afforded by the green bushes. Although I couldn't see into the room or its inhabitants, no one could see me, either, unless they opened the screen and looked down. I paused a minute to still my breathing and then pressed close to the outside wall of the cottage. A few minutes passed until I heard a woman's voice—Marnie's.

"Do you want another glass of wine, darling?" she asked someone.

The reply was muffled.

"This is a great chardonnay," Marnie said.

I heard a bottle grinding in an ice bucket.

"Come and look at the river—it's really beautiful." She was near the window and laughed. "Oh, my, you're always ready, aren't you?" Marnie was using the sexy tone that I had heard many times.

I set my teeth. There was a lengthy silence. I thought perhaps she had moved, but then she continued.

"So, before we have some fun, we need to talk about how everything will work. After all, I have to tell Alex a convincing story tomorrow." There was a mumbled dialogue before Marnie asked, "Should we go with it as planned? I know you're impatient, but are you sure this isn't too dangerous?"

I pressed my face against the cool stones and wanted to fly away, yet I was glued to the spot, waiting for an explanation. Standing very still, I strained to hear her partner's response and couldn't.

Marnie chuckled. "Oh, all right. I'll put on the air-conditioning. You always like to be cold, don't you?"

With that, the window shuddered in its ancient tracks, and the air-conditioning unit rattled to life in the other window, producing an uneven drone. Since I could no longer detect voices, it was time to leave. Silently, I crept around the corner of the cottage, fighting the urge to bang on Marnie's door and accost her and the unknown partner, but I needed time to weigh the situation. The path around the cottage led to the driveway where a black Japanese sedan with New York plates, a light-colored Saab convertible whose plates were hidden by a boxwood hedge, and Marnie's Solara were parked. Since I didn't want to be discovered, I hurried to the main road, my breath coming fast.

In the Jeep, I opened all of the windows and the sunroof to purge the heat of my anger, but the more I analyzed the brief bit of overheard conversation, the hotter I became. It seemed incontrovertible that Marnie was having an affair. Was it with someone she'd recently met or someone she'd known before me? Although it seemed impossible that she could have started a relationship so soon after ours began, Marnie and I had fallen for each other instantly, so perhaps the same thing had happened with someone else. Still, nothing had seemed wrong until the Baltimore trip. Was that where the two connected? Or had she never gone to Baltimore and had instead arranged a tryst in another city where she might wear the black dress?

I dredged through the memories from February, when Marnie and I had first encountered each other at a New Brunswick art gallery reception. It had been a blustery day, but the place was mobbed because of all the publicity and the attendance of loyal fans of an aging sculptress, whose work was featured. In a side room, along with another artist, twelve of my original gouache paintings were exhibited as part of a mini show devoted to the decorative arts—in my case, creations for wallpaper and fabrics. In addition to the art connoisseurs, there was the usual crowd who migrated from one opening to another, scooping up canapés and gulping wine from thimble-sized plastic glasses.

Because I wasn't the primary attraction, I sat on a stool near my work and answered questions and fielded a few compliments. During a brief lull, an attractive, red-haired woman approached and said she was a great admirer of my wallpaper and fabric patterns, mentioning an article written about my work in *Interior Design*. Since it was rare for someone in my business to be known outside limited circles, I was flattered. We chatted until the gallery owner asked me to speak with a potential buyer. When I returned, the woman was gone. On my stool, I found a folded note:

How about a drink? I'll be across the street
at The Scarlet Knight.—Marnie

The reception was scheduled to last another forty-five minutes. As soon as it was over, I grabbed my coat, thanked everyone, and stepped outside. Snow was beginning to fall as I walked to the popular Rutgers' bar. Its interior was painted black with crimson trim, the university's colors. In the entrance, a dusty suit of armor greeted customers, its helmet festooned with a red plume and a cheerleader's pom-pom tucked under one arm. I searched through the crowd, worrying that my mystery woman had left, but as I moved toward the rear of the brass bar, I saw her in the faded gold light, her hair softly glowing. As if she sensed my arrival, she turned and smiled, a radiant smile I will never forget.

A perfect moment. Even now, as mad as I was with her, I could feel the magic of the memory. No, Marnie couldn't set me up, but how could I reconcile her present behavior?

When I arrived home, I opened the garage, parked the Jeep, and slammed the car door. The house was dark, so I switched on the lights and began to wander around in the living room, replaying the sentences I'd heard outside the cottage. My initial reaction had been a response to the infidelity. The more I got past that unhappy territory, the more I wondered about "the plan" Marnie had mentioned. A "dangerous" plan apparently centered around me. Whatever intrigue was being hatched, it sounded menacing and as if it had been devised some time ago. But, if Marnie had been involved with someone before me, why had she been so eager to make a commitment and buy a house?

Unfortunately, it didn't take long to arrive at the sickening answer: the wills we both wrote up with the lawyer—her lawyer. In order to protect our investments, we had bequeathed our respective ownership and our estates to each other, an arrangement

Marnie had suggested. If something happened to me, all my money, possessions, and my percentage of the house would pass to her, with no one left in my family to question her right to the inheritance or her role in my death or disappearance. Since I had subsidized $25,000 of the deposit and $60,000 at closing to reduce the mortgage, she would garner a nice amount, which she knew, and much more, which she didn't. As compensation, Marnie had offered to cover more of the monthly mortgage—her income was higher and more regular than mine—a fact that had helped us to secure the house loan and had allowed me to avoid disclosure of my full assets.

In recent weeks, I had paid for most of the improvements because her $5,000 down payment had drained her funds. Marnie had promised to reimburse me from her next sales' commission in July—which she hadn't—but kept records, as if to convince me of her good intentions. Like an idiot, I had trusted her to make amends. Now, after what I had just overheard, it seemed as though Marnie was scheming to profit from the house, which meant I had to die and my estate legally transferred to her.

If this was the plot, then I was in serious jeopardy. It did no good to keep on about how I had been duped, how she didn't love me and perhaps hadn't ever. I had to concentrate on the end game, if, in fact, I had analyzed everything correctly.

It was very late. I was exhausted and needed sleep in order to find my way through this quagmire. Marnie was safely tucked away in a cottage nearly two hours distant, unlikely to leave before breakfast. I changed into pajamas and went to bed, telling myself that I would awaken early in the morning and find an attorney.

Chapter Seven

WHEN I WOKE the next morning, Marnie was staring at me, her green eyes blinking behind her tortoiseshell glasses. I recoiled, surprised to see her.

"I didn't expect you." I tried to keep my tone steady, to sound casual, but I heard the quaver in my voice.

"I needed to change clothes."

I rose to my feet, which made me feel more in control since I was taller than Marnie. "Look, I want to know what's going on."

She blinked at me again.

"Can't we talk? Maybe have some coffee?" I suggested, though I wasn't feeling at all companionable.

She started to turn toward the closet and reconsidered, as if caught between two strong impulses. "Oh, Alex, this is such an enormous mess." As she approached me, tears began to roll down her cheeks. "I'm so sorry I lost my temper the other night. I had too much to drink." She removed her glasses and wiped her eyes.

I didn't know what to say and stood there, speechless. Was this genuine remorse?

"Things just snowballed," she said. "I feel absolutely horrible."

Before I knew what was happening, Marnie placed her arms around my neck and kissed me. Instinctively, I embraced her. My mind was whirling with confusion, outrage, and, worst of all, a sexual response to her touch.

"I missed you so much," she whispered.

Though my brain was tossing verbal protests at a blitzkrieg rate, I replied, "I missed you too," and then wondered why I had said it, whether it was a lie or the truth.

"Really? Do you mean that?" Hopefulness spread across her face.

I was quiet, skeptical of Marnie, but then she kissed me again and led me to the bed, a treacherous place for us to be at the moment. I tried to step away, but she held me until I surrendered and sat on the mattress.

"I want us to get back to where we were, Alex. I really do. Tell me what you want. Anything…" Her voice ambled back to Virginia, slow and smooth.

"I don't know, Marnie." A weak response if there ever was one. I was disgusted with myself, disgusted with her transparent manipulation. I felt like a trained seal waiting for fish.

She brought her ample chest closer. "Oh, come on, let's just forget about everything," she pleaded, massaging my neck.

Though I wasn't persuaded by her apology, sexual sparks were flying.

"Marnie, I have some real concerns—"

"Oh, Alex, you still love me, don't you?"

She had me there. A black-and-white question. "Yes," I replied, trying to disguise my uncertainty.

"I knew it!" Her expression brightened. "We'll work this out. Maybe everything was too perfect before, and we had to go through a little rough patch. Yes, that's all it was."

Was she attempting to convince me or herself? Or was she acting a part? Observing her carefully, I could see no trace of fakery, yet only last night this woman had been drinking wine in a romantic cottage and making plans that threatened me. It was possible she still loved me and was in some kind of trouble involving the person at the B&B. I considered confronting her with what I knew and then, just as quickly, decided against it. Though it felt absurd to do so, I hugged her. Marnie hugged me back and began removing my pajamas, almost ripping off the buttons. Her frenzied excitement was at once manic and also frightening, as if intensified by a "last time" quality.

"Oh, yes…" she moaned, tossing her dress and underwear on the floor. Within seconds, she lowered her naked body beside me. "Oh, you feel so good!"

Her flesh was soft and curving in contrast to my angularity. She ran her hands over my hip.

"Take me, Alex." Marnie pulled me on top of her, wrapped her legs around mine, and pressed her hands against the small of my back. "Hurry!"

Her voice steamed my cheek, heating the space between us. I wanted to stop, to honor my reservations, but I was swept along with her passion despite my belief that this was a staged production. Or perhaps my anger was turning into aggression, goading me forward.

"Do it," she murmured.

I pinned her against the pillows and kissed her hard and deeply, without love or tenderness, wanting to punish Marnie for her infidelity. Despite the bitterness I felt toward her, I was equally upset with myself. As if sensing my conflicted mood, she grabbed my hand and placed it in her mouth, her green eyes feral, like those of a large, dangerous cat. She began to bite and suck my fingers, alternating between hurting and soothing me. Then she forced my hand in the space between us.

"Take me," she ordered again.

*

Later, we lay on the bed, silent and separate. The few spoken words of endearment uttered by Marnie sounded rote. I said almost nothing and made no promises of love. I felt miserable, unable to share my torment with Marnie, who seemed bent on maintaining the illusion of closeness.

"Come on. It's time for coffee. I'll make it," she offered.

I didn't answer.

"Alex, honey, are you okay?"

"Yeah, sure. Coffee is fine," I lied, wishing for her to leave the room.

Marnie glanced at me, then put on her eyeglasses.

Detecting her suspicion, I changed the subject. "Aren't you going to work?"

Sunlight struck the surface of her lenses. "I'll tell them I'm sick." Marnie headed toward the closet, her large breasts swinging easily. "I'll phone after breakfast."

I thought this was odd since it was so late already, but I let it go. As she donned her bathrobe and walked toward the kitchen, I settled in the sheets still warm from sex, but after a moment, I couldn't tolerate lying in our bed and rushed into the bathroom to take a scalding shower.

*

When I entered the kitchen, the teakettle was whistling. Marnie looked askance at my shorts and blouse.

"Dressed already?" she asked.

"Yeah." I grabbed my mug and added some sugar. I felt anxious, particularly since she kept watching me.

Marnie poured water into the white Melitta filter and gave me a glass of juice. Instead of moving away, she stepped nearer, placing her hand on my arm. "Really, Alex, we're fine."

I stared at her, stunned by her optimism.

Her lips brushed my cheek, then lingered by my neck, trying to provoke me. When I didn't react, she drew away. "I just had some stuff to deal with."

"Like what?"

She shook her head at my unfriendly tone and returned to the coffee pot. "Just things. Maybe we went too fast…buying the house and all. Maybe I needed a little time to catch up to where we were. Oh, I don't know. But I feel better, like everything is good again." As she said this, she turned and smiled at me.

Unsure of what to say or how to behave, I nodded and reached for the cereal bowls.

*

We spent the day gardening, an activity we could do together and maintain our separate thoughts. Mine were as convoluted and confused as the creepers circling through the forsythia bushes. I berated myself for not leaving Marnie, but the situation seemed increasingly gauzy and surreal. At five, sweating from the heat, I came into the house to shower while Marnie prepared a chicken for the oven. Later, as I was slipping on khaki shorts, she came into the bedroom bearing two tall whiskey sours.

"Oh, thanks," I replied, "but I should have water first or this will go straight to my head." I then noticed the liquid level in

Marnie's cocktail glass. She had skipped the water and made considerable inroads on her drink.

"My turn for the shower," she said, smiling. "You make the salad."

"Okay," I replied, relieved we would have more time apart.

I headed into the kitchen, drank some ice water, rinsed a head of Boston lettuce, and sliced some tomatoes, all the while analyzing how to confront Marnie. After shaving some parmesan cheese and adding green olives to the salad, I dressed it and placed the bowl on the table. Marnie appeared, her auburn hair damp and brushed back. She was wearing black shorts and a white, low-cut, knit top. Marnie held up a Nike box.

"Hey, Alex? Are these shoes for me?"

I'd forgotten about them. "Yeah. There was a sale. Have a present."

"Got some for yourself too, I see."

I nodded.

"Well, thanks. I'll try them on later." She made another drink and walked into the living room.

I delayed joining her by measuring water and rice. Suddenly, I felt weary, but not too weary to stop worrying. Waiting for the water to boil, I sipped my whiskey sour, all the while trying to determine if last night's fears were reasonable or ridiculous. Our morning activities had done nothing to clarify how Marnie felt about me. If anything, I was more unsure of her now, having glimpsed an emotional void disguised by her seductive behavior. Of course, I could also be accused of acting with little feeling or at least little positive feeling. However, we had arrived at this chilly place, it was apparent our relationship had become a charade, one I had to fix or end.

This realization brought me to one of the urgent questions I'd been wrestling with all afternoon: should I consult an attorney tomorrow to change my will, or should I wait? Changing my will meant altering the mutual agreement with Marnie about the house and tacitly breaking the commitment we'd made. On the other hand, at the very least, Marnie had been cheating on me and possibly was intending to do something much worse. Thinking about the conversation I'd heard below the window of the B&B, my resentment was rekindled. What had I been doing having sex with her? Revulsion roiled my stomach. And why hadn't Marnie called the office to report her absence from work? Because she'd already taken the day off as part of the plan with her partner? And, more importantly, was I in danger?

I resolved to be very observant tonight and to call an attorney when Marnie left in the morning. If I had misconstrued her conversation with the unknown partner, I could always nullify the revised will and Marnie would never know.

*

Marnie's *coq-au-vin* was fine as always and the wine was too. After we finished dishes of lemon sorbet, I told her I was going upstairs to check my answering machine and e-mail. It took me about fifteen minutes to erase all the spam advertisements, plus answer a few short notes from Gregory Reynolds and another client. Then I stretched, stood, and headed downstairs, the thick carpet cool on my bare feet. Nearing the laundry room, I heard Marnie talking quietly in her study. I stopped, hoping I hadn't made too much noise.

"Look, this may not work out—" she was saying. Whoever it was on the other end of the line seemed to cut her off. She was silent for a few seconds.

"Mmm. Yeah, I know, I know." She sounded like a chastised child, but a moment later her voice acquired a decisive edge. "Okay, listen, you're right, we'll go with it as scheduled. Let me think about it...see what I can arrange. No, she doesn't suspect. Good. Day after tomorrow is fine. See you then."

A bolt of anxiety shot through me. I hadn't misunderstood Marnie's intent after all. She was plotting something, but what? All I knew was when, not why, how, or with whom. I retreated a few steps and then walked more loudly toward the kitchen and slowed near the wine rack.

"Marnie, should I open another bottle?" I asked, not that I wanted any.

She hurried from her study. "Huh? Did you get everything finished, Alex?"

I decided that two could play the same acting game. "Yes, just a lot of nonsense as usual. No one called or missed me all day. I guess I'm not that popular."

Marnie didn't skip a beat. "You're popular with me," she drawled, encircling my shoulders and kissing my cheek. "I don't think we need more wine, do you?"

Chapter Eight

I RETRIEVED MY WILL and two other documents from the safe deposit box at the bank and arrived promptly for my one o'clock appointment. The receptionist ushered me into an expensive office. The attorney, Mr. Reilly, came in almost immediately. He was beefy like a football tackle and dressed in a conservative gray suit and maroon necktie. His thinning dark hair was combed back to emphasize a protruding forehead. Half glasses perched on his large nose.

We shook hands.

"Alexandra Wyatt? Hi, I'm Jim Reilly." He sat behind his gleaming mahogany desk, which smelled faintly of lemon, clasped his two big hands together, and observed me with a patient expression. "What can I do for you?"

"I need a revision to my will and to my power of attorney and health proxy." I handed him the documents that had been drawn up with Marnie before our house closing. "I hope it will be possible to have them changed and signed while I'm here or at least by the end of the day. Your secretary told me you might be able to do it."

The lawyer studied me attentively, probably wondering why I was in such a rush, though he didn't ask. Instead, he gave me a practiced smile. "We can do that if the will is simple."

"It is. My previous document is fine as a model except for a few changes."

He examined the contents of the envelope and raised his eyebrows when he saw the date. "These have been done very recently."

"Yes, I know. My circumstances have changed rather suddenly."

"I see. What must we amend?"

"The beneficiary, the executor, the power of attorney, and

holder of the health proxy."

He concentrated on the will first and read the appropriate sentences, moved a yellow legal pad to the center of his desk, and unscrewed the cap on a black Mont Blanc pen. "May I have the name of the new executor?"

I gave him Copelia's name and address.

"Is she a relative?"

"No. Everyone in my family is dead."

"I'm sorry to hear that," he said, jotting the information down. "And who would you like as a secondary executor?"

"No one."

"Are you sure?"

"You can list yourself."

He nodded, then read the part about the house. "And the beneficiary and contingent beneficiary?"

"Just Copelia. Please specify that she will inherit my estate and my part of the ownership of the house, the one listed in the old will."

"Perhaps you'd like to name your current beneficiary as a second? Marnie Hardwick?"

"I expressly don't want that," I replied with some vehemence. "I'm sorry. There really isn't anyone else. And also stipulate that in the event of my death, the house must be sold since I own a majority interest, and that Copelia Bye will receive my percentage of the net profit or the co-owner—"

"Marnie Hardwick?"

"Yes, the co-owner," I repeated, "may opt to keep the house and reimburse Cope for my investment plus my percentage of any rise in appraised value."

"Not that you expect to leave us soon," Mr. Reilly said with a bland smile. "I assume, since you have joint ownership, that the two of you signed a legal agreement detailing this arrangement?"

"No, not exactly. She has listed me as first beneficiary of her part ownership." At least that's what she agreed to do, though I hadn't seen the final signed document. I felt my cheeks color, thinking how dumb I'd been. "At closing, it was recorded that my down payment was $85,000 and hers was $5,000 and what percentage of ownership each of us had."

"I see. That's certainly a step in the right direction, though it doesn't spell out what your intentions are regarding any future sale of the house and the consequent loss or gain on the property. Or who will pay the monthly mortgage or for any improvements…things of that nature."

"I suppose it doesn't."

"Perhaps it would be wise to create a more comprehensive agreement between the two of you concerning the house. Just as you are changing your will, there is nothing to stop Ms. Hardwick from changing hers."

"That's true. I wish I had such an agreement, but it's too late."

Mr. Reilly reflected on this elliptical statement. "Too late?"

"Yes."

He raised an eyebrow and cleared his throat. "Well, in the event of your demise, Ms. Hardwick might contest this revised will or make it difficult for your named beneficiary to be fully reimbursed for your percentage of the property. She might argue that the two of you had an oral agreement, or she spent money on improvements."

"I know, but I can't control what Ms. Hardwick may or may not do." I reflected for a moment, staring at the fox hunt reproductions gracing the wall behind his head. "I'll tell my friend Cope to consult you should there be any legal issues with the settling of the estate or problems with the house sale. There will be ample funds to cover your expenses. In addition to the primary residence I own with Marnie, can you specify that a second property should be included in this will? The existence of this house must remain confidential and should only be revealed to my beneficiary upon my death." I provided the address.

"If you wish me to assist Ms. Bye, I would be delighted to do so, although I'm sure nothing untoward will come to pass. Rest assured that if it does, however, your instructions will be carefully followed. And the second house will never be mentioned in the interim. Since Ms. Hardwick has no financial interest in the property—"

"Or knowledge of it."

"Yes, well, then there's no reason for her to be made aware of your ownership. If that is all, I'll draft the corrections."

He wrote some notes about my previous will and then asked about my Living Will and Power of Attorney documents.

"Copelia Bye should be named on both, with you as contingent on the Power of Attorney. No second person on my health proxy."

"All right." He turned to his computer and began to type. After about twenty minutes, the attorney sent the documents to the printer. As it was spitting out pages, Mr. Reilly faced me and stroked his chin thoughtfully. "Not that you need to explain, but it might be helpful to know why you're changing your will and other papers in such a sudden manner." He raised his eyes to mine. I could see curiosity lurking under his professional gaze.

I thought for a moment, considering the vast swamp that lay before me. "Perhaps I'm only being cautious, but I have reason to believe Ms. Hardwick entered into this real estate arrangement with the intention of—"

"Receiving gain not due to her?" Mr. Reilly cut in.

I leaned against the chair, a little startled by his perspicacity, and nodded. "Possibly. Recent events have led me to doubt she...well, let's just say that I wish to protect my interests."

He twirled his pen around his fingers as if it were a miniature baton. "The way your current will is written, how all wills are written, Ms. Hardwick could only come into complete ownership of the house and your assets if you died while this will is still in effect."

"Exactly," I replied as evenly as I could.

"Or if you became incapacitated."

"Yes. That's why I need both the power of attorney and the living will revised."

"I understand." The lawyer leaned against his high-backed chair and fingered the lapel of his suit jacket. "I don't mean to make assumptions, but if you are suspicious of Ms. Hardwick, have you notified the police?"

"No, I haven't."

"Although this is the first time we've met, and I am acting as your attorney for the first time, I must advise you to do so if you have a belief that you're at risk or might potentially be the victim of some kind of scam."

"I may report her when I have more concrete evidence. As I said, this has arisen rather precipitously and I might be incorrect about her intentions, in which case, it would be a mess if I changed an agreement without consulting or notifying Marnie. I'm doing this as a precaution until I can appreciate everything more fully."

He nodded at this, gathered the printed sheets, and handed them to me for review. Everything was in order. The documents were signed, witnessed, and notarized.

*

After paying Mr. Reilly, I drove to the post office, where I mailed one set of copies to Cope. Then I went to the bank near my father's house and placed the originals in my second safe deposit box. If anything happened to me, Cope could contact Mr. Reilly, who had kept an original of the revised will. I had also provided the attorney with the name of my financial advisor, two banks, and the location of the keys to my security boxes, one of which housed the deed to my father's house. Marnie had retained the deed to our property, a request she made after closing and another telling indication of her nefarious intentions. I had explained this to Mr. Reilly and believed he would remember our conversation and act on my behalf.

On the way home, I congratulated myself for keeping my finances private. Even when Marnie wanted to do renovations and I was tempted to pay for them, I didn't offer, saying I didn't have cash. She knew I received a modest income from Gregory Reynolds, with an occasional bonus for new work, which was enough to cover my share of the utility bills, groceries, and a little over. I told her I paid most things on credit, hoping to make more money when I achieved national recognition in the design market. Last week, Marnie had suggested we apply for a home equity loan to pay for the modifications we had discussed, but I asked for a delay. At the time, I'd chaffed at my misrepresentations to Marnie; now I blessed myself for upholding the promise to my mother.

When I returned home, I sent Cope an e-mail.

Dear Cope—

Thanks for calling. It was good to speak with you. FYI, you'll receive an envelope within a few days: copies of a revised will, health care proxy, and power of attorney that I drew up today. They name you as executor and beneficiary (rather than Marnie), POA, and holder of my living will. After our conversation and a few new happenings, I have a slight suspicion Marnie may be intending to profit from our purchase of the house and is seeing someone else. I'm probably jumping to conclusions, so don't worry. Very likely this is only a temporary arrangement. More later—

Love, Alex

I sent the e-mail just as the phone rang—a telemarketer. I treated him to a fine litany of four-letter words and disconnected. Annoyed, I turned off the computer and slid my coffee cup in front of it so that I would remember to take it downstairs. Then I picked up a Dover book on Japanese stencil drawings and leafed through the illustrations. Before long, I heard the garage door rise. Feeling somewhat guilty for all my legal activities, I hesitated before going downstairs. When I finally did, Marnie greeted me with a hug.

"Hi, Alex. What did you do today, honey?"

Something I wasn't going to tell her. "A few sketches."

"That's great. I can't wait to see them."

"And how was your day?" I asked, eager to divert the conversation.

"Oh, a boring staff meeting and a client this afternoon." She put her briefcase in her study and removed her suit jacket. "Sometimes being in sales is a drag, but the commissions are nice."

"Wish my situation was like yours." I couldn't resist reminding her of the disparity between her salary and my lack of one. "Marnie, speaking of commissions, I hate to ask, but could you reimburse me for some of my down payment on the house and the improvements we've made? You said you'd do so in July."

Marnie tucked in her chin, as if surprised. "Oh. Yes. I'm sorry. I forgot to tell you that my commission was postponed until the end of this month. I complained to my boss, as did three of my colleagues, but the decision was made by the home office."

The lie was smoothly delivered.

Without giving me a chance to comment, she added, "As for your income, I'm sure your work will be in all the stores very soon. Oh, it will happen. I believe in you, Alex."

She was very convincing. It was one of the reasons I had been attracted to her, though in retrospect, perhaps her interest was intended to attract me.

"I hope I merit such confidence." I glanced at my wristwatch. "Now, maybe I should cut the grass before it rains."

"Good plan. I'll change and begin dinner."

Chapter Nine

AT BREAKFAST, I couldn't find my coffee mug and then remembered it was in my office. I selected another from the cabinet, filled it, and went upstairs, where I discovered my mug was no longer in front of the monitor.

"Oh, no!" I moaned.

Turning on the computer, I checked my "sent" e-mails and saw the one to Cope. How careless I'd been! Marnie knew I didn't use a password; in fact, we had disagreed on the subject. She liked her privacy, she said, and had refused to give me hers. Now, it was very likely Marnie had read my note to Cope—perhaps while I was mowing the grass—and knew about the changes to my will and my suspicions, although last night she had acted as if everything was fine.

My predicament was becoming more disturbing. Unless I grilled her, Marnie would continue her Academy Award performance—that is, until she put her plan into effect. According to the phone conversation I'd overheard, she was supposed to meet her partner today. A sense of foreboding flooded over me. Should I go to the police as my attorney suggested? They might think I was crazy, but it would deter Marnie from whatever she was plotting. Yet what if I was wrong about Marnie? If I reported my concerns and had misunderstood her intentions, my error would be embarrassing at best and would destroy her trust in me at worst. And it was possible she had only noticed my incoming e-mail and not the one sent to Cope. Another reason also existed for me not to call the police—curiosity. This was a dangerous motivation, but I wanted to know what her scheme was. I told myself to improvise for a while longer.

Three hours later, Cope answered.

Dear Alex,

Received your note and was instantly worried. What's going on? Are you in danger from Marnie? Pay attention to how you feel! Certainly, I will be happy to help in any way I can, and I understand the legal documents are temporary. I guess the name of your attorney will be on the will, etc., when it gets here? Let me know more, will you?

Love, Cope

I had a powerful urge to board a plane this afternoon and visit Cope, but I needed to resolve the tangled mess with Marnie, one way or the other.

Dear Cope,

Thanks for your concern. The legal changes are probably precautions—sorry to involve you in them. Unfortunately, Marnie may have logged on to my computer after I sent you the last e-mail, which means she might be aware of the new documents. I don't know how this will affect her behavior, but I've protected my computer with a password and deleted our correspondence.

Don't worry too much, okay? Maybe if she learned all financial benefits to her are gone, she'll lose interest in whatever she had in mind. In other words, I think the motive is now missing.

I'll keep you posted. The attorney's card is in the envelope—consult him if necessary.

Love, Alex

The point about motive was worth considering. If Marnie could no longer gain from our legal agreements, it was logical for her to break up with me, sell the house, and recoup what she could. If she had entered into the connection as a way to bilk money, it should be clear to her now that she wasn't going to get any—that is, if she had read my e-mail to Cope. But this was the rational approach, and this situation was not necessarily rational. Even though her motive had probably been removed, something told me she wouldn't give up. And who knew what her partner's interest was.

I felt a growing tightness in my shoulders. Although Marnie didn't intimidate me physically, her unstable emotional state, quick personality changes, and combustible anger did. The smart thing was to pack as many suitcases as I could fit in my car and move to my father's house immediately, but I hesitated. For the first time in my life, I'd made a commitment. The thought of failing, as I had before in less serious relationships, was depressing. Although my lack of success in the past could be blamed on the lousy role model provided by my parents—they divorced when I was seven and neither remarried—I still accepted most of the responsibility. I'd prevented connection by my incessant traveling and had interrupted problematic affairs by leaving, wandering around Europe like a nomad, drawing and painting, absorbing all the color and beauty of these countries as a way to ignore the absence of beauty I felt in myself.

At the moment, I fervently wished I were in Venice or Tangiers or Istanbul or anywhere else. Instead, I was in a real mess, with no one nearby to call for help—no family and all of my few friends and ex-lovers scattered around the globe. My impetuousness was also keenly embarrassing. How could I admit how foolish I'd been to become financially involved with Marnie after such a short time? As always seemed to be my lot, I would have to go it alone.

I erased all of my e-mails to and from Cope, glad I hadn't saved any that revealed our business connection.

*

All day I kept the doors locked and sat in my studio by the windows, glancing frequently at the driveway, looking for any strange visitors. No one came. When Marnie arrived, she brought a bottle of Moët to celebrate a commission she'd received, saying that when the check cleared, she would pay me two thousand dollars.

"What's the commission for?" I asked, certain the promise was another lie.

"A new account. A manufacturer of X-ray equipment in New York."

At the mention of New York, I thought about the black car and its plates. Perhaps she was involved with someone connected to work?

She reached for two flute glasses and set them on the counter, placing cheese and grapes on a plate. I uncorked the bottle and poured, thinking it was bizarre to drink with someone who was plotting to do me harm. Nevertheless, I toasted her success and remained wary.

We sat in the living room and chatted. The sun was pouring gold on everything in its path, including Marnie's red hair, which glistened. Though I hated to confront her when she was in a good mood, I hoped the mellowness incurred by the Champagne would soften the effect of my questions.

Trying to sound nonchalant, I asked, "Marnie, did you use my computer last night?"

Her eyes flickered for the briefest second. "Yeah, I did."

"How come?"

"I don't want to tell you, darling." She attempted a mischievous look.

"Why?"

"Because it's a surprise." Marnie stared at me. "Well, if you really must know, I was trying to find that office catalogue company you use, the one you told me was bookmarked."

"Why didn't you just ask me for it? Or look it up yourself online."

"I couldn't remember the name." She shrugged. "I thought it would be quicker, and because it's a present—"

"A present?"

"For you." Marnie took a last swallow of her drink. "We need some more." She took my glass and went into the kitchen even though my glass was half full.

I didn't know what to do. If I pursued the matter, everything would erupt.

When Marnie returned, she sat beside me, a little farther away than before. "Alex, what's wrong with my using your computer? All of a sudden you're acting odd."

This maneuver caught me off guard. "I'm fine." I hesitated, before adding, "I guess I was amazed you did, that's all. Remember we had that discussion about privacy? You were the one who insisted on a password for your computer, which you didn't give me."

"That's a habit from work, but you're right. I shouldn't have logged on without your permission. I just didn't think anything of it. Lord, I am so sorry!"

"Well, it's okay. I guess you found the bookmarked website?"

"Yes, I did, thanks." She drank more from her glass and reached for a grape.

Should I tell her that the bookmark had been deleted several weeks ago? Some instinct warned me not to provoke her. Since her comment about my behavior was still hanging between us, I said, "I suppose I have been a little uneven. When I'm in the middle of a new illustration, sometimes I'm distracted."

Marnie nodded and seemed willing to accept this explanation, though it sounded lame to my ears. Maybe we were both avoiding provocation. She leaned over and kissed my cheek.

"Guess we better start supper." Marnie grabbed her glass and walked into the kitchen.

*

She was quiet during dinner. After we finished the Champagne, Marnie opened a bottle of pinot grigio and drank half of it herself. Then she looked at the wall clock and suggested we take a walk. I declined.

"Oh, come on. It's a beautiful night." She glanced at her watch.

The fact that she had checked the time twice and seemed so insistent caught my attention. The property, surrounded by thick trees, would make an ideal location for someone to hide or for activity Marnie might want hidden.

"I don't feel like it tonight, Marnie."

"Oh, honey…tell me why you won't go for a walk?" Whether from the alcohol or annoyance, her face was growing red.

"I'm a little tired."

"You never do what I want."

She wasn't just sulking; she was stoking the fire. I could either agree to an outing or face another derailment. Neither choice was appealing.

I stalled. "I'd like to catch the news."

"That's an excuse."

"How about we do it tomorrow night?"

This attempt at appeasement had as much of an effect as a rowboat's wake on an ocean liner. Marnie stood and threw her napkin on her chair. "Why don't you want to be with me?"

"I do."

"Liar! I'm really sick of this!" She began to stride briskly up and down the kitchen, arms tightly crossed. "Jesus Christ! You're so selfish! All I want is to be together, to go out and enjoy our garden."

The fact that we'd been together for several hours already and were planning to spend the evening with one another seemed to have eclipsed her notice. "I don't see why you're getting so upset. We just had a nice time with the Moët you brought home and—"

"That's not the point."

Though I thought that was exactly the point, I remained silent. This infuriated her. Marnie grabbed her plate, brought it to the sink, and violently scrubbed it before shelving it in the dishwasher.

"Oh, go look at your damned television! You care more about what's happening in…in…" Words failed her as her irritation rose. "*I* am going for a walk and won't be back anytime soon." She tossed the tea towel on the edge of the counter. It fell to the floor. She glowered at its insubordination, snatched it, and threw it at me. "You finish the dishes." With this, she turned sharply, slashed the slider open, slammed it shut, and stormed onto the deck.

After she left, I sat at the table, stunned. Locking her out of the house crossed my mind. The thought was tantalizing, but I needed to know what she was planning because this scene felt contrived, as if Marnie had a schedule.

I decided it would be wise to check the other doors and rose to do so. As I turned the knob on the front door, to my astonishment, it opened. The slide bolt was also drawn back, neither of which had been the case this morning. Had Marnie unlocked the door when I was in the bathroom earlier or before I'd come downstairs from the studio? Had someone entered the house while we were eating in the kitchen? Or was she trying to entice me through the deck door so her partner could sneak in from the front? It was also possible Marnie was on her cell phone, warning her partner that I was on to their plan and it should be revised. Whatever the case, the urgency with which she suggested the walk was very worrisome, as was her abrupt flare of anger.

Quickly, I slid the bolt, twisted the lock, returned to the kitchen, and peeked through the screen. Marnie was nowhere to be seen.

My options were wrenching. Sit and wait for the unknown to happen, go out and find her—thus leaving the house unguarded—or call the police. The last seemed the least comfortable of my choices, though I knew it was the most sensible. But how could I relay my suspicions to someone who didn't know me and didn't know her? Marnie was a superb actress and could easily devise a new plot: I had become violent, and she had run out of the house. I could see the situation unfold and didn't want to risk it. And what about the possibility that someone was already in the house? I was unwilling to check the basement or the upstairs because this would cut me off from fast avenues of escape and take me too far away from the deck door.

It was nearly nine o'clock and growing dark. Marnie had been gone for over twenty minutes. Suddenly, I wondered if she had a weapon hidden somewhere. On impulse, I rushed around the corner of the kitchen to her study, found nothing, then searched the garage. When I tried to open the door to Marnie's Solara, the car was locked, something we never did because our cars were safe within the enclosed garage. I peered through the driver's side window and noticed a red knapsack, one I'd never seen before, and her straw handbag. I ran into the kitchen to check for her set of keys—we usually left them on hooks near the refrigerator—but hers weren't there or in her study. And why was her pocketbook in the car? To facilitate a speedy getaway?

And the knapsack? Did it contain a gun? The thought made me feel sick and dizzy. Although my father had taught me to shoot at a young age, sometime after that, I had developed an extreme abhorrence to guns. Even seeing them on television made me anxious, though I'd never admitted this phobia to anyone. The possibility of a weapon and a person hiding in the house were edging me into panic. I stood by the kitchen table, trying to slow my breathing and get control of my nerves. Just then, Marnie stepped through the trees onto the deck.

Chapter Ten

"I THOUGHT YOU WERE going to look at the news," Marnie reminded me, her face still flushed.

I resisted wiping the perspiration from my forehead because doing so would call attention to my agitation. "Well, I might."

We stood there, staring at each other like two boxers awaiting the starting bell. Finally, Marnie passed by, closer than she needed to, as if trying to intimidate me. My hands tightened, but nothing occurred. I locked the slider, which made me feel safer.

She poured some pinot grigio into her glass. "Want any?"

"No." I waited for her to turn in my direction. "So, what the hell is going on, Marnie?"

She took a swallow of wine. "I could ask you the same damned thing."

"We need to talk." I kept my voice even.

"Yeah, talk. Whatever." Another sip.

Although I hated confrontations, my temper was rising. "I don't think our relationship is working."

Marnie laughed derisively. "You don't, do you?"

"No, I don't." I came around the table. "I'm concerned about a lot of things that have been going on lately. I'm very uncomfortable."

At this, she snorted. "Uncomfortable? My, my. It's always about you, isn't it?"

"How can you say that?" This slipped out despite my determination not to be defensive. "It seems to me that your behavior, your *very changed* behavior, is the issue."

Marnie glanced at me, her eyes hardening. "My behavior?"

"Your drinking, for one thing."

"Come off of it, Alex. You drink as much as I do."

"You're wrong. Besides, when I do drink, my personality

doesn't change. I don't get mad." I knew it was pointless to pursue the conversation.

As if to annoy me, Marnie refilled her glass. When she raised it to her lips, she spilled a few drops, cursed, and added more wine. Disgusted, I walked into the living room and sat in my chair. Marnie followed and perched on its arm.

"So, what do you want to do, Alex? Cut and run? That's what you always do, isn't it?"

I regretted telling her about my past lovers. She hadn't been forthcoming about her own, leaving me to conclude she had lived alone most of her life except for a series of short-term affairs, which she described as abusive and controlling. In hindsight, the total of what I knew about her from fact was painfully slight.

"That's not fair, Marnie. And the situation isn't the same."

"Damned right," she said, swirling the wine in her glass. "You made a commitment to me. We bought a house together."

"How could I forget?" I retorted. "Yes, we did make a commitment, but I don't like what's happening."

She laughed. "My goodness! You don't like what's happening? Well, stop the world, I want to get off." Marnie set the wine glass on the table.

"Let's not argue about this."

"Argue? We're not arguing, are we, honey?"

This dialogue was futile. "I think we should admit we made a mistake, list the house for sale, and go our separate ways."

"You do, do you? Just like that?" She snapped her fingers, the sound loud and sharp. "Well, what if I don't feel like going my separate way, huh? What if I don't want to sell the house?" She smiled, but the smile was at war with her eyes, which glowed with hostility. "I like this place. I really do. We're staying here until I say."

I stared at her, repulsed by so much that had previously attracted me: her over-wide, loose mouth, full breasts in the tight knit blouse, and rounded bottom in clinging pants. "I'm calling a realtor in the morning. We can probably get most of our money out."

I started to rise out of the chair, but she shoved me back and laughed harshly at my shocked reaction. "And then you're going to call your new attorney? No, dear, I don't think so." Her smile disappeared. "I think you're going to call your attorney all right, but not about selling the house." She took a lock of my hair and set it in place gently, yet with so much menace that a chill fluttered down my back. "No, sweetie, we're good." She brushed her fingers across my forehead.

There was an eerie mix of malevolence and desire in her expression, as if some part of her wanted me in bed and another part wanted me dead. And I had been correct. She had read the e-mail to Cope.

"We're not fine, Marnie. I'll phone Sarah in the morning."

She draped her arm around my neck and reached down and nuzzled my ear. "Oh, come on, baby. You love me. I know you do."

"Stop it!" I pushed her away. "Yeah, I did love you. Or I loved what you pretended to be. Christ, you're sick."

She slapped me hard on the side of the face. I clenched my fists, trying to control the urge to hit her and was astonished at the blazing rage I felt. I wanted to break her in two. The fact that I could had a somewhat steadying effect.

"You had no right to do that," I told her coldly.

Marnie caressed my cheek, mimicking concern. "Oh, darling, I'm sorry. Alex, look, let's just talk."

I came to my feet so fast that Marnie was forced to stand. "You don't know how to talk, Marnie. I'm through."

Her seductive smile became laced with malice. "No, you're not through. Not yet."

I took a step toward her, drawn in, regardless of a powerful desire to fly from the room. "I'll write you a check for my half of the house bills—for four months. That should be enough time to sell the place. Or you can give me a check for what I paid and the money you owe me for improvements, and I'll transfer the mortgage to you. Whatever you want. I'm done."

"You know I can't pay that much."

"Then the damned house goes on the market, Marnie. That's

it!" I yelled.

"Well, I have another alternative in mind." Her voice slowed to a creepy drawl. "Maybe you'll buy me out. I was thinking of a sum in the neighborhood of $500,000."

"What do you mean? The mortgage company owns most of the house. Just reimburse me and do what the hell you like."

"Oh, but the property value has risen, Alex. There are closing costs. Stress." She shrugged and finished the wine. "And I should get something for my inconvenience." Marnie smiled suggestively at me. "A great deal of inconvenience. Besides, you've got the dough."

"I don't have that kind of money. I used nearly all of my savings when we purchased the house." This wasn't true, but thankfully she didn't know that.

She wagged a finger at me. "Oh, I think you're fibbing just a little."

"You're crazy! I haven't received any commissions since we moved in. I would've told you if I had."

Marnie looked smug and laughed. "Oh, yes, but you own all those nice bonds, don't you, Alex? And you've got, oh, let's see, 600 shares of IBM and a nice pile of Exxon, Microsoft, GM, GE, and lots of cash waiting around on hand. How much was that? Oh, maybe, as I recall, around $65,000, give or take the checks you write off the account." She smiled. "In fact, the last time I looked, you were worth over a million—and that's not including this house and your car."

I was outraged. "You went over my financial statements?"

"I didn't think we had any secrets from each other. Besides, I had to protect my investment."

I howled at this. "Secrets? You've plotted this from the very beginning, haven't you? Obviously, you searched through all my things."

"Now, now, honey. There's no plot. I just need to come out of this with some money. I don't have tons of it lying around like you do."

"A little money? Do you call $500,000 a decent return on your investment? I call it robbery!"

"Oh, dear, you are not seeing this in the proper light. I guess you'll learn the hard way that you should be more generous."

I ignored this comment. The sooner I left the house, the better. It was very fortunate Marnie didn't know about my father's place. I'd pack some clothes, my work files and computer, and then ditch this nightmare.

Quickly, I walked through the foyer, my shoes resounding on the marble tiles. The bedroom door was ajar as I strode into the hall next to the closet. Suddenly, from the corner of my vision, a dark form rushed out behind me. Before I could spin around, a large cloth was thrust into my face, the last thing I remembered before I lost consciousness.

Chapter Eleven

THE BIRDS were chattering in the trees when I awoke. I was facing away from the center of the living room, sitting in Marnie's wing-backed, green-plaid armchair, bound to it with white laundry line. My feet were tied with the same rope, my hands were duct-taped together in front of me, and my wristwatch had been removed. A fierce headache was pounding a war-drum beat, my mouth was horribly dry, and nausea churned my stomach, but as bad as I felt physically, my mind was in worse turmoil.

Noises emanated from the kitchen. Marnie was telling someone that I was awake. I heard a second set of footsteps, but the person didn't speak, or at least the voice wasn't audible from where I sat. The windows opposite didn't reflect anything because the blinds were down.

Marnie brought me a cup of coffee. "Here, Alex." She held it to my lips and laughed when a little dribbled down my chin onto my white polo shirt. "Oops, a spill. How clumsy of you." She returned with a bowl of soggy oatmeal, food she knew I detested.

"I don't want any of that," I said.

She shrugged. "Sure? We have to keep you in good shape. You have a lot to do."

I looked at her with revulsion. "Let me loose right now."

Marnie called to the person in the kitchen. "Alex says we should untie her. Imagine!" She giggled unpleasantly. "No, sugar, I think we have other activities in mind. First on the agenda: shopping, and then we'll check your finances. Now, what's your computer password?"

"I'm not going to tell you what it is, and you'll never guess."

"Hmm, that's a problem that requires a solution."

Marnie walked away to have a discussion with her accomplice, then returned holding a .38 Smith & Wesson Police Special, a snub nose model. I gasped in shock and clamped my eyes shut.

"I think you better not refuse." She smiled, quietly triumphant. "Now, what's the password?"

My mind raced, spinning with panic. Even with my eyes closed, I saw an after-image of the gun, its black center surrounded by silver. I willed myself to forget about the revolver and deal with the predicament, one without much likelihood of rescue. Besides the attorney, who had only met me once and had no reason to call the police, Cope would worry when she didn't hear from me, but she lived in California, and it would take days or even a week of silence before her suspicions would be aroused. If Cope then reported my absence to the authorities, Marnie could easily produce explanations to waylay their curiosity.

I opened my eyes and observed the resolution on Marnie's face. "The password is Pushkin," I replied, as the coffee burned in my gut.

"Very clever, Alex. You're right, I never would have thought of it. Oh, and your brokerage account User ID and password? It's Saturday, but we need current information to finalize our plans. And in case something happens to you." Marnie stuck the tip of the gun in my right ear.

I shivered as the cold metal touched me. Sweat rolled down my temples and along the length of my neck.

My terror turned her on. "That feels good, doesn't it? You like that, don't you?" She traced the side of my face, set the gun down, and stood in front of me. "Come on. Tell me."

I let out a slow, shaky breath and whispered the password and the digits and letters that accessed my account, praying my broker would balk at any strange requests when he read them in an e-mail on Monday morning.

Marnie wrote the information on a notepad. "That's better, dear. Now, shopping. You sit tight." She took the paper and gun to the bedroom, telling her partner to follow.

I let my head fall against the back of the armchair and waited. When Marnie began speaking on the telephone, I tried to loosen the duct tape around my wrists and wriggle my feet out of the rope, but the bindings were too tight. About twenty minutes later, Marnie walked into the room alone.

"Well, Alex, we certainly had fun."

"What did you do?" I asked angrily.

"Bought some things. My word, Alex, you have so many nice credit cards! All paid off and ready for action. And shame on you for giving the impression you were behind on your Visa, MasterCard, and American Express. Really, sweetie, you've been secretive. We selected two great Rolex watches. Of course that blew your maximum credit limit on one card. Watches are easy to hock if you know the right people, but I may keep mine. I think we'll have plenty of money, don't you?" Marnie grinned at me. "More shopping later. First," she dangled my car keys in front of my face, "my friend is taking your Jeep for a little spin. You won't need it any longer." She sat across from me, laying her cup of coffee on the table beside me. "You know, it was difficult timing all of this. Two days ago, we began running an ad in the paper to sell the Jeep, listing my partner's cell number. I was worried the ad might be premature, but we guessed right." Marnie smiled at me and then stared at her burnished crimson nails. "You'll never find the ad, by the way, and even if you do, the number is listed to someone who doesn't exist. We were lucky to get a buyer immediately, someone who didn't ask questions and was willing to meet us at the mall. We could probably get more for the car, but it's being sold for cash. Pity. I liked the Jeep, but it isn't red, and you know I always have red cars. Oh, and I found your title in that gray metal box you keep upstairs behind your books."

Silently, I cursed my laziness. I had intended to put the title in my safe deposit box several months ago and had forgotten about it. The Jeep was new, purchased shortly before we met. It would fetch about $25,000.

"Why don't you sign the title now, okay, dear?"

"No."

"Come on, what's a car compared to your life?" Marnie rose, set the gun on the table, removed a matt knife from her pocket, and placed the blade against my neck until I acquiesced. She then used the knife to slice enough tape to free my right hand. I could barely hold a pen but managed to sign the title. "Don't fret about the sale. We'll take care of the details. And while we're at it, Alex, let's make out a few checks, maybe three, two to yourself."

I gritted my teeth, furious at Marnie and furious at myself for being so trusting. She produced my checkbook and studied the balance.

"Hmm. We can withdraw $2,000 at one time at the drive-through. Let's see. Write one check for $1,950 with today's date and one for $1,975 for Monday—both to you. Then make another check out to me for $1,200, for today, which I'll either cash or deposit at my ATM. That will leave about $100 in your account."

I followed instructions, though my handwriting was unsteady, and my palm was sweating from nervousness about the gun, which she now tucked in the waistband of her red shorts, and the matt knife, which she held in her left hand.

"There," Marnie said with pleasure. "That ought to help with the cost of doing business."

I endorsed the back of the two checks and watched as she placed all three in her pocket. "I have to use the bathroom," I said, wondering if this would require her partner to enter the room. I'd assumed the person was female because of Marnie's sexual orientation, but so much about Marnie had proved false, it was possible the accomplice was a man.

"Do you? Well, all right. No puddles on the expensive carpet." She went into the kitchen and returned with a pink cotton bandana, tying it over my eyes. I heard the second person approach and felt someone loosening the ropes around my feet and the chair. With one of them on each side, I was abruptly lifted up and hauled through the foyer. They pushed me into the bathroom, unzipped my pants, thrust a wad of toilet paper between my fingers, and retreated into the hall.

After I finished, we returned to the living room, the rope was replaced at my feet, more tape was secured around my hands, and the rope was tied around my chest. I tried to sense the identity of the second person—a scent of perfume or after-shave—but without any success. Then I heard keys jingling over my head.

"My friend is going to meet the car buyer and visit your bank on the way. You don't mind, do you?" Marnie asked. "We have your license for identification."

I didn't reply, though I was now more certain Marnie's partner was female—someone who resembled me sufficiently to safely pass the drive-through's security cameras and also satisfy the car buyer if he or she inspected the limited description on my driver's license—age, height, weight, and eye and hair color. Knowing the gender made me optimistic about my chances if an opportunity arose to fight, even though the gun provided them with an overpowering advantage. I was also hopeful that I might be able to persuade Marnie to abandon their scheme.

A few minutes later, I heard the garage door open and the Jeep's engine. As the cranking of the pulley chains signaled the door was being closed, Marnie loosened the bandana around my eyes and used it to gag my mouth. "By ourselves at last. Now, I don't want you yelling for the mailman."

The mailbox was on the street, a considerable distance away, and I was sitting in the living room, on the far side of the house. Our rural location precluded the possibility of anyone being close enough to hear my shouts for help, especially with the windows shut because of the air-conditioning. I was beginning to appreciate why Marnie was so enchanted when she saw this place. Or had she discovered the house ahead of time and driven me to it deliberately? Yes, of course Marnie had.

"I think we'll do some more shopping. What do you say to that?"

Nothing, since I had a gag in my mouth.

"Let's see: L.L. Bean, Tiffany's, Coach, and so many others. What would you buy, Alex, if you had your money?" She laughed and fanned an array of catalogues on the table. "I'll only order what can be shipped express mail to arrive Monday or Tuesday and will insist they send without requiring a signature. I don't want the delivery guy to knock on the door. He'll drop off the packages just like he does for your business. Isn't that a good idea?"

The rhetorical questions were irritating. I was also worrying about the credit card and checkbook joined to my brokerage account. I rarely used either, but as far as I could recall, the card was in the closet, in my winter pocketbook, and the checkbook was in my office filing cabinet. To withdraw money or buy anything using that account, they would need one of them.

Marnie plopped merrily on the couch with the portable phone and began examining a stack of catalogues. With my other two credit cards in hand, she ordered a London Fog raincoat, some summer dresses, blouses, skirts, a silk suit, and a Coach handbag. Then she concentrated on jewelry catalogues and spent thousands more until the limits had been reached on the two remaining cards.

"Oh, dear, my mistake," she told the person on the phone. "Just send the first three items, thanks." She ended the call. "Too bad I had to stop." She sighed and walked into the kitchen to prepare lunch while I totaled the credit maximums on my cards. Marnie had spent at least $28,000. I felt sick.

Lunch was miserable. Cheese sandwiches with too much mayonnaise and a glass of tepid water. After I finished, Marnie left the gag off, probably because the mailman had been by already.

"What are you going to do with all of this stuff you're ordering?" I asked.

"Keep some of it. Sell some."

"And what are you going to do about me?"

She shrugged. "Don't know. We'll have to see how things turn out. Oh, by the way. I applied for our home equity loan."

I was astonished. "How did you do that?"

"No problem. I got the forms, finished the application, forged your signature as co-owner, and brought the papers to the bank last week. The manager was an absolute darling and promised everything would be ready on Monday." She stretched contentedly. "And I upped the amount to $35,000 rather than the $15,000 we were planning and asked for the check to be written in my name. So much more expedient."

I wasn't sure how long it would take the home equity check to clear Marnie's account once it was deposited. Perhaps two business days, which meant Marnie and her partner would stay in the house until Tuesday or Wednesday, and hopefully I would too. They also seemed intent on liquidating my stock investments, which couldn't be done until Monday. A few days would be required for transactions to settle and the catalogue deliveries to arrive, even with express service. I might get lucky and a UPS or Fed Ex delivery man would come to the door, but they were accustomed to leaving packages in the drop-off box. Help from that quarter wasn't likely unless someone new was on the route.

*

The afternoon sun poured through the skylights, illuminating Marnie as she drank from a bottle of beer. "Mmm, this is good." She ripped open a bag of Fritos and pressed one against my lips.

I twisted away.

She came closer, put the bottle of beer to my mouth, and tipped it so I had to drink to avoid spilling. I coughed.

"Pretty good, huh?"

Marnie leaned over, licked my lips, and tried to force her tongue into my mouth. I kept my teeth clenched.

"So, you want to play coy?" She gave me a flirtatious glance and sat on top of my bound hands and began to rock back and forth. "Oh, baby, that feels good!" She leaned over and nipped my neck, at first playfully, but as I turned my head away, Marnie bit harder, drawing blood that dripped slowly onto the collar of my shirt. Staring at me for a minute, she bit me again, and with long sweeps of her tongue, followed the line up to my ear. I shuddered involuntarily.

"Getting turned on, Alex? Me too. Hey, just like old times." Marnie tried to kiss me again, but I jerked away. Standing up suddenly, she punched my stomach. "That's what you get, and that's just the beginning." She glared at me and stalked off to the kitchen. The refrigerator slammed shut. I assumed Marnie had removed another beer.

An hour or so later, I heard the front door open and close, the rustle of grocery bags, and the sound of bottles being placed on the counter. Had her accomplice gone shopping near the mall and taken the bus to the house?

Dinner was pre-cooked veal parmigiana, never a favorite of mine. Marnie and her pal were enjoying themselves, if the clicking of glasses and the pop of a cork were indicative. Marnie fed me, though the tomato and cheese lay heavily on my stomach. Sometime later, I was escorted into the bathroom, then returned to the hated armchair, and my face covered with a chloroform rag until I passed out.

Chapter Twelve

ON SUNDAY MORNING, I felt sick and groggy. When Marnie walked into the living room, she didn't look so hot, either. After she covered my eyes with the bandana, she and her partner led me to the bathroom and then back to the chair.

"Too bad you woke up, dear, 'cause we have some things to attend to." I smelled chloroform. "And too bad this is the last of it. Sweet dreams!"

*

When I came to, I couldn't see because of the bandana, but Marnie must have noticed me stirring.

"Hungry?" she asked, as she removed the kerchief.

I nodded, though I had doubts about eating anything. Marnie scrambled some eggs and used a fork to bulldoze them into my mouth. After washing the dishes and allowing a bathroom break, she disappeared until late afternoon.

*

Dinner was a fried hamburger and baked beans.

"Are we having a picnic?" I remarked.

"Shut up, Alex." Marnie jammed a spoonful of food between my lips and began chatting about nothing in particular. Her speech was slurred, probably from wine, which I could smell on her breath. The accomplice remained in the kitchen, most likely sitting at the table. Although I was extremely curious as to the other person's identity, all I could hear were occasional murmurs after Marnie joined her or him and the rattle of silverware. The lights were off to give the impression that no one was home.

After dark, I was blindfolded again and brought into the bathroom. I surmised Marnie's partner was stronger because of the tighter grip on my arm. Both reeked of liquor. The sweet odor added to my troubled stomach. I told them I felt ill. Marnie must have moved her friend into the hall because she took off the bandana as well as one strip of tape so I could hold more toilet paper. Just in time, too, since I was violently sick. Marnie left, though I heard her whispering in the foyer. Even though I feared I was going to vomit again, I used the tips of my fingers to open the drawer by the sink and ease out a small nail file. After closing the drawer, I shoved the file between the duct tape and my wrists and prayed it would be obscured from view in the dimly lit room. Then I hurried to the toilet before another bout.

Marnie returned, flushed the toilet, and wiped my mouth with a damp cloth. She gave me a swallow of water to rinse.

"Are you done?"

"Let me sit here for a minute. Got to pee."

This annoyed Marnie, but she agreed. When I finished, she helped me brush my teeth, replaced the blindfold, and led me into the living room, where I banged my shin against the coffee table. Marnie pushed me into the chair as her partner bound my chest and feet with laundry line. After she or he left, Marnie untied the bandana. Because of the high back of the chair and its angle, I couldn't see the kitchen, though I heard another bottle being uncorked. Who the hell was Marnie with? Evidently the person wanted to prevent me from making an identification if I got free, hence the bandana and the position of the chair. Although this explanation was logical, I couldn't shake a feeling of familiarity, as if I knew the person, but who would perpetrate a crime like this?

Sometime later, chairs shuffled on the kitchen floor, and there were faint whispers, none of which revealed the gender of the other speaker. Marnie entered the living room and stood beside me. Even in the muted light, I could see high color on her cheeks.

"Nite-nite, Alex," she said. "Sleep tight!" She laughed at her cleverness and left.

Soon, I heard water running in the sink, dishes and glasses being placed in the drain rack, and more unintelligible conversation before Marnie moaned sexily.

"My, my! We're going to have fun. In our great big bed." Her voice was loud, as if she was speaking for my benefit. "Mmm. Oh, you are so damned hot!" More noise. Marnie's throaty laugh. "Alexandra? We have urgent business to attend to...and it simply cannot wait!" There were sounds of foreplay and Marnie chuckled. "We'll leave the door open so you can hear everything."

True to her promise, they went into the bedroom. Marnie moaned again, either for her partner's sake or mine. She cried out several times before all became silent. I supposed a night of drinking had impeded a night of lengthy lovemaking.

After waiting until I thought they were asleep, I worked the nail file out and held it in my right hand. With as much force as I could muster at such an awkward angle, I thrust the file into the tape and sawed until my fingers went numb. I switched the file to my left hand and bent my right as far as it would go, trying to restore circulation. For what seemed an eternity, I continued this tedious process, goaded by anger, until the layers of duct tape were cut. Then I drew up my legs until my fingers could reach the rope's knots. When I was able to release the laundry line tying my lower legs together, I was still bound under my arms, across my chest, and tied at the back of the chair below its flared wings, which prevented me from sliding the rope upward. The nail file would take too long to slice the rope, but there was a pair of scissors in the kitchen. Could I lift the chair on my back like a turtle carrying its shell? This feat had to be accomplished quietly so Marnie or her partner wouldn't hear me banging around.

I rested for a few seconds and tried to stand but nearly toppled over to the side because the chair was much heavier than I had imagined, and my method of carrying it was incredibly clumsy. When I regained my balance, I tucked into a crouch and shuffled forward, listening for sounds from the bedroom.

The pocket entry into the kitchen was narrower than a standard door and not wide enough for the chair. I cursed in silence, feeling exhausted and frustrated, until I remembered the carving set in the dining room cabinet. Though I nearly knocked over a side table, I spread my feet wide for balance, eased open a drawer, and lifted the lid of the cherry box. After selecting a short bone-handled knife, I hobbled to the end of the living room so

Marnie couldn't see me from the bed. My knees and back were burning from the effort, but I managed to lower the chair onto the floor with me in it. When I landed, a burst of air blew through my lips. For a moment, I sat there, catching my breath, and then began attacking the ropes with the sharp knife until I was free.

Now what? I couldn't hang around because either Marnie or her friend might wake. I snuck into the kitchen and saw my checkbook and credit cards. I pocketed everything, furious at Marnie's cold-blooded abuse and itching for revenge. From a hook, I removed her car keys, thinking to steal her Solara, even though she might hear the garage door open. Then I realized her partner had a car. I peeked out the window and any hopes of an automotive theft and getaway died: a black sedan was parked in the driveway, blocking the garage. I searched for its keys in the kitchen but couldn't find them.

I left Marnie's keys on the counter and stood there, shaking, as adrenaline juiced my nerves, and a lethal mix of fight-or-flee urges bombarded me. I had to get out of the house immediately.

I slipped the carving knife under my shirt and belt, against the small of my back, hurried into the kitchen, noted the time—2:26 a.m.—and stepped to the slider. After lifting the dowel rod from the track, I unlatched the door, crept outside, and took a welcome lungful of cool air that smelled of grass, pine, and freedom. I savored this for a second, then dashed around the house and peered through the window of the sedan. No keys were in the ignition.

"Damn!" I muttered. What should I do now?

It was still dark, but the house and garden were illuminated by the moon, which spread its silver light across the yard and cast black shadow-tentacles from the oak and chestnut trees on the white concrete driveway. The night hummed with sounds from the nearby forest, and a breeze filtered through the leaves. I bent low, rushed down the path toward the front door, veered to the right, and edged through a row of bushes. Just as I did, I felt something brush my face. Startled, I jumped backward and then realized a spider had spun a web in the shrubbery. After waiting for my heart to stop pounding, I inched toward the bedroom window. The blinds were down, but one slat was twisted, through which I spied Marnie's hand draped languidly over the bed and the revolver on the table next to her, lit by the green light from her digital clock. The Smith & Wesson seemed to glow, repelling and attracting me at the same time. For a moment, I hesitated until a fiery anger was ignited. That gun made the difference between us. If I had it, I'd be in control.

An intelligent person would have run to the nearest neighbor and called the police. Part of me wanted to do just that, but there was the question of settling the score with Marnie and her unknown friend. If I left them and they woke and discovered my escape, they could flee before the police arrived and avoid punishment. I couldn't let that happen. I needed to avenge the hours sitting helplessly in the chair, the humiliation I'd endured, the havoc they had inflicted upon my credit cards and checking account, and the theft of my Jeep. I was boiling mad at Marnie, that traitorous seductress who had turned me into a love-struck, gullible sucker. I clenched my jaw. No, I wouldn't leave. I was obsessed to learn the identity of the person abetting Marnie and to have the satisfaction of trussing both of them in chairs until the police arrived and carted them away.

After retreating to the path, I sprinted around the house and stood by the slider to steel my nerve. Then I entered through the deck door, slipped through the kitchen and foyer, and stopped in the hall leading to the bedroom. The room was almost dark except for the faint light from the window on Marnie's side. As far as I could see, her accomplice was buried under a mound of bedding.

Grateful for the thickly padded carpet, I knelt on both knees, retrieved the knife from under my belt, and crawled around the corner of the bed. When I approached the end table, I switched the knife to my left hand and reached for the Smith & Wesson. My fingers were trembling as I grasped the gun, which felt like burning metal in my palm.

A wave of dizziness swept over me, and I rested my forehead on the carpet until the room slowed its tornadic spinning. Finally, holding both weapons, I inched backward until I was by the foot of the bed. I swerved, rose to a crouch, exited through the foyer, and hurried into the laundry room. There, I nervously checked that the gun's safety was on and inspected the swing-out cylinder: fully loaded, six bullets. I stared at the heavy piece of steel and heard the sound of gunshots reverberating in my head. For a moment, I thought the gun had fired, but it hadn't.

Scared by this hallucination, I staggered against the wall, my legs weak, and tried desperately to think. I had seen enough crime and police shows to know it wasn't a smart idea to put fingerprints on a weapon in circumstances like these. After donning two latex gloves from a shelf near the washing machine, I removed a towel from the laundry basket, dampened the cloth in the utility sink, added soap, and rubbed the revolver and the knife clean of prints, then rinsed and dried the outsides of the gloves, leaving them on. I repositioned the knife under my shirt and picked up the .38, feeling more confident, although the gun made me feel queasy. I reviewed the option of barricading myself in the studio and phoning the police; however, the connecting door was hollow, with a flimsy lock, and easy to kick in, nor did I know who was with Marnie. It was possible he or she also had a gun.

The more I analyzed the situation, the more fixated I became about the second person. I retraced my steps to the bedroom. From the hallway, I saw that Marnie had turned over and now faced the center of the bed, with her foot on top of the cream-colored sheets. As I came closer, I looked at the cluster of covers on the left side and was stunned to see no one there. Had Marnie shifted the bedspread in her sleep or had someone thrown them off and hidden?

I wheeled around, the gun held in front, and checked the closet and the bathroom. Although it was disturbing to leave Marnie behind me with someone else in the house, someone who might be armed, I had to find her partner.

It was prudent to assume he or she knew the weapon was in my possession. I looked through the bathroom window at the black car. If the partner meant to run, exiting through the front door while

I was in the laundry room would have been simple, though I might have heard the door open. Did my enemy intend to stay and fight?

I edged down the short hall and glanced into the foyer. The front door was still locked and bolted. In the living room, nothing appeared changed. Was someone hiding behind the chair or by the end of the sofa? If I entered the foyer for a better look, I would be exposed in the open space. Have patience, I counseled. My adversary would risk a peek eventually.

After a few minutes, I decided no one was in the living room. This left the upper-level bathroom and bedrooms as the most likely places because my studio was only accessible via the stairs by the laundry room, where I'd just been. The basement could be ruled out because a case of wine was pushed against the door and hadn't been moved.

Quickly, I covered the distance to the staircase and ascended. Every tread seemed to groan, making me wonder whether I would have been alerted if anyone had climbed to the second floor. At the top, I checked around the corner. There was no one in the hall. The only noises were the air compressor whirring outside and the soft rush of air through the vents. I stepped into the doorway of the larger bedroom, where I could see most of the room and under the tall four-poster bed. The mirror over the chest of drawers reflected the other section. Empty.

I knew Marnie had crammed the closet with clothes and boxes, making it impossible for anyone to hide inside. Turning sharply on the hall carpet, I tiptoed to the bathroom and entered. Perhaps I'd seen too many scary movie scenes in bathtubs, but I felt a formidable dread about pulling back the shower curtain. If someone was there and armed, I would be an easy target. I slid a towel off the rack, balled it up, and threw the towel into the curtain using my left hand. Nothing happened. After suffering through a bout of breathlessness, I forced myself to draw the curtain. No one was there.

Just then, I heard Marnie downstairs.

"Alexandra?" She sounded frightened.

I didn't know what to do. Should I tie her in the chair or keep looking? She was unarmed and couldn't drive the car out of the garage because of the sedan. I decided to finish my search for her accomplice before dealing with Marnie. Silently, I slipped into the other guest room. The spaces between the twin beds and to the side of the right one were vacant. The beds were too low for someone to fit underneath. That left the closet and the far side of the twin bed or next to the armoire.

It was now or never. I crashed my shoulder against the dresser, sliding it several feet, but nothing stirred. Then I tore open the closet door. I was alone.

"Where are you?" Marnie was mounting the stairs.

When she walked into the room, she stopped abruptly. I pointed the revolver at her, my arms growing inexplicably weak. For some reason, she laughed, as if the scene was wildly amusing.

"Alex, there's no one here."

I didn't respond because I felt foolish charging around in an unoccupied room.

"Come on. Let's go to the kitchen, have a cup of coffee, and talk everything over." She said this calmly.

"Marnie, there's nothing to talk over. Where is your partner?"

She shrugged. "Gone."

"I doubt it." I gestured for her to exit the room ahead of me. As we went downstairs, she kept saying my name, over and over. I wished she would be quiet so I could hear other sounds in the house.

In the foyer, she said, "Sweetie, put down the gun."

This last comment was spoken loud enough to warn her partner that I had the Smith & Wesson. Did she know where the other person was?

"Go and sit in the chair," I told her.

"Alex, don't do this. We can cancel all the stuff, put the house on the market, and go our separate ways like you wanted."

I laughed. "I would love to do that, but the milk of human kindness has curdled just a bit." I pointed at the spot on my neck where she had bitten me. "You seem to have a very short memory."

"Okay, so I got carried away. It was sort of sexy, you know, having you all tied up. I thought you liked that sort of thing." Her voice took on the smoky tone I had previously found alluring. She started to close the distance between us. "Sugar, I couldn't help it. I got turned on. You know how I am."

"I know exactly how you are. Sit down."

Her expression turned sulky. "This is ridiculous. Let's just forget about the whole thing."

"No. Sit."

Marnie finally did as I asked. I picked up the rope, and just as I managed to form a slipknot while holding the revolver, a voice came from behind me.

Chapter Thirteen

"DON'T TURN AROUND." It was a man. Standing very close behind me. "Marnie, take the gun."

I froze. The voice was familiar. I pointed the Smith & Wesson at Marnie, who had risen. "No, don't move," I told her. There was no way to miss Marnie if I took a shot.

"A classical standoff?" the man said. "Checkmate? I don't care if you shoot her. Go ahead. You'll take a bullet as soon as you pull the trigger. Now, put the gun down."

Crows were waking in the pine forest, their raucous voices calling to each other. My legs felt weak, like I might collapse.

"And don't turn around," he repeated.

I believed he would kill me. Slowly, I placed the revolver on the end table.

Marnie smiled. "See there, now we can have a nice little chat." She rose, picked up the weapon, and pushed the armchair to face the windows. "Sit."

I stared at the silver barrel, which grew larger as Marnie stepped closer. I sat, wishing the chair was pointed in the direction of the man.

Marnie laughed and said to him, "That was pretty cool! I mean, you didn't even have a gun."

The man laughed with her. There had been no second weapon. I shook my head at my stupidity. I had fallen for a trick every kid has seen countless times on television.

"Good work," Marnie said. "Hiding under the bed so Alex thought you were somewhere else in the house. You even fooled me."

I ached to look at the man. "Who are you?" The feeling of familiarity was increasing. Was I connected to him because of Marnie, or was he directly linked to me?

He asked Marnie to give him the revolver, which she did. "Tie Alex up."

As she leaned down to grasp the rope, I swiftly removed the knife from my belt, jumped to my feet, and threw my arm around Marnie. She fell against my chest as I whipped the blade to her neck and turned to see my adversary. There, in front of me, stood a mirror image of myself, even wearing a white polo shirt. My mouth dropped open.

A smile slowly spread across his face, my face. "Hello, Alexandra."

Stunned, I saw my fraternal twin. The room tilted and seemed to collapse into a distorted mess of walls and windows. "Alex…you're dead…"

Marnie tried to pry herself loose. In my alarm, I almost released her but then tightened my grip. My mind was reeling with confusion, shocked into blankness.

"Nearly dead." As if he didn't care about Marnie, my brother calmly opened the blinds using his left hand while holding the gun in his right. The early morning light flooded his face.

My twin appeared to be two inches taller than me, about five-ten, with a slim, athletic build like mine. His hair was black and fairly short, with bangs swept to the right and sides brushed above his ears in a style almost identical to my own—or rather, the style Marnie had created for me and presumably for him. Alex's eyes were the same dark blue, and we shared our father's broad forehead and straight nose, our mother's mouth and coloring. His face was slightly more angular, but otherwise we were remarkably similar. And, like our features, we shared the name of Alex: his for Alexander, mine for Alexandra.

"You look pretty good, dear sister of mine. Grew a bit, didn't you?"

I was speechless.

"You really thought I was dead?" he asked.

"Yes," I whispered.

"I guess that's obvious." Alex studied me for a moment, as if my reaction baffled him. "Well, I was almost dead, wasn't I? I guess in most ways I am." He sat in a chair by the sofa but kept the gun trained on me.

I couldn't believe my brother was alive. My ears filled with noise; my vision danced.

"So, do you want to hear the story?"

I nodded.

"I'm sure you know some of it, Alex. That Father and I went hunting for lion and cape buffalo."

He was speaking of the trip to Zimbabwe, in the Zambezi Valley, when we were nineteen, a safari organized by our father.

"I don't remember much."

"No? I wonder why?" His eyes hardened, as did his tone. "We missed you, Alex. We really did, but you didn't miss us." He stared at me and waited, as if he expected me to reply. Then he smiled. "Oh, but that's right…you couldn't get out of bed that morning to join us, could you? Must have been a very special late night."

I was silent. My head throbbed with pressure. "I don't—"

"Recall?" My brother gave me a strange smile. "Maybe your memory needs refreshing. Damn, it was hot."

I remembered we had been there several days and recalled the valley's heat and how the muddy rivers overflowed their banks after the end of rainy season, how the thick, brown water cascaded over ash-gray rocks. I tried to picture Alex and my father in the bush but couldn't.

"What happened?" My voice sounded faint.

"Forgot, did you?" He snorted. "Well, I got shot."

I swallowed hard. "Who…?"

Alex's eyes held mine in a visual lock. He chuckled at some private amusement. "I suppose it was some dumb hunter who didn't see me in the tall grass…next thing I knew, I was on the ground, bleeding."

"But how…?" I seemed unable to formulate a complete question.

"How did I survive?" He gave a bitter laugh. "Three Tonga tribesmen found me. I must have been unconscious when they brought me to a dusty hut in their village. I had a high fever because the wound had become infected, and I'd been burned, lying exposed to the sun. The women covered my chest with all kinds of leaves and roots and crap. Luckily, the bullet went straight through, but it sure left a big hole." He tugged his white shirt to expose a jagged, red scar several inches long. "My souvenir of our trip to Zimbabwe."

My throat constricted. Marnie struggled against me, complaining. I pulled her closer, as if she could protect me from the sight of my brother's wound.

Alex continued. "Of course, when I got out of that godforsaken place weeks later and returned to my room one night late, everything was gone—my money, passport, clothes. Imagine how I felt when I learned my sweet sister had left with all my stuff." His eyes were luminous with anger.

"I didn't know what to do. I waited for days. The police finally told me there was no way you could survive…what with the lions and—"

"Oh, yeah, the lions. What we were there to kill. Bloody stupid idea of Father's."

I looked at the floor. "I guess you don't know about Dad, then, do you?"

My brother's face went taut, but he didn't answer.

"They found him dead."

"Really." He didn't sound surprised.

I nodded. "His body was badly mauled. They weren't even sure it was him except for his clothes and some shredded papers in his jacket."

My brother was quiet, his eyes glittering, his mouth twitching into a cruel smile. "Did anyone bother to look for me?"

His disinterest in our father's death was surprising. "Yes, a large force and some trackers. They found Dad's body and decided he had been attacked by a lion and fell and struck his head on a rock. Because more blood was nearby, they thought the lion had carried you off. However, they didn't understand why your rifles were missing. Guess the Tongas took them."

"Guess they did. So, did you search too? Huh?" he asked in a nasty tone.

"I...yes...but when we didn't find you...well...the commissioner told me it could be a long time before they located you. Your body, that is. I didn't want to leave. Mother insisted. Told the embassy to send me home. I flew on the plane with Dad's coffin. We kept hoping to hear news about you, but we never did." I reported this story mechanically, like something invented. The time felt so distant, curtained off, mostly forgotten.

"I bet."

"Come on, let me go," Marnie shouted, twisting her head to evade the knife.

In response, I touched her skin with the knife's point until she stopped resisting. With my eyes on my brother, I tried to think of what to say. "Why didn't you go to Kariba or call the American ambassador in Harare? He was a friend of Dad's."

He stared at me hard. "Couldn't do that, Alex."

"Why not?"

His expression looked slightly unfocused, as if he were remembering. After a dry bark of laughter, he said, "Because of what I did to our dear father."

I stiffened. "What do you mean?"

My twin gaped at me. "They didn't do an autopsy on him?"

"No, they didn't."

Alex laughed again and shook his head in disbelief. Tears began spilling down his cheeks. "Well, doesn't that beat all? After I hit the bastard on the head with a rock."

For a second, my vision went black. "No! Alex..."

My brother gave me a grim look and continued, his voice flat. "Afterward, he collapsed, like he stumbled or something. It was so easy, so quick. I stood there for a few minutes wondering what to do. That's almost the last thing I recall before I—"

"Why did you kill him?" I asked, desperate for a reasonable answer.

Alex shrugged. "Ha! That's pretty funny, don't you think?" As if distracted by an inner dialogue, he continued in a soft voice. "Does any of it matter? It's done. He deserved it and maybe I did too."

"All this time. You could have called…" I stammered.

"Yeah? Really? For some reason, I never thought of that." My brother stared at me as if this statement held meaning for us both.

I tried to piece together the memories from that day and couldn't.

Seeing my confusion, he said, "How was I to know the police weren't looking for me? Father and I went into the bush together. Everyone knew that because we were supposed to use the Land Rover, but oh, no, not Father. Tough guy wanted to play big white hunter on foot. He told the guides to stay in camp."

I swayed on my feet until Marnie began squirming in my arms. I cinched my hold across her chest.

Alex laughed again. "So, I could have come home again after all? The perfect crime. Well, damn! I guess I was too cautious—"

"Or felt too guilty."

Chapter Fourteen

THE HUNTING SAFARI had been my father's ill-conceived idea to turn things around for the three of us—between Alex and me, and between both of us and him. Our family story was complicated and unhappy, the problems arising soon after my parents' marriage.

They had met in the railroad station in Venice, having received each other's reserved tickets due to a mix-up of their last names—Wyatt and Wyce. This sparked a conversation that continued on the train. Before the trip ended, they decided to stay together in Rome for a few days. A few days became weeks. They were engaged two months later.

My mother described their first argument as symbolic. Just before the wedding, my father introduced her as Mrs. Wyce. My mother didn't like it and told him she intended to retain her maiden name after they were married. This wasn't acceptable to him. She became angry and threatened to cancel the ceremony, which shocked my father so much that he agreed to her terms, and the wedding was held. When she became pregnant, the matter resurfaced because my father insisted any offspring should bear his name. When they were surprised with twins, a compromise was reached: I would take my mother's last name, Wyatt, and my brother would be given my father's name, Wyce. Furthermore, since they both liked the name Alex before they knew there would be two of us, neither one was willing to cede the name to the other, as if one child belonged to one parent and the other child belonged to the other. Thus, we were both given that name, a baroque arrangement that cemented our status as pawns in our parents' battleground.

When we were four years old, my mother's mother died and left her a sizable inheritance. My mother refused to allow my father to touch her money, though he thought she should defer to his financial judgment. As retaliation, he accepted a job as a travel writer for a men's adventure magazine. The job's primary attraction—besides the incessant travel—was the handsome arrangements provided by hotels and restaurants in return for publicity and reviews. Because most of his living expenses were free, however, my father received only modest commissions that left little money to send home to my mother. When she had to shoulder most of the cost for our upbringing while my father freely wandered the globe, she couldn't deal with the inequity and petitioned for divorce when Alex and I were seven.

My father insisted on custody of Alexander, though my father and I were much closer. At first, my mother argued, but she finally agreed to it as long as she retained custody of me. This suited my father because he envisioned my brother, a male, as better able to handle an uprooted and nomadic lifestyle. Unfortunately, for most of the year, Alex needed to attend school in one place. My father resolved the issue by enrolling him in a Swiss boarding academy, which allowed my father to travel as whim and job assignments dictated. During much of his childhood, Alex didn't see either parent or myself often.

I knew my brother deeply hated boarding school and had been accused of setting fire to the science lab and stealing from students. I always suspected the problems were worse than we knew because my mother's information derived almost exclusively from my brother. She accepted his claims of innocence and became upset about his treatment. A flurry of letters crossed between my parents, but in the end, my mother—perhaps due to battle weariness—threw up her hands and didn't fight on behalf of my twin.

Whenever I saw my father, he rarely mentioned Alex, either because my brother didn't register on my father's mental radar or because he was more interested in describing his own adventures. During my brother's school vacations, Dad made Alex travel alone to be with him, navigating strange airports and stations and shipping docks. I had experienced some of the same behavior, though my mother tried to organize safe transit whenever I journeyed to meet my father.

When my brother and I did see each other, we were always astonished at our physical similarities. Until our teenage years, we were about the same height. Since I tend to be flat-chested and his build was slender, we resembled each other to an extraordinary degree. Our personalities, however, were very different. And now, at age thirty-three, my brother had confessed to the murder of our father without exhibiting the slightest remorse. I shuddered to think how enraged someone would be to kill another person, yet in some strange way, I could feel Alex's anger strangling my own heart.

*

My twin stared at me with uneasy curiosity. "So, you had quite a little fling with Marnie. I guess I was right about you being queer, huh?"

I didn't want to provoke him by responding in the wrong way. Though his question sounded homophobic, it touched upon other loaded issues that existed between us.

"I've been gay for years." Marnie shifted, and I increased my grip, wondering how long Alex would tolerate this stalemate.

"Quite the sex athlete too, I hear." He grinned at Marnie. "She had to pretend, you know. She was pretty disgusted, but she'll have a nice reward for services rendered."

"Oh, it wasn't as bad as all that," Marnie told him in a sulky voice, apparently annoyed that he wasn't doing anything about the knife held to her neck.

Alex didn't comment and neither did I. I was trying to imagine how they had concocted this intricate plot. I asked him.

"We just sort of fell in by accident. I met Marnie at a bar in New York, in the Village. We had some interests in common and hit it off right away, didn't we, Marnie?"

"Yeah. Though at the moment, I kind of wish we hadn't."

He smiled, as if her plight didn't concern him. "Turns out Marnie had a computer and an online connection. She entered your name and up you popped, with a link to the Gregory Reynolds website, an article about your upcoming exhibit, and a newspaper interview that mentioned the town where you lived."

"Why didn't you just telephone me?"

"I thought it would be more entertaining to prepare a unique introduction," he said in a sly voice. "Besides, after what happened, if I arrived on your doorstep, I didn't think you'd welcome me with open arms or cough up any of the money you inherited from Mom…or Dad, if he had any." He shrugged. "And I didn't know whether I had to be careful because of the police, even after fourteen years. Anyhow, Marnie decided you were probably queer—the way you looked and all—and I remembered you telling me about some affair you had in high school. So, we went for that angle."

"Come on, let me go…" Marnie twisted her shoulders, trying to loosen my hold.

My brother ignored her. "When we read the announcement about your exhibition at the New Brunswick gallery, we knew it would be a perfect opportunity. Marnie arrived, flirted, you reacted, and there we were. Right in your bed. Once the two of you got involved, she tried to find your checking and brokerage statements in your apartment, but whenever she was there, you were too, so Marnie couldn't snoop around much. However, she did peek at the front page of your monthly stock portfolio and knew you had money. We talked it over and figured a long game might work, a real estate scam, which would give us a few months to plan everything and time for Marnie to gain your trust and investigate your financial accounts more thoroughly. She had a few bucks saved and so did I. Together, we had enough for a small house down payment—at least enough to look credible. Her company had a branch office in central New Jersey and agreed to let her switch sales territories. I have to say, I was amazed how simple it was. Once she set the hook, it was no problem reeling you in." He appraised the house as if seeing it for the first time. "And a nice little place we have here too. A bit offbeat, but I like it."

"This is a great homecoming reunion but let me loose!" Marnie demanded.

"Yeah, isn't it?" Alex replied, chuckling. "Why don't you put down the knife, Sis. She's nothing to you."

"And she mustn't mean anything to you, either." I squeezed the knife tighter, though my hands were slippery inside the latex gloves.

"You're right," he said to me, rising to his feet, the gun pointed at us. "She doesn't mean anything. You might as well slit her throat, for all I care."

As much as I didn't like relinquishing the few cards I had, my brother had the better hand. I couldn't hold Marnie forever. My legs were shaking, and my fingers were cramping from gripping the knife. Then, too, if he could kill my father without compunction, he could kill both of us just as easily. "Okay, you win." I lowered my knife and took a step away from Marnie.

Marnie rushed to my brother's side. "Thanks a lot, Alex!" she told him angrily.

"I was only kidding, hon. You know that. She wouldn't have let you free otherwise." He draped an arm around her waist and drew her close. "We're good." He smiled and turned to me. "Okay, put the knife on the floor and push it my way with your foot."

Reluctantly, I did as he asked.

"Marnie, pick it up and move it out of my sister's reach."

She grabbed the knife, returned it to its box, and stuffed the box in the highest kitchen cabinet. When she rejoined my brother, he gave her a kiss, and her face softened, though I could tell that she was still upset with him.

"How about some breakfast?" Alex suggested, taking a seat.

Marnie muttered something under her breath but walked to the refrigerator.

"So, what did you do all this time?" I dropped into the armchair and ripped off the latex gloves. "Did you stay in Africa?"

"For a while. I didn't have any money or clothes—as you know since you took everything—so I stole stuff from a guy at camp. Then I went south to Durban and hung out. Did some waitering in a hotel, which gave me a chance to improve my jewelry collection. Lots of dumb, rich tourists think leaving stuff under their beds is the same as putting it in a safe. After a few months, I found work on a ship bound for Marseilles. I did a stint in Cannes, working in the casino. Much better pay and more opportunities. Unfortunately, one of my opportunities didn't work out…an old guy who got upset when I tried to help him carry his winnings." Alex laughed. "I had to leave town a little faster than I intended. I transferred operations to Trieste and did the hotel gig again. Nearly got arrested there. Some woman caught me checking out her suitcase, but she was so drunk she couldn't scream before I…well, I had to get out of town again. Seems like the story of my life!" He yawned and stretched.

"What happened after that?"

"I met some guys who were crewing on a yacht. They let me stay on board if I agreed to do the cleaning and cooking. When the owner asked them to sail the boat to Brindisi, I went too. My pals and I had a blast, but when we came into port, the owner wasn't thrilled by the boat's condition or the state of his liquor supply. He threw a fit, called the police, and I hightailed it to Greece via the ferry. After hitchhiking to Piraeus, I found a job loading cargo and registering incoming freight…pretty dirty work. A few months later, I was promoted upstairs because my language skill and education were assets. I did a lot of traveling for the company, overseeing shipping operations in the Mediterranean. Got to know a lot of useful people, the kind that can get you fake credit cards, passports, and driver's licenses. Last year, I took one of the fleet's ships to Lisbon. By then, I'd saved money, had papers—some not in my real name—and told the captain I wanted to go home to see my sister. He found me work on a ship bound for New York, and there you have it. Goal accomplished."

"How long have you been here?"

"Eight months. I tried to find Mom first, but other people were living in her house. The post office told me she died years ago. They didn't know your address. I drove to a bunch of places, but no luck."

"I've moved around a lot," I replied dryly.

"Family disease."

We were silent for a moment. "Why did you wait until now to show up?"

Alex frowned. "I had a few special jobs to do for friends in New York. Off the payroll. Kept me busy while Marnie was working you over. I wasn't in any hurry. I was getting my revenge every day that Marnie made a chump out of you."

I gritted my teeth in exasperation. "When you found me…why the blindfold and everything?"

"Oh, I don't know. I guess I wanted to observe you without you seeing me. One thing I learned over my life is to maintain all my options. I also thought it might be a good idea to keep a low profile, just in case I was still on a wanted list. Besides, it's sort of hard to be revived from the dead." He smiled, a wry expression on his face.

"I can imagine."

"So, here we are."

"Yeah, here we are."

I studied my twin, trying to understand what kind of man he had become. "What do you plan to do with me, Alex? Make me disappear?"

He chuckled. "Well, we thought you might have a disaster happen. Natural or unnatural."

"You're the expert on that."

"Yeah, kind of," he replied. "Anyhow, once Marnie found out how much you were worth, the idea of receiving my rightful inheritance appealed to me."

"Mother left everything of hers to me. I had nothing to do with it."

"Because she thought I was dead. And if you hadn't left Zimbabwe so fast, you would've known I was still alive. But you didn't care, did you?"

I could tell my return to the United States was a sticking point, one that had goaded him all these years. "I stayed as long as I could. I already told you that. What was I supposed to do? They said you might never be found." I shook my head. "Mother wouldn't have left you anything anyway. You know their weird arrangement, Alex. Dad was supposed to name you as his beneficiary, and I was Mother's."

"Yeah, and as usual you got the better end of the goddamned deal. He didn't have much, did he? Just a little run-down shack in Tangiers where he kept some stuff between jaunts. Hell, there probably wasn't enough money to fix it up to sell. Besides, I was afraid to make a claim because I didn't know if the police were after me. I wasn't even positive dear Dad was dead."

My father had never confided the extent of his finances to Alexander because he didn't trust him. Thus, my brother had no knowledge of his true inheritance—the seaside house bought before my father died and several hundred thousand dollars. Another family disease. My father hadn't been trusted by his father, either. Four months before our African hunting trip, my grandfather had suffered a fatal heart attack, and though he expressed hesitation in the letter accompanying his will, he left his estate to my father, a complete shock to Dad because Grandfather had always been critical ever since my father abandoned my mother. On the morning before my brother killed my father, Dad revealed to me that he'd bought a house on the coast of New Jersey and that Alex was his first beneficiary and I was named second. Dad explained why he hadn't told Alexander—that knowing money was in Alex's future would only encourage irresponsible behavior. It was therefore horribly ironic that my father died at Alex's hand, and my brother had no idea the murder—if no one discovered who'd done it—would have netted him a sizable amount. I could tell Alex about this inheritance, which had been bequeathed to me after my brother was deemed dead, but here he was threatening to kill me so he could get his hands on my money, including some that wasn't rightfully his.

I looked my twin in the eye and lied. "I'm sorry. I know Dad wasn't good at saving money, but how can you blame me for that? He spent what he had and enjoyed life. Until you ended it for him."

"Guess that was quite a big surprise. If he even knew what happened," Alex retorted. "You know, Dad never had time for me…sending me to the Swiss school and traveling constantly so I never knew where he was. I couldn't even call him because he was always in a new place, some place where I wasn't."

"That must have been hard," I replied, torn between derision and honesty.

"Don't give me that sympathetic bullshit. You had it easy." A smile lurked around his mouth. "I think considering everything you've done, a large payback is overdue, don't you?"

I didn't answer.

My brother settled his feet on the coffee table. The gun rested on his knee.

"How's breakfast coming?" he called to Marnie.

"Almost ready." Her voice still sounded annoyed. As if to punctuate her mood, she threw some silverware in the sink.

"And after we eat?" I asked him.

"Well, we plan to have an e-mail chat with your broker. Instruct him to sell your stocks and maybe some mutual funds so you'll have a nice, fat cash account."

"He won't do that unless he hears from me in person." My broker and I communicated via online but confirmed trades on the phone. I had no idea how he would behave.

"We'll see…" Alex replied.

*

"Well, my word, you have one sharpie broker," Marnie exclaimed. "He fell all over himself to be helpful."

"What did you do?" I asked.

"You told him that you desperately wanted to buy a vacation house in Maine—a great deal—and you needed money immediately or the cabin would be sold to another buyer. So, bye-bye to GE, IBM, and most of those stodgy stocks. Really, Alex, you could have done better with other stuff anyway. Now we have $427,000 to add to the existing cash."

I didn't answer because I was calculating that my account, once the trades settled, would contain about half a million. I knew, too, that with my bonds as collateral, an on-margin feature was designed to automatically cover shortfalls.

Marnie noticed my preoccupation and said to my brother, "Alexandra is doing math." She faced me. "Yes, dear, you have about $495,000. At some point, we might sell your mutual funds."

I wished I'd given her the house and left. We were talking about a lot of money.

"And you're going to the bank later?" Marnie asked my brother.

"Yeah. When I comb my hair like this, I really look like my sister. You did a great job with the cut, Marnie, but I hope I don't have to impersonate her. I'd have to get that lesbian swagger down better. Even so, I guess I could pass." He laughed at the thought.

What did he intend to do with me while he did his errands? Would he leave Marnie alone with the revolver? Could I manipulate the triangulation of Alex, Marnie, and myself so that Marnie was on my side? She was piqued about his earlier comment regarding her expendability, despite Alex's attempts to reassure her. From what I could observe, the coldness in his personality ran deep. Had Marnie detected this, or had the promised largesse overcome her judgment? Or did she suffer from the same absence of feeling? Whatever the case, Marnie should have been very afraid of Alex. I was.

Chapter Fifteen

ALEX AND MARNIE moved the chair to face the room and trussed me tightly. When they walked into the kitchen, Alex looped an arm around her neck.

"Who's my girl, huh? Hey, today is Christmas! Some stuff arriving."

Marnie's dour expression lightened at the thought of the incoming deliveries. She kissed Alex on the mouth. Whatever doubts she had earlier were apparently forgotten.

"Should I call the bank to see if the home equity check is ready?" she asked him.

"Yeah. Good idea."

Marnie telephoned and returned, grinning. "All set. I can get the money and deposit it. I'll also cash the $1,200 check."

"You do your trip first. Take my keys and use my car—it's blocking yours. Meanwhile, my sister and I will continue our family reunion."

Marnie exited through the deck door. A minute later, we heard the rental car leave.

Alex sprawled on the couch and crossed his legs at the ankles. "Ah, what a great place you two bought. Good to get some equity out of it. Thirty-five thousand will come in handy. Hope the bank doesn't screw up."

Of course, I hoped they would. I had hoped, too, that Alex planned to accompany Marnie so I might have an opportunity to break free. This expectation dashed, I wondered at the hold my brother had on her. He seemed confident she wouldn't take the money and run, yet Marnie would soon have $36,200, including my personal check. Perhaps Alex had planned the spending spree, knowing the attraction of all those purchases would entice her to return.

I reassessed the time required to accomplish their various maneuvers. The brokerage transactions would take a few days to clear, as would the home equity check Marnie planned to deposit in her account. With express mail requested, most of the packages would arrive tomorrow. Whether I needed to be alive during this process was unknown.

"So, Alex," my brother began, "how are you feeling now?"

I didn't respond to his smug question.

"You know, I think you should call and cancel that new will, don't you?"

My brother was aware of the revised documents because Marnie had told him about my e-mail to Cope, but the attorney's name hadn't been mentioned. Could I misdial Mr. Reilly's number and fake a conversation with him? I doubted Alex would fall for this ploy. He would surely listen on our portable phone in the same room, ready to disconnect if I said something he didn't like. And if I really spoke with my lawyer and he voided the new legal revisions without my actual presence, what would Alex and Marnie do then? It would require patience to accomplish the house scam. First, Alex would need to stage a realistic accident for me, wait for my old will to be read, my estate established, and the title transferred to Marnie before listing the house for sale. All of this would take time, nerve, and solidarity between the two of them. I didn't underestimate Alex, but could they maintain their relationship for months?

I stated the obvious. "If I cancel my new will, you'll have to kill me to inherit my share of the house."

"And if you don't cancel it and we kill you, we don't get a cent. In either case, you're dead." He said this in a matter-of-fact manner, as if my life meant nothing to him one way or the other. "Hey, I've got a great idea. You could just give Marnie the house, and then we could kill you later." He laughed.

"To accomplish an ownership transfer, you'd have to bring me to a lawyer's office. You can't do that at gunpoint, can you?"

"No, not very easily. I suppose it's curtains for you no matter what." His lips curled into a mischievous grin. "Of course, after your death, I could move in with Marnie, impersonate you, and gradually deplete your portfolio until we're able to sell the house." He shook his head and sighed. "But that's too much trouble."

"I could refuse to call the attorney…if you're going to murder me anyway. At least you would lose your $5,000 house down payment."

"Hmm. Maybe, but I think you'll make the call, or else we'll have to take a trip and see your pal, Cope. To persuade her that the house and money are rightfully ours."

He had me there and knew it. No matter what I did, the net effect was the same. Suddenly, it seemed pointless whether I canceled the will and he killed me to get the money, or whether I refused to cancel the will and he killed me. The threat about Cope tipped the proverbial scales.

"I guess I'll make the call."

"That's more like it, Sis." He found the phone book and the portable phone, then untied the ropes around my chest. My feet were still free. "Come into the bedroom."

I tried to think quickly as I walked. How could I alert Jim Reilly? He was already aware of my concern about Marnie. I sat on the edge of the bed.

"What's the name?" he asked.

I told him. He thumbed through the directory for the number, dialed it on the table-top phone, and jammed the receiver between my fingers. As the receptionist answered, my brother clicked on the portable.

"May I speak to Mr. Reilly? This is Alexandra Wyatt."

"Let me see if he is available. Please hold a minute."

The Smith & Wesson was aimed at my face.

"Jim Reilly speaking."

"Mr. Reilly, this is Alex Wyatt. I came on Wednesday to have you revise a will for me."

"Yes, Ms. Wyatt. I recall the matter well."

"I'm sorry, but I've changed my mind and would like to cancel this new will and power of attorney so that the original ones I left in your office remain valid. And I won't make our appointment today. The one to create a new health proxy. You know, to fix your secretary's mistake. The old proxy is fine."

He was silent for a moment. "Well, okay, but—"

"Also, please destroy your copies of the revised will and the health proxy I was supposed to sign and notarize this afternoon." I hadn't left the POA or the old will with him, the health directive was already complete, no appointment had been scheduled, and I'd met with him last Thursday, not Wednesday. His secretary hadn't typed anything.

To his credit, after a few seconds, Reilly got the message something was wrong. "The health proxy for today? Yes, I have it here as well as your previous legal papers. And I see your appointment on my calendar, which I'll cancel. Now, are you sure you're comfortable with reverting to your earlier documents?"

"Yes, I am. Please send a bill for the cost of creating the new will, since it's no longer necessary for me to come in today." I had already paid him.

"Sure. Again, please accept my apologies for not having everything finished while you were here." His tone was even, but I was confident Mr. Reilly had received my distress signal.

"No problem."

"Ms. Wyatt, excuse me for asking, but I assume from your request that your original beneficiary is back in your good graces?"

I was silent for a few beats too long. Alex's eyes widened, and he gestured that I should end the conversation immediately.

"Actually, everything is fine, Mr. Reilly. I'm optimistic the relationship will work out. Thank you for your time."

Alex clicked off the portable, grabbed the receiver, and slammed it on the cradle. "That was a little close." His face was mottled with anger. "I don't think you quite realize your place in all of this. You're expendable, very expendable, or will be shortly."

I exhaled an uneasy breath. "Alex, I understand my situation very well."

"And while we're at it, give me your checkbook. It's gone from the counter."

"In my back pocket."

He prodded me off the bed and took it and my credit cards. "Back to the living room."

"You don't have any reason to be upset with me." I slumped into the wing chair.

"No? You really are quick to forget." He shook his head and, with one hand, wrapped the laundry line around my chest and snugged the rope. After inserting the .38 in his belt, he threaded the line under my arms and tied the ends behind the chair. "Who's profited from our parents? Who's sitting here in a big house? Who got the fancy education?"

"A big house that the mortgage company owns. And now the equity company," I said. "We were born with equal chances. You went to a good Swiss school while I was going to public school. You could have done anything you wanted with your life. You can't blame anyone except yourself for the way things turned out. You weren't interested in going to college—"

"I was only allowed in that private school because Dad did a deal with an administrator, who was a pal of his. They charged Dad room and board—no tuition—in exchange for some travel comps he wangled. If Dad had to pay for an apartment and a full-time woman to stay with me, it would have cost him a lot, and he would've needed to be around more often. So don't think sticking me in a Swiss academy was generous or thoughtful. And there was no way Dad could afford college. I never even asked him."

"Maybe Mother might have helped."

"Mother? Ha!" he scoffed. "Not likely. She divided us up. You were hers and I was his. She didn't want anything to do with me."

"That's not true. She cared about you, Alex. You know how it was between them. They got locked into opposing each other. We were just pieces in their game. Besides, did it ever occur to you that I wanted to be with you and Dad?"

"Like you were in Africa?"

The tone of his voice disturbed me, but I was mad. "Yeah, like that. Going to places the two of you went."

He lowered himself onto the couch. "You might not have enjoyed it after years of tagging along behind him. It didn't matter if I wanted to spend time with my friends during vacation, I always had to come when he whistled. And school? I remember when I was ten. I was sick with pneumonia, and no one could reach our dear father on the phone. They finally put me in the hospital because I needed oxygen. Four days after I got out, Father comes rushing to my dorm room like he just heard, even though I knew the school received a telegram from him ten days before. I learned later that he was shacked up with a Moroccan woman. He could have arrived in a day, if he'd wanted. And not a word from you or Mother."

"Mom didn't hear you were sick until after you were well, and she had no authority to do anything anyway."

He snorted. "So much for maternal and paternal concern."

"I'm sorry, but that situation wasn't Mother's fault or mine." I thought for a minute. "Maybe I did have it easier than you did. At least I had a parent who lived with me."

This seemed to mollify him slightly. "Yeah, you did, and you had all the spending money you wanted. I bet Mom even gave you a car."

"Hey, that's not true! I always had a part-time job in high school. I worked for the Playhouse painting sets, ushering, doing odd jobs. And a car? I didn't get a car until I was nearly finished with college. Mom's old Buick Regal that she couldn't drive any longer." My irritation was boiling to the surface, the intensity frightening me. "Instead of being angry at our parents, look in the damned mirror. Neither of them turned you into a murderer and a thief. A guy who's running scared, who thinks everyone owes him something. No, who you are is your own creation, Alex."

My brother didn't like what I said and growled, "You wouldn't know anything about it. What it's like never to have money. A man needs cash to take out girls and stuff. It gets expensive."

The "stuff" was to pay for abortions for two girls he had impregnated. I'd overheard phone arguments between my parents on the subject.

"Why didn't you get a job during school?" I asked.

"Nobody wanted to hire me, an American. All the jobs went to

French or Swiss or Italian students."

I doubted Alex had attempted to find employment. From what I'd heard, he spent his summers hanging out along the Costa del Sol, unsupervised, unless my father forced Alex to join him somewhere.

"Pretty tough, I guess," I replied with a hint of sarcasm.

"I don't need your sympathy," he retorted.

"No, you don't. But listen, Alex, you could start over. Get a decent job—you're good at languages—Spanish, French, some Italian, right?"

"A little German and Greek, too, but I don't have a college diploma or any legit work experiences. And, besides, there are easier ways to make a buck."

"Yeah, stealing from me."

"You won't mind for long." We exchanged hostile looks. Finally, he stood. "Think I'll have one of your beers. Want one?"

"No, thanks."

"Don't move from that chair." He laughed, knowing I couldn't.

As he walked into the kitchen, I tried to think of how to influence my brother before Marnie came home, but Alex surprised me when he returned with two beers. After removing a strip of duct tape on my wrists, he inserted the bottle between my fingers.

"Hey, do you remember when I came to visit? When we were twelve?" He sat on the sofa. "We went up to the Poconos with Mom."

"Yes, I remember." I didn't want to talk about it.

He took a gulp of beer. "The hotel had that enclosed area of the lake where we played water volleyball. You and I were a great team. What, we had one guy on our side and stood against five?"

"They wouldn't stop playing, insisting we would lose the next game, but we never did, did we?"

"No, we didn't. Went on most of the afternoon." Alex smiled at the memory.

"You got a terrible sunburn." I eased the bottle to my lips and swallowed some beer. "Well, come to think of it, so did I."

My brother nodded. "You were beet red."

We both paused, sorting our thoughts. Alex observed me in silence, as if I might reveal more about our trip. When I said nothing, Alex crossed his legs and adopted a relaxed posture, one at odds with the nervous twitch of his foot.

"The cabin was boiling hot that night, with our sunburns and all," he said.

"Yes, it was."

I recalled the evening vividly, though I didn't say so to Alex. The sound of crickets, the whine of mosquitoes, the rickety twin beds, the coarse blankets against red, burned skin. It all came back, the shame and the confusion. After Mother had tucked us in, she left to have a drink with a man she met during the afternoon. Alex and I talked for a while, and then he climbed out of the covers and suggested we remove our pajamas since it was so warm. I looked at him as he pulled off his shirt and noticed how his body was shaped like mine. Next, he removed his pajama bottom, smiling strangely as he fell back against the cot. Through the open window, the moonlight flooded over him and his rising erection. I remember being stunned, uncertain what to do next. When Alex asked me to come to his bed, I became even more frightened. As if in a trance, I found myself beside him. He unbuttoned my cotton top and slid it off my shoulders, brushing my protesting hands away and working down my shortie pajamas. Before I knew what was happening, he kissed my lips, exploring my mouth with his tongue. As he moved on top of me, he began to rub my nipples with his fingers. Though I had discovered some simple sexual pleasures on my own, it was astonishing how exciting and frightening this felt, lying together naked, the light from the window bright as day on our slender bodies, the insistence of his penis pushing damply against my stomach. Although I begged Alex to stop, he didn't. Instead, he whispered, "We're so alike. We'll be together. Always."

I remembered bracing my hands against his shoulders, struggling to create space between us, but my brother was intent on uniting us, or as he said, completing our union.

I often wondered what would have happened if Mother hadn't ended her date early. We heard her stumble on the gravel path near the road. By the time the cabin's screen door slapped shut, we were dressed and rushing under the covers in our individual beds. Alex had made me promise not to tell our mother.

"I never told anyone," I admitted.

His eyes narrowed and he sighed. Did the memory make him sad or nostalgic, or did it revive other feelings that were best forgotten?

"That was a long time ago," he said.

I swallowed some beer. "Yeah, it was."

Alex's gaze wandered as if he was lost in memories. "You won't believe this, but that was one of the best moments of my life."

This announcement had a shattering honesty to it, made all the more powerful in the present circumstances. He tipped the bottle and drank more beer. "Do you ever think about that night?"

I knew the question wasn't quite accurate. He wanted to know whether I ever thought about him. I felt a flush creep up my neck.

"That was my first sexual experience," I whispered.

"Me too."

These admissions lay suspended between us. We exchanged glances, and then Alex finished his drink and wiped his mouth. "Do you want another beer?"

I didn't want more alcohol but sending him into the kitchen might reroute the conversation. "All right."

When my brother returned with two bottles, he unwrapped more of the duct tape, improving my range of motion. Smiling, he said, "We were pretty good, weren't we?"

This renewed my anxiety, but his mood seemed changed. More fraternal than sexual, reminding me of the twin I once loved. "Yes, we were." As I said this, I realized how similar he was to Marnie—the same magnetic, sexy persuasiveness that flowed so naturally.

"You know, it was hard for me to listen to Marnie talk about you. She did, too. Talk." He took a drink. "I think she was attracted to you. Maybe because we resemble each other so much. Maybe she thought of me when she was with you—"

"And maybe she thought of me when she was with you." I gave him a measured look and sipped some beer.

My brother raised his bottle in salute. "Yeah. You're probably right. Strange, huh?"

"Yeah," I agreed. "So, what are you going to do about her?"

The question bothered him. His eyes sharpened, and he set the bottle down on the table loudly. "What difference does it make to you?"

I shrugged. "Just curious, I guess." I tried to sound offhand.

"Actually, you should be asking what I'm going to do about you."

I refused to ask, partly because I was afraid to know, and partly because I didn't want to give him the satisfaction.

Chapter Sixteen

MY BROTHER WAS on his third beer, and I was halfway through my second when Marnie came home. She stored some food in the refrigerator.

"Did everything go okay at the bank?" my brother asked.

"Smooth. No problem. The home equity check is deposited in my checking account, so we're in great shape." She giggled. "And I have a wonderful treat!" Marnie went into the garage and returned with two bottles of Dom Pérignon. "One's cold, the other will be shortly. We have to celebrate!" Without asking, she pulled two glasses from the cabinet and slowly released the cork.

Alex tossed off the last of his beer and accepted a glass. "Give Alex some. She's paying for it."

Marnie sighed and clucked at him. "Oh, my. I suppose you're right. We must be hospitable." She walked into the kitchen and returned with a third glass.

Alex stood, removed my beer bottle and the rest of the tape, and handed me my drink. Then he sat in my leather chair, nestled the gun next to his thigh, and made a toast. "To Alexandra! May she rest in peace!" He chuckled at his joke.

I hesitated, not wishing to toast my demise, but finally took a swallow.

"So, dear sister, we need to reduce the cash in your brokerage account."

"I have her checks right here," Marnie said. "Thought they were hidden in your files, didn't you?" she asked me. "Well, I found them."

"Excellent!" my brother told her.

My hopes plummeted. They could access all the cash and the money from the stock sales and, if they were clever enough, tap into the on-margin account. If they ran an overdraft, however, my broker would certainly become alarmed and telephone or, at the least, stop any activity until he spoke with me.

"Remember what we talked about?" Marnie reminded my brother. "Buying something expensive using checks drawn on Alex's account and then selling it later for cash?"

My brother nodded. "Yeah, as a matter of fact I got in touch with two diamond dealers. We're all set." He sipped the Champagne, his face wreathed in appreciation. "Damn, this is fine! I have to give the French credit. None of that sparkling wine garbage. How about some more, Marnie?"

After she refilled their glasses, he continued. "Ah, diamonds. They're small, easy to transport, and negotiable. I doubt the first dealer will look closely at my ID if the check is good. I have an appointment to buy these diamonds this afternoon and the second batch in a few days. By the way, where does Alex keep her canceled checks?"

"In the desk in the bedroom."

"Go get one so I can study how she writes the numbers. Alex can put in the dealers' name and sign the checks. I'll take the same pen with me and fill in the dollar amounts when I'm closing the deal."

He gave me a pen, and I did as he said.

*

After Alex studied my writing, he gave Marnie the gun while he went to the bathroom. Upon his return, they escorted me there to freshen up. Unfortunately, Marnie kept guard so I had no opportunity to search for useful tools. Alex then bound me in the chair, adding duct tape around my wrists and rope around my feet. He inserted my driver's license in his wallet to use at the bank's drive-through, although they didn't always ask for identification. Even if they did, there was no photo on the license, and Alex could easily pass a cursory examination. My brother seemed surprisingly sober as he left.

Marnie finished her Champagne and kept the second bottle chilling because Alex had been emphatic that she shouldn't drink more. She walked outside to the delivery box and brought in several packages, which she carried to the coffee table. Marnie angled the revolver toward the wall, which was a relief, and began opening boxes using a pair of scissors. She moaned with pleasure, stood, and held up an expensive green silk suit.

"I'll give you a fashion show!" She flung her jeans and blouse on the floor, stepping into the skirt, buttoning the jacket, and twirling around the room like a model. From another package, she removed a pair of chocolate-colored slingbacks that she tried on. "What do you think, Alex? Is this me?"

"Very nice, Marnie."

"Is that all you can say? What great presents you gave me! I love presents."

Two small packages were next. A man's silver Rolex Submariner watch, which she admired and returned to the box, and then a woman's gold Rolex, which Marnie gleefully slipped on her wrist.

"I've wanted one of these for ages. It's a little loose, but once we're out of the country, I'll visit a jeweler."

"Pretty flashy to wear in the meantime." I decided to begin my strategy of dividing Marnie from my brother. "I doubt Alex will let you keep the watch."

Marnie frowned. "He has nothing to say about it." She went into the garage and returned with an enormous yellow suitcase with wheels and a pop-up handle. "Bought this a few days ago. I'll use my old one too, and my overnight bag."

"Three things to carry?" I shook my head. "Alex won't go for that."

"Well, I don't intend on leaving all my clothes behind."

"My brother likes to travel light. I imagine now more than ever."

"Nonsense! He wouldn't have let me buy this stuff if I couldn't bring it."

I could understand Marnie's logic, but it was unlikely Alex meant for her to be so overloaded with luggage that she couldn't handle it all at one time.

"It probably doesn't matter. You won't get far anyway."

"Oh, enough already! Alex has everything under control. I'm not worried."

"You should be. Where are you going?"

"None of your business," Marnie snapped. "Let's just say we plan to travel. I can't wait."

"You'll have to wait if you need to sell the house."

"We might not bother. Nice to have the money, but maybe it will take too long. Actually, I'm not sure what your brother intends to do."

"He hasn't shared his plans?" I asked. "Like what's going to happen to me?"

Marnie snickered in a girlish manner that was annoying. "You'll see."

I surmised she didn't know. "Don't you realize we're both in danger? My death has to be arranged, but he'll get rid of you the second you aren't useful."

"Be quiet!" And with that she picked up the bandana from the floor and gagged me. "You can shut up for a while."

I sat and did just that while Marnie paraded her new outfit down the catwalk of our living room. After she changed into her shorts and blouse, the doorbell rang. Marnie jumped and covered her mouth. The front door was across the living room and foyer from where I was sitting. If she opened the door, I was directly in sight.

There was a forceful knock. "Ms. Wyatt, this is the police."

Marnie grabbed the Smith & Wesson, bent low, and slipped through the kitchen, probably to peek through the narrow window in the pantry, one that looked out on the entrance. I tried to yell and rock the chair, but the amount of noise I made with the gag was minimal.

The police rang the bell again and thumped on the door. I prayed they would come around to the deck and break in, but after a squawk from the patrol car, they left. Marnie waited a few minutes and then walked into the living room, looking pale but relieved.

"All gone," she said. "Thank goodness."

Jim Reilly's handiwork. He must have reported our suspicious conversation. With a little luck, the police would return, particularly if they saw the black sedan in the drive later. I hoped they would be persistent and that Jim Reilly had impressed them with the gravity of the situation. I also hoped they had noticed the air-conditioning was on, which meant someone was in the house or would be soon.

*

Marnie went upstairs to access my portfolio online. When she entered the kitchen, she called my brother to warn him the stock sales hadn't cleared and not to exceed the cash in my account. Then she spent several hours in the bedroom, probably cramming clothes into her suitcases. At one point, the matter of the air-conditioning occurred to her and she switched it off, turning on the living room's ceiling fan instead. Eventually, she made sandwiches and removed the bandana so I could eat. I felt really foolish being fed, though I was glad to have something in my stomach. Despite the police visit, Marnie seemed chipper.

"I think I'll take some of your mother's jewelry," she said brightly.

"Come on, Marnie. Those pieces have special meaning to me, you know that."

"I don't think what you want matters, do you? In the overall scheme of things? And, anyway, your brother would probably like the jewelry."

"I doubt he intends to wear her pearls any time soon."

Her attention was now on this newest enterprise. Marnie trotted into the bedroom and came out with my rosewood jewelry box, tipping its contents onto the coffee table. With a careless finger, she picked through the costume items and set aside my grandmother's diamond ring, some gold bracelets and necklaces, my mother's rings, and her strand of Mikimoto pearls. The most expensive items were scooped into a plastic sandwich bag.

*

By early evening, Marnie announced she had almost finished

packing, though a trace of uncertainty accompanied this statement. We were in the living room, staring at each other, when we heard Alex return. This time, he drove the car into the windowless garage. With the lights and air-conditioning off and the blinds drawn, the police would assume the house was empty and probably wouldn't knock again unless Jim Reilly persisted. I wasn't sure he would.

Alex had a big smile on his face when he entered the room. "Boy, did we strike it rich! They gave me nine cut diamonds and never asked for ID because a friend had vouched for me. I'll pick up the other stones from the second dealer on Wednesday. Also cashed your check for you, Sis."

"I want to see the diamonds!" Marnie was excited.

Alex took a small manila packet from his shirt pocket and waved it in the air. "Got them right here." He poured the gemstones carefully into the palm of his hand and pinched one between his thumb and forefinger. Even in the dull light, it sparkled.

"Wow!" Marnie's eyes gleamed almost as much as the diamond. "Can I hold them?"

"Nope. They stay right here on me," Alex replied. "For safekeeping." He returned the gems to the envelope.

She pouted. "You don't trust me."

"I don't trust anyone. Besides, you don't want to get caught with these, do you? And take off that Rolex. It has to be in perfect condition when we sell it."

Marnie scowled at him, stared lovingly at the watch, and unclasped it from her wrist.

Chapter Seventeen

ALEX OPENED the second bottle of Champagne to celebrate. I could hear Marnie and my brother in the kitchen, discussing the price and quality of the diamonds. He had apparently heeded her advice and only spent some of the cash. Most likely, more money would be available tomorrow, and the bonds and mutual funds remained. I was fairly positive my broker would balk at any additional online orders to liquidate those holdings after the unusual request for money to buy the vacation house—or not without a discussion. Alex was smart enough to realize this and probably wouldn't press his luck. On the other hand, my broker had already responded to Alex's previous e-mail directions.

As I stewed over this, Marnie informed Alex about the police visit. He wasn't pleased and immediately decided to speed up their schedule. He warned Marnie about standing in front of the windows where she could be seen from the road. A few minutes later, when they began to cook pasta, throwing in tomatoes, garlic, olives, celery, and other leftovers, they seemed amused about sneaking around to stay out of sight, or perhaps their mood was because of the Dom Pérignon. They ate dinner in the dining room and then brought a plate in for me, serving the pasta cold, fork by fork.

About 7:45, the phone rang, startling us all. Marnie let the machine pick up, though we could hear the message. It was the police department. For Alexandra Wyatt. They reported their visit to the house and said they wanted to speak to me as soon as possible. A number and the officer's name were left.

I felt deflated since this meant they were unlikely to make another house call tonight. I was tired of sitting in the chair and tired of being tied. My back ached and I desperately needed to stretch my cramped body. It didn't help my mood that Alex and

Marnie were in the dining room, drinking wine and eating popcorn while discussing the house sale. Marnie wanted to wait and sell it; Alex countered with the obvious: the police were alerted and would be distrustful if anything irregular occurred, especially if I died "accidentally," which would be necessary so Marnie could inherit the house. But what if Alex was concocting a different scenario wherein Marnie would be blamed for my death, and her plan to rob my estate would be exposed, thus nullifying her claim? He could wait a short time before swooping in as my long-lost brother, who had survived in Africa, unbeknownst to me, and had only recently returned to America and learned of my tragic death. He then could insist the estate was his. He probably possessed identification in his real name, made by his shady contacts, and his appearance would clinch his fraternal assertion.

I thought about this and decided there was no guarantee a judge would honor his request because Cope was a legitimate second beneficiary on my original will and, of course, first beneficiary on my revised will. Even if Reilly had ripped up the newer one, Marnie knew about Cope months ago when we created our legal documents. She would have informed Alex of every detail, so regardless if Alex deleted Marnie from the equation, Cope was still blocking his path. However, if my brother murdered Marnie and then me, Cope would have no inkling of Alex's connection to Marnie, and, being an honorable woman, she might agree to give him some of the estate. Or—even more horrible to imagine—Alex could fly to San Francisco and dispatch Cope, leaving three dead women, and no one who could incriminate him. Marnie's death would need to precede mine by a few days and be properly documented by the authorities so her estate would legally revert to me prior to my death. With no legal beneficiaries in my will still alive, the state would decide whether my brother was my legitimate heir. It would take a lot of time and expense, but he might prevail. Or he could abscond with the money he already had—probably the safest solution.

About ten, Alex came in to see whether I needed to use the toilet, which I did. He untied me and, with Marnie in tow, pushed me into the semi-dark bathroom. I brushed my teeth and washed my face. Even in the low light, I was startled at how drawn and weary I looked. For the hundredth time, I cursed myself for returning into the house instead of escaping. Had I been stupider then or in February when I fell for Marnie?

Alex seemed worse for the drink, as did Marnie, who stumbled as she led me to the chair. The gag, duct tape, and ropes were replaced, but not the binding at my feet. As fatigued as I was, this gave me hope. Since they couldn't risk turning on the television, the two of them were soon bored and went to bed. I gave them an hour, as best as I could judge, and tried to do my turtle act again. Whether due to the way I was tied or my fatigue, I could only sidle the chair a few feet. I looked for something sharp on the adjacent bookcase, but everything useful had been moved.

I must have dozed for several hours. From my new position, I could make out the time on the kitchen wall clock: 3:10 a.m. My energy slightly renewed from my nap, I began inching the chair forward, hoping to find a tool in the dining room. Frustrated with my slow progress, I tried to stand with the chair balanced on my back. After a few steps, I staggered and pitched sideways, crashing onto the floor, and narrowly missed banging my head on the coffee table.

Alex rushed into the room with the gun. When he saw my predicament, he laughed, put the revolver on the table, and came over to right the chair with me in it. He removed the gag.

"Pretty dumb, Alex," he whispered. "I didn't think you were so clumsy."

"I had a bad dream," I replied with irritation. "Someone was tying me to a chair and robbing me."

He shook his head. "No one is robbing you. I'm just getting back what you owe me."

"Let's not go through that again."

Alex sat down, looked at me, and stroked his chin. I couldn't see his expression well, even with the ambient glow from the skylights, but I sensed a subtle change. The night was very still, except for the whir of the fan overhead, yet his silence had a loudness that palpitated in the air between us. Then, in a wistful voice, he whispered, "It's been a long time."

I didn't know how to respond because I wasn't sure where he was going with the conversation. Alex had always been like that, ideas or statements coming out of the blue. When we were young, sometimes I intuitively understood him; as he grew older, I understood far less.

"Fourteen years. A lot has happened."

He was quiet, with his eyes closed, so I thought he might be asleep. Suddenly, he stared at me. "So, tell me about Mother."

"What do you mean?"

"Did she try to learn what happened to me?"

"Yes, of course. She called the ambassador and all sorts of people. She was told you were missing and presumed dead from a lion attack."

"Missing and presumed dead? That's a laugh." But he wasn't laughing. He seemed downcast, almost morose. "How did she die?"

"She had a small stroke first. That changed everything immediately."

"When?"

"A month after I returned from Africa. I don't know what brought it on, but Mom was really upset about you and about our father's death. The stroke forced her to use a walker and impaired her speech, but we managed with the help of an aide and some of her friends. I came home from college on weekends. Then, as I was packing to leave school at the end of my junior year, she had another stroke. After the hospital, she went into rehabilitation for a month. When she was released, she was a little better. Mom could use her left hand to feed herself and to scrawl a few words, but her right side was paralyzed. I spent the summer at home, and in August, she had a third stroke and needed full-time care. I wanted to stay with her, but she had already made me promise to finish at Bard. I moved her into a nursing facility near campus and sold her house."

"And you kept the furniture, didn't you?" He glanced at my

mother's table and chairs. "Father's things could've fit into a goddamned closet."

I was quiet for a moment, letting his jealousy dissipate.

"And then?" he asked.

Talking about my mother always made me sad. I stared at Alex and realized he felt the same way. "After the last stroke, her speech was severely affected. I did what I could, but she was miserable being stuck in a wheelchair. I think she didn't want to live any longer. A cerebral hemorrhage killed her."

"So, I guess she really couldn't try and find me." He sounded like a lost child.

"No, not after Mom became sick."

"But what about you?"

"What could I have done? I was a kid…alone in Africa."

He grunted and looked away, as if I had misunderstood him.

"Besides, after what occurred the night before…" I shot him an angry look.

Alex lifted his head as if startled. "Yes. The night before. I remember." He rubbed his thigh. "Things just got a little out of hand, Alex."

It was my turn to be silent.

"I told you, I never forgot that first time," he said softly.

"And I never forgot that last time," I countered, which was not altogether true. Much of what occurred in Africa had been traumatic, but my memory was incomplete, with large gaps missing.

He stood wearily, untied me so he could move the chair to the end of the room, then I took my place again, and Alex restored the bindings. "Good night, Sis." He kissed my forehead and left the room.

*

The whistle of the teakettle woke me. Marnie was dressed in a flimsy nightgown that covered very little. I twisted to relieve my stiff muscles, but the bindings constricted most movement.

"Alexandra, here's your coffee." She exited the kitchen hunched over so she couldn't be seen through the window. I began to feel as though we were hunkered down in some kind of war zone with snipers in the trees.

"Thanks," I told her as she held the coffee to my lips.

"What were you and Alex talking about last night?"

I took another sip. "He wanted to know how Mother died."

Marnie studied me for signs I was being untruthful, then returned to make breakfast. When Alex walked in, he gave me a moody look and crouched to avoid the windows. The two of them ate. Shortly after, Marnie brought fried eggs that she fed to me.

"Is my sister okay?" my brother called from the kitchen.

"Yeah, everything's still tight," Marnie answered.

"Good. I'm taking a shower."

Marnie cleaned the kitchen and started to run the dishwasher but turned it off probably because the noise might be heard if anyone came to the door. Of course, the same could be said of the shower since it was on the wall near the front entrance. Marnie must have realized this because she went into the bathroom, and the water stopped. Laughter emanated from the hall. It soon became clear what Marnie and my brother were doing.

Their fun contrasted with my mounting frustration. I was unable to get free and unable to insert a wedge between Marnie and my brother. As much as I didn't like to consider it, the police were unlikely to return because they had no solid evidence of wrongdoing, only my attorney's concern, and he probably believed he'd done his duty by calling them.

A half hour later, Alex and Marnie entered from the bedroom. My brother was wearing khaki trousers and a long-sleeve linen overshirt. Marnie was in a flowered tank top that revealed still-aroused nipples. Alex noticed this and slid the tank up so that he could take her in his mouth. She giggled and swatted him on the shoulder.

"Come on, not in front of your sister," she teased.

He glanced at me and grinned. "Hey, I think my sister likes it. Getting turned on over there?"

"No," I replied.

Alex lifted his head to laugh and then gave Marnie's nipples a squeeze that sent her backing away in mock protest. He laughed again. "No more fooling around, hon. We have work to do."

She attempted to look annoyed but couldn't resist a smile that sparkled with post-coital pleasure. "I think we've already done a lot for one morning."

He smiled and, with a relaxed and easy stride, strolled over to my chair. "Too bad my sister isn't having any fun."

"I'm fine, thank you. I've had enough of that for a while."

"I bet you have." He turned to Marnie. "I've got a dealer who's willing to sell some gold Krugerrands and other coins—legitimate. He said he'll take Alex's brokerage check if I have identification, which I do. The deal's on for this afternoon."

"I love gold!" Marnie replied.

"I noticed."

"Hey, you promised me the best, baby." She gave him a feline arch of her back that emphasized the skimpy length of the tank top.

"And you're getting it, aren't you?"

She laced a flirtatious hand around his ear. "Yeah, sweetie, I'm getting it good."

This display of affection was turning disgustingly saccharine. I decided to change the subject. "So, what are you going to do after you buy the rest of the diamonds?"

My brother turned to me. "You have big ears. Well, today we have some stuff arriving, right, Marnie? Then we'll see."

She brightened at the thought of more packages. "Can't wait!"

Alex glanced around the room. "It'd be nice to sell the TV and stereo system. Probably haul in a thousand or so for everything."

"How will you do that?" I asked him. "Another trip to your crooked friends?"

"No. Maybe at a flea market."

"Someone might remember you."

"No, someone might remember *you*," he replied. "I could go in drag. Maybe I'll practice this afternoon, what do you think? Wear some makeup and jewelry? This coin dealer's more likely to be fussy about my credentials."

I wasn't sure if he could cover the remnants of his facial hair no matter how closely he shaved, but with several layers of liquid makeup and powder, it might be possible.

"What about selling the computer and printer upstairs?" Marnie asked.

"Not worth the bother, but come to think of it, I should check the hard drive to make sure there's nothing on it that incriminates you. Keep an eye on her, okay?"

He handed the gun to Marnie and stuffed the gag in my mouth.

Chapter Eighteen

WHEN MY BROTHER RETURNED, he announced that all mentions of Marnie had been deleted from e-mails or files on my computer.

"Oh, Alex, you received a nice note from your concerned friend Cope," he said. "I answered and told her everything was fine. That Marnie was great and there was nothing to worry about. I also asked her to destroy the papers when they arrive."

"What if she calls?" Marnie asked him.

"We don't answer the phone. Besides, I wrote that the two of you were going to Vermont for ten days on a romantic vacation. That should buy us enough time."

Marnie chuckled. "Good idea. And, like we discussed, I told my boss I'd be out for a week or two because of a medical procedure. I've already cleaned my computer at work and the one here."

They fixed ham sandwiches and ungagged me so I could eat, replacing the bandana when we heard the sound of a truck in the drive.

Alex risked a peek through the window. "Fed Ex. He's putting stuff in the box." After waiting until the truck turned onto the main road, he went out the sliding door and carried in packages. "The driver must think you've won the lottery."

"Probably," Marnie replied. "And I guess we can't get the mail. It's going to pile up."

"No, it isn't. I emptied the mailbox three days ago and then called the post office to hold all mail for thirty days. They wanted me to fill out a form, but I explained I was going out of town due to a sudden death in the family and couldn't."

"Brilliant!"

"Now, before I leave you to your fun, Marnie, will you help me with the makeup?"

They headed for the bathroom. A second shave and some dampening and styling of Alex's hair? Marnie and my brother were enjoying themselves, chuckling at their handiwork.

"You're prettier than your sister," Marnie teased. "Hey, try these clip earrings."

He approximated a high, feminine voice. "Oh, dear, look how glamorous! What shade of lipstick should I use?"

"For god's sake, Alex. Don't overdo it. You can't play this too flamboyantly, otherwise you'll draw too much attention to yourself. And we need to add a scarf to hide your Adam's apple. Might look a little weird in this heat, but a turtleneck would be really silly at this time of year."

"What about shoes?" he asked.

"Your feet are bigger than your sister's. Hmm. Why don't you stop and buy some slip-ons? Something that looks feminine. Pink or with beads or something."

Alex did the swishy voice again. "Shoes are so important. A girl has to have lots of shoes."

"Okay, cut it out. You're just playing your sister, not Marilyn Monroe. I'll give you directions to one of those cheap shoe stores that's on your way. If they don't have a size large enough in the women's section, get something nondescript. And thank goodness you wear baggy pants. They'll hide your, well, you know what."

They both laughed. "Let's hope the coin dealer isn't cute!" My brother was getting carried away with his witticisms.

When the two of them came into the living room, I was shocked. Alex looked more convincing as a female than I did. His fine skin and neat features had allowed Marnie to transform him successfully. With some mousse and spray, she had created bangs that softened the angle of his forehead and covered his ears. His beard was now invisible, and his cheeks glowed with a faint blush of color. Marnie had applied modest shadow and liner, enhancing his blue eyes. The gold hoop earrings were a nice touch, along with gold bangles and Marnie's watch; his nails had been shaped and buffed. A flowered kerchief was tied around his neck, and Marnie's straw bag rested in the crook of his elbow.

"How do I look, Alex?" he asked in a falsetto voice as he slipped my wallet, brokerage checkbook, and his cell phone in the bag.

Because the gag was still in my mouth, I shrugged my shoulders.

Before he left, my brother untied the laundry line and let me use the bathroom under Marnie's scrutiny, the Smith & Wesson in her hand. It felt good to move, but no opportunity presented itself to grab anything useful, though the bathroom counter was awash in cosmetics and hair products. They returned me to the chair and carefully re-tied the ropes.

"Do you need anything while I'm out?" he asked Marnie.

"Maybe some more wine and beer and something for dinner."

"Okay. Too bad we can't use the grill outside. If someone came to the door, they might smell the smoke. I'll buy something from the deli."

"Fine. Good luck and, well, just don't be too feminine." She cast an eye in my direction. "Your sister isn't, after all."

"Don't kiss me," he told her. "You'll spoil my lipstick."

Marnie gave him a whack with a magazine. "Get out of here!"

The room had grown warm without the air conditioner running, and I was growing even hotter. Anxiety was producing an acid bloom in my stomach, and when Marnie left to clean the bathroom, I agonized over every possible means of escape, arriving at the miserable conclusion there were none. No one was coming to my rescue, Marnie had the gun, and I was bound tightly.

After twenty minutes, Marnie untied the bandana. I thanked her and watched as she sat on the couch amid the delivered boxes, her eyes sparkling with anticipation. She opened each one eagerly and placed the clothes and expensive jewelry on the coffee table. Some of it would be difficult to unload, but some of it was part of Marnie's reward.

"Where are you two going dressed in style?" I noticed a men's single-breasted blue blazer and green silk necktie.

"Maybe Spain or Greece."

"So, you expect to get rid of me and waltz out of the country? You can't live forever on these clothes and the diamonds, two Rolexes, and a few gold coins."

"We'll have plenty with the $24,500 from the sale of your Jeep and another $35,000 from the home equity loan, a couple of thousand from your checking account, and the coins and diamonds. I have a buyer for my car. Someone who worked at my former office in Perth Amboy. Alex's car is a rental."

"I see. I guess you no longer plan to sell the house?"

"I'm not sure. Probably we won't." Marnie seemed more interested in unfolding a cream-colored cashmere sweater set. "We may need to leave soon."

"You don't honestly think Alex is going to take you to Europe, do you?"

She stared at me, then blinked. "Yes, we're going to Europe. Alex has our passports and everything."

"He has his, but have you seen yours?"

"No, but several weeks ago Alex asked me to get passport photos taken. He said he was having my papers created."

"And you fell for that?"

Marnie didn't like this. "I know he's taken care of them. He told me everything was ready."

I smiled. "Sure. Now think about it. Everyone believes Alex is dead, right?"

"Yeah."

"Well, unless someone knows who he is, he's basically invisible. Alex entered the country under another name, maybe not even using a U.S. passport. He leaves, and no one is aware that Alexander Wyce was here."

"So?"

"So, if they find my murdered body, they won't look for him. The police will think someone else did it, and they're already suspicious of you. Do you know why?"

"No."

"Because my attorney called them. I tipped him off when Alex made me phone him."

"Alex didn't tell me that."

"Because he didn't catch on until the police came to the door."

Marnie returned the cashmere sweater into its box. "Okay, so what?"

"The attorney knows I was changing my will because I was afraid for my safety. When I called to cancel the revisions, he deduced something was the matter and correctly assumed you were meaning to harm me. I'm sure he told this to the police."

She gave me a stony glance. "Then I would be Suspect Number One, huh?"

"Exactly. Alex is unknown. Who're they going to look for? You. Not him."

Marnie chewed her lip. "But if I don't kill you and he does, then I can tell that to the police, and they'll have his fingerprints on the gun and everything."

"He won't be careless and leave prints. Besides, his fingerprints probably aren't on record because he grew up in Europe and wasn't arrested anywhere. Face it, Marnie, the police won't find Alex. He's used to disappearing, which he's done for fourteen years. He'll get away, leaving you. You ordered all these things on my credit cards, deposited the home equity check in your account—"

"There's nothing wrong with the home equity loan. It will appear legal," she protested, an angry flush rising on her face.

"But if you're discovered with the items you bought with my credit cards, you'd be charged with theft. Once that door is opened, the sales in my portfolio will be examined, as well as the use of my brokerage checks. At the least you would be considered my brother's accomplice, yet this is all an imaginary hypothesis. The ending might be different."

"What do you mean?"

"Alex might kill you too," I offered in a quiet voice. "And take the money and go. Maybe he's buying his plane tickets right now."

"Alex wouldn't do that!" Marnie stood and paced the carpet, her arms across her chest.

"He murdered my father. I don't know whether he planned to

do it or whether he did it in a fit of temper. He plans to kill me, right? Seems like killing you wouldn't matter much to him."

"You have it all wrong!" She grabbed the pink gag, jammed it in my mouth, and knotted it tightly against the back of my head. "You'll see!" With a backward glance glowing with hostility, she stalked from the room.

A surge of hopefulness spread over me. I had planted some doubts in Marnie's mind.

Chapter Nineteen

MARNIE IGNORED ME for most of the afternoon. She was probably rearranging her suitcase because I heard her complaining about leaving things behind, although what she planned to do with all this stuff on the run, I had no idea. As she rolled her new yellow suitcase to the garage, Marnie continued muttering to herself, sounding quite unhinged. After reentering the kitchen, she uncapped a beer and sat on the living room sofa, drinking in self-absorbed silence and fanning herself with a magazine. The temperature in the house was close to eighty degrees.

By evening, Alex hadn't returned. Marnie began drumming her fingers on the table, tapping her foot against its leg, and drinking one bottle of beer after another. Each crash of glass into the recycling container was louder. By my count, she had finished five beers. This wasn't enough to make her seriously drunk, but her judgment would be impaired, which might not be so fine for me, because I was one cause of her anger.

It was growing dark early. A summer storm was brewing in the west.

"We'll have some cheese until your brother gets here." She lurched into the kitchen. I heard the cutlery drawer open and a clatter of a knife on a dish. "Do you want a beer?"

I couldn't answer because of the gag. Marnie entered with a block of cheddar cheese and some apple slices on a plate, which she set on the table. After loosening the bandana, she again offered a beer. I told her a soda would be fine. She scoffed but returned with ginger ale in a glass. After cutting the cheese, she loaded a slab with a piece of apple and fed it to me along with a sip of soda.

"We're going to have some thunder and lightning," she said.

"I know, but it's miles off yet."

She nodded, not really interested in the conversation, and ate some cheese.

"Did you fit everything in one suitcase?" I asked.

"No. I need a second one."

"You really think you're going to drive out of here with all that luggage?"

"Look, I don't want to hear any more about it, okay?"

I shrugged and decided to let her drink without interruption, which she did. Soon, the sixth bottle was finished. In the far valley, muffled thunder rolled and the wind rushed through the trees. Marnie gave me another swallow of ginger ale and some apple and began to pace the floor in earnest, finally heading into the liquor closet for something stronger. Instead of sitting with me, she waited for Alex in the dining room, a bottle of vodka and the .38 propped beside her.

The storm soon overwhelmed us. Amid the thunder, neither one of us heard the garage door opening. When Alex entered the dining room, Marnie jumped in surprise. He came to a standstill under the skylights; bursts of lightning illuminated his face. He stared at Marnie, the bottle, and at me. With makeup and earrings, Alex was a macabre sight, but the rage exploding across his features was the most frightening.

"What the hell are you doing?" he yelled at Marnie.

"What are *you* doing, coming back this late?" she shouted.

"I was getting the gold coins. The guys didn't open the shop on time. What was I supposed to do? Blow the whole damned deal?" He laid a grocery bag and Marnie's straw handbag on the pass-through's counter.

"It took you eight hours!"

"I had other things to do."

"Like what?" she demanded.

"Getting tickets," he retorted, nearing the dining table.

Marnie laughed scornfully. "I bet. Did you get two?"

"Of course I did."

"And where are my passport and identification papers?"

"I have them."

She gave him a look that blazed even in the darkness. "Where are they?"

"In a safe place."

"In the car? In your purse?" This last was said with venom.

Alex approached her, his face tight. In a low growl, he said, "I told you. I have them. Everything is taken care of." He thrust the gold bangles from his wrist and slammed them on the dining room table.

The alcohol was driving her now. "Are you sure? Are you quite sure?"

He looked at me and then fixed on Marnie. "What ideas has my sister put in your head?"

"Nothing. But you know, Alex, here we are. You're dead, or at least that's what everyone thinks, and I'm involved with your sister. The bank knows it, her friend Cope knows it, the realtor—everyone. And her new attorney thinks something is wrong since Alex tried to change her will and then told him to cancel the changes. All of this connects me to Alex. Who'll be blamed if something happens to her? Who?"

My brother turned in my direction, recognizing the source of Marnie's provocation. "You should learn to keep your mouth shut."

His eyes flashed and his mouth tightened. He took a step toward me but stopped when Marnie raised the revolver from the table and aimed the gun at him.

"What do you think you're doing?" Alex demanded.

"Protecting my interests."

As gripping as this scene was, I was thinking about the paring knife on the plate. It was about three feet away, to my left, near the edge of the table. My brother's back was turned, and Marnie was angled toward him. The light in the room was dim.

Summoning all my strength, I lifted the chair a few inches and scooted it toward the knife. Once, then four times. I worried an argument between my brother and Marnie was about to erupt, but their dispute drew their attention away from me.

"Look, Marnie," my brother said, "I don't know why you're so upset. This is all nonsense. Nonsense from my sister. Think about this morning, after the shower—"

"I don't want to think about that. When I'm no longer useful, I'll be as expendable as she is. No, I have other plans."

"Come on, hon," he said in a reasonable voice, ignoring her tirade. "We're going to fly out of here with lots of money. We can live a nice life in Greece or Spain." He took a step toward her. "Babe, I want you with me. We've set this whole thing up. It's taken months to plan. You're great, amazing. I need you."

"Get back, Alex. I don't believe anything you say." She waved the revolver at him. "I think I'll kill you, then your sister. Make it look like she shot you, you wrestled the gun away, and then you shot your sister. Sounds good. My car is almost packed. I'm ready to go."

I raised the chair again and tipped forward. Wrenching my hands to the side, I grasped the handle, tucked the knife between my fingers, moved the chair to its original location, and slipped the knife under the seat cushion.

"You can't leave the country without a passport," Alex said. "And the police will look for you. That red car of yours is easy to spot. Hey, come on, I have the documents you need. To get away just like we planned."

Marnie remained silent, but she seemed to be weighing her options. At last, she asked, "What kind of passport did you get me?"

"Irish. With your red hair, I thought that would be the best."

Despite her anger, this detail seemed to impress Marnie. "What else?"

"A driver's license, a couple of phony cards from Dublin."

"What name did you use?"

"Megan O'Connell. Born in Ireland, raised in America, and now living in Dublin, in an apartment. You're a science teacher."

She liked this. Her shoulders relaxed.

Alex pressed his advantage smoothly. "Yeah, we've got tickets from JFK to Shannon and a rental car booked there. We'll take a scenic tour for three days, drop the car at the airport in Dublin, and catch a flight to Athens, using different names and passports to throw off the trail."

A huge clap of thunder made them both flinch.

Marnie regained herself. "And once we get to Athens, then what?"

Alex replied in a gentle voice, "Then we disappear. I have a friend with a boat in Piraeus. He'll take us to one of the islands, no questions asked. Everything is cheap. All the wine you want, fresh fish, blue skies like none you've ever seen. We'll rent a car or buy two scooters...whatever you like. And get a cottage on a hill overlooking the sea."

Marnie still seemed dubious, but the lilting cadences of his voice had softened her. The gun point drifted downward. "When are we going?"

Alex smiled. "Friday night." He tried taking a step toward her and this time she let him. "I want you to come with me, Marnie. You're the sexiest woman I've ever known. Besides, what have you got here? Nothing."

"Nothing, thanks to you," she said bitterly. A strike of lightning reflected on her face.

"Marnie, Marnie, we have money. We can get out of here and travel to beautiful places. There's no reason to return. We're good together. We've earned this. You've earned it."

I could think of a lot of reasons why Marnie shouldn't trust him, but it appeared that Marnie was retreating from her hostile position.

"Friday night?" Her voice held a tinge of hope.

"Yeah. We'll sell your car in Perth Amboy like you've arranged and drive my rental to the airport. It'll be great. An adventure," he cajoled. "Come on..."

My brother closed the space between them. He reached for the gun and turned it aside without resistance. After he took it away from her, she placed her arms around his neck and began to sob.

"Hey, everything's fine." Alex kissed her cheek and wiped her tears. "That's my girl."

"Oh, Alex, this has been so difficult. I'm sorry," she cried, holding him tightly.

"Easy does it. It's okay," he told her. "Now, would you like to see the coins I bought?"

From the straw bag, Alex removed three small display boxes. Marnie sniffed, but as she reached for one of the plastic cases, her downturned mouth raised upward into a happy smile.

Chapter Twenty

AFTER ALEX SCRUBBED the makeup from his face and changed, they ate in the dining room and talked quietly, making it impossible for me to overhear their conversation. The storm moved toward the east, with only an occasional murmur of thunder. When they finished, Marnie complained of a headache and went to bed. My brother brought in a plate of cold leftovers and a glass of water, removing the duct tape from my fingers but keeping my wrists bound.

I took a bite of ham. "So, Marnie had too much to drink again."

He snorted. "Yes. It's getting to be a real habit."

I mused on his own alcoholic intake and wondered if he had a problem himself. I could smell the liquor on his breath. "What are you going to do about her?"

"You might want to be concerned about yourself." A grim expression settled over his features. He helped me with a forkful of coleslaw so I wouldn't spill.

I chewed for a minute. "Yeah, I know. Believe me, I'm concerned."

"What happens between Marnie and me, well, that's none of your business. Don't put any more garbage into her head, either."

"So, what's next?" With a shaking hand, I lifted a glass of water to my mouth.

"Well, you might be taking a ride."

"Why?"

"You'll see. Maybe on a sailboat. You'd like that, wouldn't you?"

His tone darkened as he said this. At this time of year, the waters around New Jersey were crowded with boats, but it wouldn't take long to reach the ocean or a secluded inlet to do whatever he had in mind. I thought about the knife hidden under the seat cushion and wondered whether an opportunity to use it would present itself. My luck so far had been atrocious, and the one time I'd been lucky, I made the wrong choice.

Alex went to scrape the dishes and open a bottle of beer. After he returned to the living room, he set the beer on the coffee table and stared at me, his face inscrutable in the low light.

"Do you need to go to the bathroom?" he asked.

I nodded.

Alex untied the ropes around my chest and pushed me toward the foyer. In the bathroom, he sliced one strand of tape and pressed a wad of toilet paper into my hands. Then he undid my belt, button, and zipper, and let his fingers rest against my thigh. I backed away from him and was relieved when he left the room, though the door remained ajar so he could glimpse through the crack. A cold wave of fear washed over me as I used the toilet.

"Okay to brush my teeth?"

"Yes, but hurry up."

It was difficult to squeeze the toothpaste onto the brush, but I managed. When I'd finished, Alex escorted me into the hall. Marnie was snoring loudly in the bedroom.

My brother jerked a thumb in her direction. "I'll never sleep in there. Maybe I'll try the couch. Wait while I grab some pillows."

He tucked two under his arm, prodded me toward the living room, closed the bedroom door, and threw the pillows on the sofa. After shoving the armchair closer to the windows, my brother pushed me into the seat, tucked the revolver in his belt, and replaced the laundry line and tied the knots in front, which might be helpful. He forgot the bindings around my feet and to replace the duct tape, leaving my fingers free. If only he would sleep in the bedroom, I might flee the house, but Alex's decision to camp out on the couch would make it difficult.

"Do you want anything else?" he asked.

I shook my head.

"Sleepy?"

"Sort of."

Alex yawned and pinched open the venetian blinds. When he

was satisfied no one was outside, he let the slats fall. The room was dark, especially in my corner, which was deep in shadow, though the skylights provided some faint light on Alex, who began arranging the pillows.

After he laid down, he said, "Not much to do. Can't read. No television. Might as well call it quits for the night."

He lowered the .38 on the coffee table next to his left hand—approximately ten feet away from me, a tantalizing target—and twisted a button on his shirt to the left and then to the right. When his fingers stopped their fidgeting, my brother smoothed the cotton cloth rippling over his chest.

"Sounds like you and Marnie had a gay old time, huh?" A slow smile creased his face. "You know, I was curious what two women did together. Marnie described some of the stuff. It kind of excited her to tell me."

His eyes sought mine, though I doubted Alex could see me well. I refused to engage in the conversation.

"Don't like to think about Marnie with me, do you? You're probably still hung up on her." He laughed, amused. "Well, I'd just forget about Marnie."

"I would be delighted to forget about her," I muttered.

"A little sore about how things worked out?"

"That's one way to put it." I stared at him. "You two are a lot alike."

"Marnie isn't like me. She's volatile and unstable and gets by on her looks and her flirtatious abilities."

"I rest my case."

"Come on, she's just a convenience. Sure, she's been fun in bed. I won't tell you otherwise. In fact, she's damned hot. But you know all about that. Why don't you tell me about one of your little escapades? They would make a great bedtime story."

"No, I think you've heard enough."

"Oh, Alex, just one? Maybe about the time you made it with her in the snow? Behind your apartment? You remember. She brought out a blanket, and you took off all her clothes? I didn't figure you to be so imaginative, Sis."

I hated that he knew about this, hated that Marnie had told him about those private moments. "I told you I don't want to talk about it."

"Poor Alex," he said softly. "Pretty tough to learn everything that happened between you was deliberately planned or faked."

Whether from pride or anger, I was getting steamed. "I don't believe you. Yes, you two conspired and executed this very well, but there were some moments with Marnie that were real."

My brother laughed. "Anything can be faked. Admit it, she had you from day one. You were a patsy, a pushover, a chump. I hope that makes you feel stupid because that's what you deserve." His eyes gleamed, and he licked his lips. "But remember, I haven't forgotten…"

"Forgotten what?"

"You know…" He drifted off, as if he could say no more.

We studied each other for a long time. Finally, his eyes fluttered closed, and, a few minutes later, his breathing changed, growing more regular in sleep.

*

I ached to get free. The likelihood of another opportunity to cut the tape was slim, even though the thought of making the attempt while my brother was lying on the couch was daunting. I moved my hands a few inches to see whether he would notice. He didn't. Bracing both feet on the carpet, I lifted my body and withdrew the knife from under the seat cushion. The blade was sharp because Marnie was a fanatic about keeping our knives whetted to a fine edge. Holding it by its black handle, I turned the blade and began to hack at the tape, grateful that Alex hadn't bound my fingers. After a while, the tape parted with a small sucking noise that seemed loud to my sensitive ears. I then worked frantically at the single large knot of rope, picking at it with my fingernails until it gave. Two loops of laundry line circled around my body, but with the knot untied, the ropes were sufficiently loose so one strong yank would remove them, although I probably couldn't throw the ropes over my head and snatch the gun before Alex woke. If startled, would he instinctively grab the revolver and shoot?

I rotated the paring knife backward and pressed it between my hands, which I held together so it would appear the tape was intact, and mulled over whether Alex really intended on killing me. Because the house scheme had been scrapped, the primary motive for my death was gone. If my logic was correct, if Alex had a vestige of affection for me, all he needed to do was stash me in a remote place and fly to Europe, where he would be difficult to find because he probably had several fake passports, such as the Irish passport for Marnie, the existence of which I doubted.

The more I analyzed the situation, the more I was sure he wouldn't take her with him. She would be a liability, fussing about suitcases and comfortable accommodations when he wanted to disappear into whatever hole he could find until he felt safe to surface and enjoy his windfall. Paying her way would also be expensive, cutting his profit in half. The only reason to bring her was if he cared for Marnie, and I didn't think he did. Romps in the bedroom would not be sufficiently important if they jeopardized his survival.

As I stared at Alex asleep, I sensed he still harbored nostalgia for our childhood and that a remnant of our closeness still existed, whatever its nature. How would he react if I tried to take the gun? Would he view it as an act of betrayal? Could he shoot me, or for that matter, could I shoot him? The thought made me feel like I'd been swallowed by oily blackness. For a moment, my vision dimmed like a sky before a storm. I sat there, frozen and frightened.

My psychic agitation, unfortunately, was transmitted. Alex opened his eyes and glanced at me. I hoped the darkness would prevent him from noticing the sliced tape or the unknotted rope.

He yawned. "Trouble sleeping?"

"Yes, a bit. This chair isn't exactly a bed."

He smoothed his cheek with the side of his hand. "You're right."

His agreeableness made him sound sympathetic, yet his moods tended to be changeable.

"Pretty stiff, too," I added.

He gave that half a thought, stood, and picked up the gun. "Got to pee."

I watched him round the corner into the hall and calculated the amount of time I'd need to get through the sliding door and out of the house. The dowel rod was lodged tight in the track. It would take a few seconds to remove it and pull open the slider and screen. The front door, which was nearer, would have to be unlocked and unbolted. The door was also closer to Alex, who would hear me leave and give chase. It was unlikely I could outrun him.

The toilet flushed. After he entered the room, Alex turned his back to place the gun on the table.

I shoved the ropes over my head and leapt out of the chair. Alex whirled around, and I rushed at him, slashing his shoulder with the paring knife. Stunned, he grasped the wound and glanced at the blood oozing down his sleeve, his eyes wide with alarm. Without hesitation, I aimed the knife at his chest, but he swiftly released his shoulder and parried the strike. A cut opened on the side of his hand, but when Alex realized I was about to lunge again, he jumped backward, and the tip of the knife sliced his white linen shirt.

I retreated and we stared at each other, both bent in a defensive crouch. Alex could have grabbed the revolver, yet he seemed strangely calm, almost appreciative of the chance to physically engage. Finally, he charged forward, dodging a sweep of the knife, and grasped my right wrist. Pressing his body against mine, he plowed us against the wall. The impact sent the knife flying across the room, landing beyond the couch. I kicked his left leg, but as he toppled over, Alex clutched my shoulder and brought us both crashing onto the carpet. He regrouped and struck my chin hard with his fist, splitting the skin. Blood dripped down my neck, and I was momentarily dazed until Alex began ripping at my blouse. I batted at his hands and twisted away until I was on top of my brother. I felt the sharpness of his ribs against my own; his breathing, like mine, was coming in great rasps. As children, we had wrestled, evenly matched, until one subdued the other and brought the loser to tears. Now, the game had become deadly. I scrambled to rise above him and reach for the gun on the table, but

Alex caught my belt and prevented me. He hauled downward until we were face to face. His eyes were wild with anger, yet another emotion was present, one I couldn't read. With my free hand, I punched him in the side. He flinched and hung on, then flipped me over. When I lifted my leg to kick him again, he was too fast and subdued my leg with his own. Then he pinned both of my wrists so I couldn't move.

"I have you, Alex," he whispered.

I struggled, but he held me tight. A wolfish grin spread across his face. "I have you. And you know what? I like it."

I tried to wriggle loose, but Alex pressed his full weight on top of me. I felt the hardening of his cock as he worked his body parallel to my own.

"No, please," I begged.

My brother brought his face closer, his eyes gleaming with desire. Suddenly, he kissed me hard on the lips and forced his tongue inside my mouth. I jutted backward and attempted to get free, but he moved my hands above my head and began rocking his hips up and down, pushing himself between my legs.

"Oh, god…don't do this!" I pleaded. "No!"

He laughed. "It's been a long time. Too long."

Just as I didn't want to think about what was happening now, I tried to crowd out memories of what had happened fourteen years ago, the last time I'd seen him, but he wanted to remember; he was desperate with the keenness of his memory.

"Come on, Sis. That little thatched-roof chalet on the edge of camp? It was so private. Our special place."

He kissed me again, then let go of my hand so he could raise my shirt. At that moment, I brought a fist down on his head, causing him to fall to the side, stunned. He recovered, unclasped my belt buckle, and reached for my pants zipper. I didn't have room to mount a full swing, though I elbowed him in the ribs. Undeterred, he continued, stripping off my pants and whispering a litany of phrases, speaking mostly to himself.

"You want this. I know you do."

After he slid to my right and pulled off my underwear, I thrust my knee into his groin. He yelped and clutched himself.

I needed to get the gun because I couldn't overpower Alex. I crawled toward the table and clutched its edge. As I did, Alex tackled me and flattened us both. He sat on my back and forced my right hand down to my side where he could trap it with his knee. I tried desperately to push up, but with his commanding position, Alex was able to wrench my left arm behind me. I fought him with all my strength, but he had better leverage and a male's stronger body. When I stopped thrashing to catch my breath, Alex grabbed the rope from the floor and wrapped it around my right wrist, raising my hand over my head, and then did the same with my left.

"Enough?" he asked.

I thought about this and weighed other possible moves, but I exhaled a long breath and said yes.

He turned me over, sat astride my hips, and restrained my hands. "You always were a hellcat. I see that hasn't changed." A lock of black hair curled over his right eye. "So, what's next, huh?"

"Just put me in the damned chair."

My brother ignored this and looped the end of the rope around my throat and between my wrists. If I tried to hit him, the rope would tighten across my larynx. He wiped his perspiring upper lip, smearing some blood from his hand onto his mouth, and then pulled up my blouse and bra. For a long moment, Alex stared at me, but finally he gave into his desire. He covered my nipple with his warm, bloody hand and began to stroke gently.

"You like this, don't you?" Alex murmured. "Yeah, I know you do. Just like you did that night."

"No, Alex, please!"

"Oh, you were great! I loved being the first man inside you." He drew closer. "No one else has meant anything. No one. Do you know that?" Alex paused after this revelation, perhaps taken aback by the admission. "Come on, Alex, kiss me." He brought his lips near mine, waiting for a response.

I averted my face. Alex ignored my rejection, took me in his arms, and kissed me with passion and desperation, as if I were the last person on earth. His emotion was palpable, frantic, electric. He unzipped his trousers and removed them and his briefs. His erection jutted against my thigh.

"Don't do it…" I began to cry.

Alex stopped, his hand suspended between my legs, and gasped. His gaze was unfocused, as if he was staring into a void, somewhere between the far past and the present. When he lifted his gaze to my face, tears were welling in his eyes. My brother shook his head, then crushed his body against mine. Shaking with anguish, great sobs broke from deep inside of him.

"I'm sorry," he moaned.

He was unable to say more, just repeated this whispered apology over and over, as he cried and swayed us back and forth. Though certainly no such memory exists, our embrace seemed reminiscent of our pre-natal position. It felt as if his loneliness and overwhelming need were passing into my skin by some kind of osmosis. All the years of being without family had been so painful, so utterly sad, that I understood my brother's emotions, as much as they terrified me.

We lay there on the floor until Alex eased to my side, his arm cradling my head, and fell asleep. I was so uncomfortable and upset that I couldn't close my eyes, as tired as I was. Slowly, almost imperceptibly, dawn filtered through the blinds and the skylights. I knew this night's happening would change the situation, perhaps would serve to erase some of his anger and guilt, but I didn't believe it would deter him from his goal: to get what he felt was due him.

A while later, the door to the bedroom opened—closed, it had probably muffled most of the noise. I listened for Marnie's steps in the hall and heard her intake of breath when she entered the living room and saw us lying on the floor, blood soaking the rug and our clothes. Though I couldn't see her, the gun clanked against the table as she picked it up. When she stood in front of us, her hand trembled and her eyes opened wide as she gazed upon our semi-naked bodies.

"What happened?" Her voice quivered with anger.

I had no idea what to say. I shook my head. My brother woke

and jumped when he saw Marnie with the revolver aimed at him. Then he quickly glanced at me before focusing on Marnie.

She sank into the chair. "What did you do?" she asked Alex.

He raised himself, wincing from the pain from his shoulder and hand. "Marnie, it's a long story."

"Goddammit, Alex, what did you do?" she shouted.

Alex sighed. "My sister got a knife somehow."

"From where?" she demanded of me.

"The paring knife from the cheese platter," I replied. "You forgot about it when Alex returned last night."

My brother took this in and threw a furious look at Marnie. "I guess you were too drunk to notice," he said bitterly. "Alex cut the tape and untied the ropes while I was sleeping. She stabbed me with the knife."

Marnie nodded and then, with the tip of the revolver, pointed at his trousers. "And your sister did that too?" She didn't wait for an answer. "The inseparable twins," she said, throwing her head back and letting loose a torrent of manic laughter. "Oh, I get it now. What I don't get, Alex, is why you bothered with me when you wanted your sister all along."

"Marnie, this…this just happened. I don't know why."

"You don't know why?" She gestured at his cock. "And that just came out all on its own? Come on, Alex. How stupid do you think I am?"

I had no idea whether my brother really cared for Marnie or whether he was just concerned for his own safety, but clearly Alex was as apprehensive about her incensed mood as I was.

"Marnie, this wasn't about sex…" I began, although this wasn't altogether true.

"You're lying there tied up with your blouse around your neck and you're telling me it wasn't about sex? Look at your brother!"

I did as she suggested and then fixed my eyes on her. "No, it was about having no family left."

Alex stared at me with a wistful expression, as if he shared my feelings. Slowly, he started to pull on his underwear.

Marnie waved the revolver at him. "Oh, Alex, why quit now?

Maybe you two should go another round. Actually, I'd like to observe. You know, just to compare styles? Besides, you might knock her up. Wouldn't that be interesting? Which of you would the baby look like?" Her laughter once again veered into hysteria. Abruptly, she came to her feet. "You were so interested in your sister and me, what we did together. Now I know why. It turned you on, didn't it? You wanted to do it to your sister the entire time you were with me."

"No, I didn't." He started to rise.

"Stay where you are, Alex. Your blood is already on the floor. More won't matter."

"Please, Marnie," I said. "Let's talk about this. Can I get up?"

She made no response. My brother ignored her and untied the rope around my throat. "This got out of hand. I didn't intend it. I didn't want it."

"I don't believe you."

I hurried to straighten my bra and shirt. "He's telling the truth." I had no idea why I was supporting him.

Marnie examined my face. "Put her in the chair, Alex. Tie the rope from the back and use the duct tape like before. And for god's sake, get dressed."

He staggered to his feet, eyeing Marnie with caution, and slipped into his slacks. "Can't we clean up?"

She watched me fumble with my pants' zipper. "Okay, but make it fast."

Alex steered me into the bathroom. After a lingering look, he traced the angle of my shoulder with his finger. I shivered, scared by my brother's dangerous attraction. He retreated into the hall but kept the door ajar. Knowing his eyes were on me, I removed my clothes, covering myself as best I could until I stepped into the shower. When I came out, a button-down shirt, tan cargo pants, underwear, socks, and the new pair of Nike sneakers sat on the countertop beside a box of Band-Aids. I dried off, stuck two bandages over the cut on my chin, and dressed while Alex stood in the hall. I held his gaze until I finished, as if by doing so, I could stop him from touching me again.

After we returned to the living room, he pushed me into the chair, and before I knew it, I was in the same position as before.

"My turn to take a shower," he said to Marnie.

Marnie gave him a brittle look. "A quick one."

When the bathroom door closed, Marnie turned to me, her green eyes blinking. "I just have one comment for you, Alex." And with that, she slugged my cheek with the handle of the gun.

Chapter Twenty-One

WE ATE BAGELS with cream cheese for breakfast. Everyone was quiet, nervous, wary, and warm. Last night, the situation had been raw, stripped to the roiling feelings between my brother and myself. Though I couldn't imagine Marnie forgiving him, it seemed Alex had miraculously coaxed her into his intimate graces. Since I was exhausted, I fell asleep after eating. When I awoke, the sun was high in the sky, and the room was empty. Shortly afterward, Marnie came in from the garage with her suitcase, probably because Alex insisted she should bring less. Grumbling, she piled some clothes on the dining table and then walked into the living room. After glaring at me, Marnie took a seat on the sofa and began aggressively flipping pages in a magazine.

Dressed as me, Alex left to complete the second diamond deal, which meant Marnie trusted him even though my brother had the cash from the sale of my Jeep and from two checks, my brokerage account checkbook, the coins, and some of the diamonds in his possession—soon to have them all. After the events of last night, why would he have a reason to return?

"Alex might not come back," I said.

Marnie's head rose. "Don't start again. Yes, he will. Of course he will."

"Why?" I explained that my brother had most of the money and valuables. "You have a home equity check deposited in your bank, new clothes, and some cash, which he probably thinks is payment enough for your contribution. And, oh yes, Marnie, you have me. What are you going to do with me if he doesn't show up? And how are you going to get away? The police will come when someone wonders where I am. The house will be searched, and this mess will be the first thing they see." With my toe, I pointed to the bloodstained carpet. "When that happens, if I'm found dead, they'll reach the conclusion you murdered me, whether or not you did. My will provides the motive. Your accounts will be frozen and a description of you and your car will be broadcasted."

"I'm not concerned. Alex will be home soon, and everything will go as planned."

"You're dreaming! If he doesn't abandon you, maybe he'll kill us both. We're the people who know he's alive, who could jeopardize his escape."

Marnie stared unseeing at the magazine in front of her, and then her jaw tightened. "I could just shoot you and wait for him. How about that?"

*

Marnie had nothing to drink other than a glass of milk. I didn't know whether I was relieved about this abstemiousness or not. After our earlier conversation, she avoided me and stayed in the bedroom. I slept again, partly due to fatigue and partly from boredom. When I woke, Alex was coming through the door with a bucket of fried chicken and two bags in hand. After stuffing the chicken in the refrigerator, he opened a bag full of cheeseburgers and fries and called to Marnie, who brought the food to the dining room table and sat with him. He showed Marnie sixteen large diamonds he had purchased—presumably the cash from the stock sales had become accessible and mostly depleted. Again, Alex refused to let Marnie have the stones. He picked up the .38 and tucked it into the small of his back. Alex was now in charge. I doubted Marnie would have the gun again.

I ate cold fries and a cheeseburger and wished I hadn't.

As the sun was setting, I heard Alex tell Marnie to empty her bank account the next day if the home equity check had cleared.

"Do you think that's safe, Alex?"

"They don't care what you do with your own money. If you're worried, leave ten bucks," he told her.

I could tell she disliked his tone, but also that she was willing to do as he asked, probably because it was to her advantage, which appeared to be her main reason for doing everything, regardless of immorality or illegality. In this, she was cunning and cold, greedy like my brother. She also possessed his explosive, unpredictable temper.

As a child, Alex had been quick to fly into tantrums if he wanted something. He had never shared toys, and, though we lived apart for most of our growing years, when he visited, Alex insisted my mother buy him duplicates of any toys of mine that he coveted. If she didn't, he'd treat us to angry tirades that lasted hours. My brother was also obsessive about his looks, endlessly combing his hair and becoming furious if his clothes weren't pressed to his satisfaction. The irony was that my parents thought he might be homosexual. My brother, as I well knew, was completely heterosexual.

*

The fried chicken and biscuits were served late. When I finished, they allowed me to use the toilet, then checked my hands before taping them again. My brother slept in the bedroom with Marnie. I dozed fitfully in the miserable chair, shuddering awake often when nightmares about being bound and gagged beset me.

*

The next morning, there was action. Marnie was in the laundry room folding clothes while my brother made sandwiches. Alex was wearing white pants that emphasized his strong thighs and slender waist and a blue-and-white striped Oxford shirt with the sleeves cuffed above his wrists. He looked handsome, crisp, like a navy captain. His "boat ride" comment came to mind. Were we off for the high seas?

After Marnie completed the chores, she left. About noon, my brother carried a suitcase to his car and then brought a black carryall bag into the kitchen and packed napkins, plastic knives and forks, paper plates, cups, and two rolls of duct tape inside. Ominously, he laid a coil of nylon rope on the counter before entering the living room.

"All set?" I asked in a falsely jaunty voice.

"Yeah, I guess. I don't need much."

"What happened to the 'we' in that sentence?"

He gave me a tired smile. "*We* won't need much."

"When is Marnie returning?"

He shrugged and looked at his watch. "Soon."

"Then off to the boat?" I was being flippant, though I didn't know why.

"Yeah. Do you want to freshen up a little?"

"Last chance?"

Alex gave me a sour look. "Just answer me 'yes' or 'no' if that isn't too much trouble. We won't be leaving until dark."

"Okay."

My brother walked me into the bathroom, leaving the door open. I washed with a cloth and combed my hair, observing the bruises on my face and removing the Band-Aids on my chin. The cut was healing, but it still looked nasty. When I came out, Alex was standing there, lost in thought.

"Thanks," I said.

"You're welcome."

He escorted me to the chair. Alex pieced together strands of laundry line to re-use, swearing because his bandaged hand hurt.

"What's with the extra rope over there?" I asked him.

"Just a precaution. The way you squirm out of things, I don't want to take any chances."

I surmised from this that I was joining them for a sail. The very immediate future, therefore, posed no threat. "What kind of boat?"

My brother chewed on his lip for a minute. "Sailboat. An O'Day '32."

"Nice."

"You like sailboats."

"Up to now.

Chapter Twenty-Two

MARNIE ARRIVED with a good head of steam. She set her handbag, several boxes, and a large envelope on the counter, and marched into the living room as if she were treading the stage of a dramatic production. "They would only let me cash $17,500! Some lunatic reason like the check hadn't entirely cleared. Can you believe it? I tried, really I did. They told me I could speak with the manager, but I didn't want to complain for obvious reasons."

"That's okay, Marnie." Alex embraced her. "You did the best you could."

This mollified her somewhat. "That isn't much money."

"No, but maybe we can withdraw the rest from another branch when we're driving to meet your car buyer. And, besides, we've done very well with the coins and everything else."

She separated from Alex. "Any risk the stuff will be found at customs? In our luggage?"

"I doubt it, but if they do, the certificates of sale and authenticity are in the name of Alex Wyatt—no sex mentioned. Did that to match Alex's name on the brokerage checks. That's also the name on my passport."

"Wow! That's clever," she replied.

I thought so too. A fascinating psychological transference by my twin.

"Are you bringing that rope to the boat?" She pointed toward the kitchen counter.

Alex gave her a meaningful glance.

"Oh, yeah, right. And I bought a tarp like you wanted."

I didn't like the sound of that at all. This was one voyage I would be delighted to skip.

Marnie faced me and gestured to her right foot. "Hey, Alex. Good work. The shoes are a perfect fit. It's our turn to be twins."

She was wearing the Nikes I'd given her. Since I wanted nothing to do with Marnie, this made me realize how far we'd fallen from the time when I loved sharing everything with her. I felt sadness mix with disgust, adding to the unpleasant atmosphere in the room. I forced myself to exhale slowly, to relax the tightness in my body, and then observed Marnie walk into the bedroom and return with an overnight bag, which she brought to her car. I assumed Alex had kyboshed the second suitcase and allowed Marnie the large yellow suitcase plus one carry-on for the flight. When she finished clearing her unpacked clothes from the table, Marnie and my brother began playing cards and drinking coffee in the dining room. They seemed to be killing time, which was fine so long as they weren't killing me.

I asked to have my watch replaced. Marnie laughed and said I didn't need it, but Alex replied it was 6:20 p.m. The question roused them to prepare dinner. I noticed both had forsaken alcohol—no small thing for Marnie. After eating and trips to the bathroom for everyone, Alex carried a red and white cooler in from the garage, and the two of them placed sandwiches, soda, leftover fried chicken, and ice inside, then inserted some cleaning supplies in a paper bag. When he went to the bedroom, Marnie added a six-pack of beer to the cooler and toted it to her car.

Alex returned, put on his green slicker, and grabbed his carryall bag. "Okay, no need to wait. A cold front is coming in. The weather will keep everyone away."

As we walked into the garage, I could hear the wind outside. The air was also cooler. Alex snatched my red rain slicker from a hook on the door, presumably for me, but Marnie took it from his hand.

"I'm going to wear that. I packed my new raincoat. Here, she can wear this." She handed him a ratty blue parka of hers that had been hanging in the garage for months.

Using a matt knife, Alex cut off the duct tape around my hands and helped me with the jacket, pulling up the zipper and tying its hood below my chin. "I don't want anyone to recognize you on the way." From his carryall, he removed a roll of tape, applied several strips to my wrists, placed the roll in the left large slash pocket of his coat and the knife in his trousers' pocket, and tossed his carryall, the nylon rope, and a tarp in the trunk with two bags of garbage. Then he nudged me into the passenger seat and fastened my seatbelt.

"Do you have everything you need in your car, Marnie?" he called to her.

She wasn't happy. "I guess so. It's a shame to leave so much behind."

My brother made no comment. "Okay, we're set. Just follow and stay close."

Alex joined me in the sedan, opened the garage door with the remote, and eased into the drive. I turned to see Marnie exit in her Solara, and the garage door shut behind her.

"Where are we going?" I asked, as we made a left onto the main road.

"You'll find out when we get there."

The evening sky was overcast, wind pinning back the leaves. A few sprinkles began to fall, enough to smear the dirt on the windshield.

"Not great sailing weather," I commented.

"No, but it'll do."

The rain, as long as it didn't turn into a squall, would probably suit my brother's purposes. It would reduce the number of boaters on a Thursday night and would certainly reduce visibility. The thought of being on a sailboat in foul weather was not a pleasant one; the thought of dying under those circumstances was even less pleasant.

"How did you get the boat?"

"Through an agency, using your ID. The day I was dressed like you."

"I see. How long is it rented for?"

"Long enough."

My brother was in no mood to provide any useful information, so I tried to recall times we had spent together, happy moments when we were young, that might invoke a positive sentiment in him. Unless I had some opportunity on the boat, psychological manipulation was my only weapon.

"Do you remember when you visited for five weeks, and we took the Blue Jay class?"

He thought for a minute, negotiating a winding curve. "Yeah, sure. The summer when we were ten. We had to participate in a regatta. During a storm."

"Yeah. Mom bought us yellow oilskins because it was raining so hard."

He laughed. "They were adult size. Way too big."

"Yeah. I had to roll the sleeves to the elbows."

"That was one brutal afternoon. Really cold and windy. Every time the boat heeled, water poured over the side. We had to keep bailing while we were sailing."

"Didn't we compete against the Shrewsbury club?"

He nodded.

"You were a captain and won the race." I knew this would please him.

My brother grinned. "Yeah, I did, but it was close. During the last fifteen minutes, I tacked sharply going around a marker and cut off the lead boat."

"I was crewing in mine. My hands were raw from holding the main sheet."

"I guess I had the easier job with the tiller. Your boat came in third."

For some reason, I was flattered that he remembered. "Yeah, which wasn't too bad because there were twelve boats."

"Thirteen," he corrected. "We had a lot of fun that visit."

"I asked Mom to buy a sailboat, but she refused. At least I had friends with Turnabouts and Comets and could go out with them. I was even allowed to skipper a thirty-six-foot Columbia a few times. I'll probably get skin cancer from all the sunburns." As soon as I said this, my brother glanced at me, and I stared back, struck silent.

Alex turned off the small road onto a highway. Marnie's red car was reflected in the side mirror, following about a hundred feet back, an easy task since my brother was driving exactly at the speed limit. The rain began to fall harder, and the wind frisked the trees. It would be an early autumn, I thought, perhaps not a pretty one. Except for the recent storm, the weather had been dry during most of the summer, with unrelenting heat until tonight's sudden drop in temperature. Though it was a relief to be out of the house and driving around, everything of beauty made me sad, since it seemed my days, if not my hours, were numbered.

I glanced at my brother's strong, angular hands on the steering wheel. His thumb was long and dominant compared to his other fingers, in similar proportion to my hand. His profile was like seeing the side of one's face that one never sees in a mirror. I looked at Alex and saw that side of myself.

The windshield wipers were touching the car's window frame on every leftward swipe, a steady beat that was both rhythmic and irritating. When the rain thinned, the wipers scraped, sending an arcing streak across the glass like a downturned smile. Lights from oncoming cars flared now and then, summer shore traffic on the move, restlessly traveling between apartment rentals, the casinos down south, boats, and beaches. We turned onto the Garden State Parkway and headed north.

I looked back at Marnie, wondering what she was thinking and whether my brother's promises had reassured her. What was the old saying? "It takes one to know one." She was shrewd and smart, even dulled by drink, and had to be suspicious of Alex because it was evident that he would fare better alone. Did Marnie have her own plan? Setting him up as the fall guy and figuring a way to take all the money, diamonds, and coins? If her ruse with me had been convincing down to the last intimate detail, why couldn't she fool Alex too? I reminded myself Alex had the gun, most of the cash, the passports and papers, and, ostensibly, so far as I knew, the upper hand.

"Are you really going to take Marnie with you?" I asked.

"What do you think?" He was fencing with me, showing a trace of a smile.

"I don't think so. I've been trying to see it from your

perspective. If she goes, she'll slow you down and will be a nuisance or worse. And she's expensive. The money is the most convincing reason not to bring her. Marnie spends a lot on clothes, food, wine, and would insist on staying at decent hotels. You would be broke in no time, even in Greece or somewhere cheap to live."

He tipped his head toward me. "Points well taken. But does it matter to you what happens?"

"Meaning I won't be around to care?"

"That's not exactly what I said," he replied, tossing me a warning glance.

"Are you asking me whether I'm still in love with Marnie?"

My brother nodded. "Yeah, I suppose."

"That's easy. The answer is an emphatic *no*. Don't get me wrong, we had a great time before everything unraveled. She seemed nearly perfect: intelligent, attractive, ready to try new things. A good cook, enjoyed going to restaurants, watching old movies, dancing, and playing tennis. I could go on and on. To tell the truth, I'm still confused about everything that's happened."

"Marnie is a very fine actress. She missed her calling."

"She's going to miss more than that it seems, isn't she?"

Alex shook his head. "Don't jump to conclusions, Sis."

"You'll have to excuse my curiosity, but my curiosity is about all I have at the moment."

"Well, sometimes life takes unexpected turns—not necessarily good ones. You haven't learned that lesson as thoroughly as I have."

"No, maybe not. Still, I lost my entire family and my home when I was twenty-two." As I said this, I felt vaguely guilty, though I didn't know why. It wasn't because my life had been easier than my brother's.

"Not my fault," he whispered.

I wasn't sure what he meant but was disinclined to ask. "To be honest, Alex, I haven't been very happy. I know my experiences don't compare with yours, but both of us have been on our own and lonely."

His expression darkened; his eyes became hooded and remote.

"You have no idea how I feel or what I've had to deal with."

"No, I guess I don't."

He glanced at me to see if I was being sarcastic or honest. "I've needed to do things to survive. I don't want to talk about them, but you get my drift."

I had no response, so I closed my eyes until the car swerved to leave the Parkway. Though I missed seeing the exit sign, the preponderance of fishing and bait shops, boat trailer sales, and other nautical stores confirmed we were close to Sandy Hook Bay, on its west or southwest corner. I knew the area fairly well—where the marine channels were, how the peninsula of Sandy Hook pointed a seven-mile finger into its center, the way the ocean poured around the Hook. It was a fine sailing location, a terminal moraine formed by one of the southernmost glaciers, with access to several New Jersey rivers, to New York City, the ports of Newark and Elizabeth, and the open Atlantic. Alex would have many choices for whatever he had in mind.

We came upon a small four-lane highway and then almost immediately entered a typical New Jersey shore town with some modern stores but more that were old. As we passed by one, it looked as if its display hadn't been dusted or changed since the fifties: the man and woman mannequins, with their limbs awkwardly flexed, sported swimsuits faded by the sun. Every few blocks there was a tavern, usually a brick building with small, high windows fogged by years of smoke and decorated with neon beer signs. The main street still had diagonal parking, a vestige of simpler times.

My brother kept driving, clearly knowledgeable about his route. At one point, Marnie missed a stoplight, so he pulled the car against the curb, swearing at her under his breath. When the light changed, he resumed his twenty-five-m.p.h. speed, though I could see it maddened him to go so slow. He was tapping his fingers on the top of the steering wheel and sighing with frustration when a drunk fisherman in navy waders attempted to cross the street and changed his mind halfway. A look of murderous impatience flashed on Alex's face, a look that reminded me how dangerous

Alex was.

Finally, we drove down a long, low hill flanked by beach grass. The car bumped over a short wooden bridge and onto a flat area cut away from the dunes and surfaced with yellow gravel. Puddles formed in deep holes so that large splashes of dirty water washed over the front of the car as we passed. The parking lot was edged by a line of horizontal telephone poles around which chicory and Queen Anne's lace grew. Alex stopped in a space nearest the marina. Before he turned off the ignition, I noted the time on the car's clock: 8:50. The trip had taken an hour. Marnie parked to our left. She looked at us through the silver, rain-spotted windows. Her eyes appeared apprehensive, but perhaps I was misreading her.

My brother came around the sedan and opened my door. As he leaned over to release my seatbelt, I noticed the bulge of the Smith & Wesson revolver in his right slash pocket. "Let's go, Sis."

Alex popped open the trunk, grabbed the garbage bags, and threw them in a nearby dumpster. Returning to the car, he lifted out the carryall, the coil of rope, and the tarp, which he tucked over my hands to hide the tape. Marnie approached, lugging the cooler and the paper bag containing cleaning supplies. Her red knapsack was slung over her shoulder. Her hair was frizzing in the wet drizzle and falling into her eyes, much to her annoyance.

"Help me with this damned thing," she told my brother.

He locked his car, took one of the cooler's handles, and together we headed toward the docks.

I shivered. The temperature had fallen and was unusually chilly. "Nice night for a cruise," I remarked.

"Well, no fair-weather sailors we," Alex replied.

Despite the cool air, I was sweating in the confines of the jacket as I trudged along, dodging puddles, and glancing nervously at the white-capped water, which was being blasted by wind and slanting rain. Around the corner of the parking area were several docks attached to a new steel bulkhead. Unfortunately, on this heavy weather night, not a soul was around, though there were over thirty boats tied up, ranging in size from small outboards to a decaying wooden yacht. By a ten-foot-square building, an ice machine whirred under an overhead light. Two soda dispensers flanked it, alongside a green mesh trash container full of empty cans. The place was bleak, pressed under a low purplish sky. At the end of the two docks, water was splashing, wetting the dark gray planks. The jingle of stays and rigging filled the air above the moan of the wind.

My brother unlocked a tall gate stenciled with a sign: "Private: Boat Owners Only." He led us to the middle of the pier, where an O'Day sailboat rocked briskly in its partial enclosure. The hull was white, the deck sand-colored. Though the boat was older, it appeared to be in fine shape.

I stood above the O'Day. The cold rain dripped down my face and beat against my pants, which were becoming soaked. The wooden dock quaked, buffeted by a northwest wind and the driving waves. Alex and Marnie dropped the cooler. He set down his carryall and the rope before descending the sailboat's ladder and stepping onto the top of the stern cabin. He then moved forward to unsnap the cockpit cover. Once the cover was stowed, he returned to help us.

"Come on, hurry up," he said crossly to Marnie.

She handed him the bag and rope, which he placed on the cockpit deck, and the cooler, which he set near the hatch leading to the main cabin. I gave him the tarp. He inserted it into a storage box.

"I hope you're going to untie me," I said.

"No, you'll just have to trust us. Marnie, hold her shoulders while I help her."

With my hands taped, venturing down the ladder facing front was a frightening challenge, particularly because the tide was low and the boat floated far below the dock. I was glad for Alex's hands on my legs and finally landed and fell against him. After he steadied me, I stepped into the cockpit, which was composed of two parallel fiberglass benches, the wheel, compass, and navigational equipment, all forward of the stern compartment—most likely the master suite. The main and bow cabins were revealed when Alex unlocked the hatch door. I turned when I heard Marnie climb into the boat, muttering that Alex hadn't assisted her on the ladder. After a slip on the deck, she sat on the starboard bench with obvious relief and parked her red knapsack at her feet.

"Alex, can't we cover this area?" she asked.

"No, it's too windy." He stared at her like she was excess baggage. "Maybe later we can attach the Bimini top but not now."

He studied the wind directional, started the engine, and turned on the running lights. "Marnie, go below and check for any knives or sharp implements my dear sister could use. This is important. There's too much that could go wrong to risk being sloppy."

Marnie didn't seem pleased with his captain's voice but nodded, grabbed her knapsack and the paper bag, and did as he asked.

"A landlubber," he whispered to me in a conspiratorial manner after Marnie disappeared into the center cabin and switched on some lamps. A few minutes later, Alex asked her to come to the ladder so he could hand her the cooler and a few items from his bag. After he did this, we heard her opening and closing cabinets in the galley before heading into the forward cabin.

I moved beside my brother. "Alex, just untie me. You need help. Unless you plan to motor around all night, Marnie won't be able to handle the sails. She'll probably fall overboard."

He smiled, as if the idea of Marnie drowning was a welcome one, and then faced into the wind, his dark hair blowing back like a mane. "Maybe when we get out into the bay. I need to study the charts and the marine forecast."

Marnie shouted, "The front room is okay."

Alex snorted derisively. "Do you hear that? Well, that's where you're going for now."

"Look, Alex, I know these waters better than you do—"

"Get going, Sis. I can manage."

I gave him a searching look, but he was determined. He eased me down the wooden ladder into the galley and sitting area, where the mainmast was anchored in the center of a long table with flaps. The head was to the left, or so I presumed since Marnie quickly pushed me into the fore cabin. In the bow, two bunks came together to form a "V." I sat on one.

"Marnie, you have to do something. He's going to kill us both. You know that."

She was wearing her glasses. Because of the moisture on them, I couldn't see her eyes clearly. "You don't know what you're talking about. We're going for a ride to get rid of you." She said the last with some satisfaction. "Alex and I will return the boat and go to the airport tomorrow."

"There will be no tomorrow for us, Marnie. He practically told me as much."

"I don't think so. Besides, I have a little insurance of my own," she said, pulling out a handgun from her knapsack.

Chapter Twenty-Three

MARNIE LOCKED ME in the bow compartment which, was dark except for stripes of light angling through the horizontal wooden slats on the door. I stretched out on the bunk and listened to Marnie bustling in the galley and Alex unsnapping the cover on the mainsail. A metallic voice from the radio was broadcasting the weather. "Four-foot seas with a variable breeze of twenty knots. No chance of thunderstorms."

After this, my brother thumped into the cockpit and called down to Marnie. "I doubt many people will be out fishing or pleasure-boating tonight. Oh, and I hate to ask, but do you get seasick?"

"I feel a little queasy. Is this going to be bad?"

"Brisk. I won't raise the jib because we're short of crew. Did you gather anything Alex could use as a weapon?"

"Yeah. On the table in the kitchen."

"Galley," he corrected.

I heard Alex descend the hatch ladder and begin stowing items in what I presumed was the boat's safe. Then he unlocked the louvered door.

"Come out, Sis, and have a seat."

I stepped close to my brother. "Please cut the tape," I whispered. "What am I going to do once we're at sea? Jump overboard?"

"You were a damned good swimmer. Better than me."

"After we leave the marina, we'll be too far from land."

Alex didn't answer. He had other things on his mind, such as the charts he unfurled across the table. I assumed from the movement of his finger on the map that we were heading past Sandy Hook and into the open ocean. I hoped he knew what he was doing.

The two of them climbed on deck. Through the hatch opening, I saw Alex instruct Marnie how to steer and control speed. He then began running up and down the gunwales, casting off lines, and pushing against the pilings to keep the boat from whacking them. Marnie remained at the helm, so it was no surprise when the starboard side received a sickening scrape.

"For Christ's sake! Slow and straight!" Alex yelled.

The O'Day lurched, and I heard my brother smack the top of the cabin and swear at Marnie. After another hit, the boat rounded the enclosure and veered to the left, past the end piling. Alex relieved Marnie at the helm, steering us into the space between the piers. As the wind caught the boat, it yawed slightly, and the rocking increased as we neared the marina's exit.

Despite the dampness blowing through the hatch, the main cabin was stuffy, although not as bad as the bow compartment. Both had been closed for some time, and the smell of salt and mildew permeated the air. My shirt was sticky under the jacket; my socks, slacks, and sneakers were wet. I felt miserable, but Alex wasn't in a good mood, either. He was shouting at Marnie because she wasn't performing some nautical duty to his satisfaction. The intricacies of sailing were unknown to her, and with the wind, the dark night, and the choppy seas, her courage was probably failing. I was wondering how long this arrangement would last when Marnie snapped at him and climbed down into the galley.

"Alex wants you." Marnie's cheeks were red with fury.

With Marnie boosting me, I made it up the ladder and sprawled onto the rain-washed left bench.

My brother's dark hair was plastered to his head. "Can you hoist the mainsail?" he hollered over the wind.

After rising unsteadily to my feet, I glanced at the huge mast. It had been years since I'd been on a sailboat this size. Mostly, I was expert in small class boats. On them, we rarely cleated a mainsail, for example, and never in a strong wind, but this was more common practice on larger vessels. I wondered if Alex intended to do this, considering the irregular gusts.

"Yes, I think so." I extended my bound hands toward my

brother.

He sighed, looped an elbow through the stainless-steel wheel, removed his matt knife, and sliced the tape. I peeled it off and put it in my pocket.

As we approached the channel, he increased speed. Holding onto the grab rails, I began loosening the individual ties that bound the mainsail. Alex came about to port and scrutinized the directional in order to maintain a neutral position in relation to the wind. He let down the swing keel, which would increase our draft and reduce lateral movement, and followed every move as I hauled up the mainsail, cleated the halyard, and coiled the extra line. Alex freed the main sheet as the sail moved to the starboard side, its great triangle luffing. The bow continued a slight drift to the right until the sail filled with wind and created forward momentum. I cranked the winch to tighten the main sheet, cleated the rope, and sat in the cockpit while my brother switched off the engine and brought us on course for Sandy Hook. The O'Day began to cleanly cut through the waves.

"Not as fast as she could go," he remarked, studying the head of the sail and squinting because of the rain pelting his eyes. Regardless of the miserable weather, a contented smile appeared on his face.

"No, but fast enough. What's your hurry?" I teased him, being infected with his sudden cheerfulness.

"I don't think this tack will take us all the way to the Hook, do you?"

"It'll be pretty close. We'll have to watch the buoys and markers. The channel runs near the tip. Sometimes the tankers and freighters look like they're going to go aground because they're so close, and occasionally they do. On the west side, immediately off the channel, is Flynn's Knoll. Between the Sandy Hook Channel and the Ambrose Channel, nearer to Coney Island, is Romer's Shoal. Both are great fishing areas but tricky to navigate with this low tide."

"We'll keep an eye out."

*

As we entered the bay, the wind increased, as did the wave heights. I adjusted the sail to reduce headway, ignoring Alex as he raised an eyebrow at my lack of daring. He countered with a change in course that brought the sailboat on the same angle of heel as before. He grinned and gave me a salute. We were on a more easterly tack.

"If you want to stay in the channel, you're going to have to head up a bit," I warned him.

After a few more minutes of eating sea spray, he did as I suggested, and I let out the sail accordingly. Marnie ascended the ladder, closed the hatch, and lost her balance. When she grabbed Alex for support, he frowned and shifted her onto a seat.

Marnie's face looked stiff and pale. "Where are we going?"

"Out to sea," he replied. "It might be a little rough for a while, though I think this cold front is going to pass over soon. It will be calmer in a few hours." Alex looked at her as if this statement held additional meaning.

Through the mist, the lighthouse at Sandy Hook and lights from the Coast Guard Station emerged. No other boats were visible, even in Horseshoe Cove, where they sometimes moored to ride out weather or to party, visiting back and forth in dinghies. During the Revolutionary War, the British fleet had done much the same thing, plying the waters between the anchored warships with lighters and barges carrying officers, men, and supplies. At one point, hundreds of ships had been huddled together around the Hook and in the bay. The area was legendary, since from the first days of New Amsterdam and the early settlements, whoever held Sandy Hook controlled the entrance to New York harbor.

I broke off my historical reverie and reminded myself to attend to the situation at hand. "We're nearly in the Sandy Hook Channel. Is it okay if I go to the bow to see better?"

"Good idea."

With difficulty, I made my way forward on the tilting, slippery deck and dropped down on top of the fore cabin, holding on to a handrail. During a break in the rain and a brief rift in the clouds, the moon appeared. With this fragile light, I saw the beach as we came abreast of the Hook.

"Hold the course, Alex," I yelled, cupping one hand around my mouth. I turned and surveyed the land as it passed by, thinking I should attempt a getaway. Alex was right—I was a very good swimmer. It was possible that I could reach the shore. Even so, distances were deceptive at night, and the water around the peninsula was rife with currents. If this was a receding tide, I might miss the land entirely and be swept in the fast outflow of the Shrewsbury River. I knew small boats had been overturned there, clammers and fishermen drowned, their bodies sometimes never found. I decided I didn't have the guts to try it.

The visibility was still poor, but I spotted the marker G "17," a flashing green gong buoy, ahead on the starboard side, and a red buoy with a bell, R "18," to port. These marked the easterly curve into Sandy Hook Channel. We would have to stay in the center channel here and not veer northward into the area of Flynn's Knoll or southward onto the tip of Sandy Hook itself, where water depths decreased precipitously.

"Alex, more to starboard!" I signaled to indicate the direction. It was possible we could round the Hook without a change of tack since the northwest wind was proving agreeable. We passed another gong buoy, G "13," on the leeward side and shortly thereafter began to feel the effects of the rip, the area where the ocean meets the bay. As the boat was influenced by the higher waves, the pitching increased. A deep-throated foghorn broke the silence as a monstrous black hulk, a low-lying tanker, materialized out of the mist, far enough away to pose no danger. We navigated the end of the Hook, skirting its hazardous shoals and those of the False Hook, which ran parallel on the seaward side and was the location of many shipwrecks.

After markers G "11" and G "7," I went aft to adjust the mainsail, letting it out in a broad reach to take advantage of the wind coming almost directly over the stern. This tack drove us into the incoming waves, so that our progress was constant but wet. When we were in deeper water, Alex steered onto a starboard tack, sailing close-hauled on the port side. The rain, which had stopped, began again for another intense burst.

Marnie had been observing our course through the channel, her face pale and anxious and streaked with rain. Once we had cleared the most hazardous waters, she stood and cursed the miserable weather, then retreated below. I joined Alex and together we studied the clouds parting, and the half-moon edging through the black storm clouds. Faint off the port side, the green strings of lights on the Verrazano Bridge were visible, soon to be astern. Manhattan was a colorful blur, with Coney Island and its Ferris wheel more glow than detail. The boat was still heaving, but the wind had notched down. I was cold and glad for the parka and its hood.

"Looks like the worst may be over," Alex said.

"Yeah. It might even turn out to be a beautiful night."

"I think so," he agreed. "Hey, why don't you get us a soda?"

I hesitated, hating to leave the dramatic view, but did as my brother asked. In the galley, Marnie was sitting at the table with a can of Budweiser and gnawing on a piece of chicken.

"So much for seasickness," I muttered. Then I remembered her gun. Should I attack Marnie and try to steal it? The noise would alert my brother, who had the .38 in his pocket.

She ignored my remark and wiped her fingers with a napkin. "Just curious, but what's the deal with the red and green colors and the numbers on the buoys?"

"Red right returning." I took two cans of soda from the refrigerator and slipped them in the pockets of my coat.

"What the hell does that mean?"

"When heading toward land, the red markers are always on the right of the channel, the green ones on the left, and the numbers increase. Sailing seaward, it's the opposite."

"Guess you two learned that as kids." Marnie took a swig of beer. "Want one?"

I shook my head, climbed the ladder, and left the hatch open since the rain had subsided. I offered Alex the Coke and sat, stunned at the change in our surroundings. The sky had turned a dark, pinky lavender below a long rill of mountainous black clouds that funneled above Long Island. The sea was silvery where the path of the rising moon spilled over it. Altogether, it was a majestic and inspiring sight. I leaned against the bench, amazed by the beauty made by man and nature, yet at the same time being cognizant of the ugliness of the situation on board.

"Isn't the channel pretty straight through here?" My brother kept an eye on the trim of the mainsail.

"Yes. It follows the coast of Long Island out to sea."

Alex's face became solemn and then he nodded.

"That's where you intend to take us?" I asked.

He ignored my question, and we remained quiet as the skyline of Manhattan passed over the transom. The cooler air was tarting up the view, revealing the two World Trade Center buildings at far left and the colored lights of the Empire State in midtown. The silver, scalloped Art Deco Chrysler Building was to the right amid the cluster of tall skyscrapers. Looming high off the water, a packed container ship was sailing toward us, its checkerboard green, orange, and white boxes luminescent in the darkness. It gained on us doggedly until it finally passed to our port side.

From his carryall bag, Alex removed a baseball cap of mine and put it on his head. He sipped his Coke, one hand firmly on the wheel and his attention on the boat's movement, as we had been taught. Even though I was idle, I, too, was inspecting the wind's direction, the sail, and the course. For some time, we sat in silence except for the creaking of the mast and boom, the wind slapping the taut sail, and the swish of water beneath the hull. The land slid by on our starboard quarter, and the Twin Lights blinked its single lit beacon high on the distant dark hill of New Jersey. An intermittent row of second-floor house lights were visible above the sea wall that ran along the peninsula. Not far off, the gathering breakers crashed onto the beach. Overhead, stars pierced the night's blackness.

"Reminds me of the night Dad took us striped-bass fishing," I began.

My brother looked up, instantly in sync with my contemplations. "Yeah. It was about this time of year."

"Remember how he traced the constellations using a flashlight?"

"I never understood why that worked. How one small flashlight could illuminate something so far away," he mused, studying the sky. "Isn't that Cassiopeia there?" With his finger in the air, he traced the constellation shaped like a "W."

"Yes. And Cepheus." I pointed to the constellation resembling a house drawn by a child.

He tipped his head so the bill of his cap no longer shadowed his eyes and the moonlight lit his face, making it seem unnaturally white. "You were always fascinated with astronomy. When Mom took us to the Hayden Planetarium, you sat on the floor and refused to leave."

"I was so excited that I made her bring me three times after you flew home to Dad's."

He laughed. "You wanted to be an astronomer until you realized how much math was involved."

"Not my strong subject. Nor yours."

"No, you're right. I did better in languages and English."

"Did you ever think about writing as a career?" I asked him.

"Not really." He looked past the softly glowing sail. "Well, maybe I did for a period of time when I kept a journal and wrote some poetry. Didn't I send you a few poems?"

"Yes, I still have them."

He chuckled, a little embarrassed. "Mostly adolescent junk. The journal was better, but it was pretty depressing stuff."

"I'd like to read it sometime." As I said this, I realized the time would probably never come because one of us or both of us would be dead.

He glanced at me but said nothing. I lowered my head and felt angry for momentarily forgetting my brother's duplicitous personality.

Chapter Twenty-Four

PERHAPS CURIOUS about the cessation of conversation, Marnie climbed the ladder. Her legs were uncooperative, an effect of the sea and beer, and she tumbled awkwardly onto a seat. From her jacket pocket, she removed a can of Budweiser. Its pop was loud in the silence. She sipped noisily to remove the foam on the top.

"Do you want one?" she asked Alex.

He glowered at her. "Where did you get that?"

Marnie shrugged and took another swallow.

Alex made no effort to disguise the rebuke. "I'm fine with soda."

"Where are we going?"

"Farther."

"Are we going to sleep out here?"

Alex ignored her, as if more important concerns were on his mind. "Sis, would you let the sail out?"

Happy to get away from Marnie, I moved quickly to do as he asked. The wind was still changeable, requiring small alterations. We would probably tack soon and head away from the coast. When I returned, Alex was slouching slightly, as if his thoughts were weighing heavily on him.

Marnie inhaled deeply. "Great stuff, this sea air," she said to no one in particular and took a gulp of beer.

I sensed my brother's revulsion rising, or was it my own? His eyes were fixed on some point ahead in an attempt to wall himself off from the conversation, but even so, I felt an inexplicable connection with him despite how much he frightened me. It was as if the three-way dynamics had shifted, aligning us against Marnie, who had increasingly irritated Alex. In fact, his disposition seemed to be hardening against her hour by hour because of her drinking and annoying behavior. If my brother truly intended to leave the country with her, how long would he tolerate Marnie? Living with her would also incur risk unless Marnie's alcoholic intake could be controlled—in a drunken moment, she could easily say something that would endanger them.

Was my brother considering this? Watching her knock back the beer, I was struck by my own disgust and realized Alex tacitly understood that I shared his reaction. Since she'd come on deck, the tension had risen significantly.

Marnie finished the can and tossed it over her shoulder into the ocean.

Alex jumped up, startled. "Don't do that!"

"What's the matter? One can isn't going to make any difference!"

He clenched his teeth, glowering at her. "Just don't throw trash overboard, do you understand?"

"Good lord, Alex, relax." When he didn't respond, she threw a hostile look at me instead, as if I had criticized her. "I think you ought to tie your sister up."

"No, I need her to help."

Marnie didn't take her eyes off of me. "I can help."

My brother snorted. "Not in your condition."

"What do you mean, 'my condition?' I'm fine."

He looked down at her. "How many beers have you had?"

She rose to her feet abruptly, steadying herself on his shoulder. He cringed at her touch and jerked away.

"Look, what I have to drink has nothing to do with you. I'm perfectly able, capable of fixing the ropes like your sister. Just tell me what to do."

"You brought a six-pack of beer, right? How many cans are left?"

"What is this? A quiz? Who do you think you are, my goddamned boss?"

"Sit down or go below. We're changing tacks."

Immediately, I moved into position, ready for the boom to come abeam and the deck angle to shift. Marnie was caught unawares and fell.

"You did that on purpose!" she shouted.

He gave her a smile that was incendiary in its satisfaction. "I told you to sit. This is a sailboat. Things happen fast. You have to be alert. And sober."

As we wore an amended course away from land, Marnie cursed and headed down the ladder. She missed a rung and landed heavily on the deck below, swearing in aggravation.

Alex glanced at me, shook his head, and tried not to laugh. I leaned over and closed the hatch, delighted to cage Marnie, but then I remembered the weapon in her knapsack. If she perceived Alex's unity with me and was jealous, she might shoot us both. Should I warn my brother? Or would his ignorance of Marnie's gun give me an opportunity to steal it, one I wouldn't have if he took it away from her? In her present deteriorating condition, Marnie might be careless but also dangerous. However, I reminded myself that my brother's friendliness toward me could dissolve. He was as mercurial as this evening's weather, a killer, who had murdered my father and might do the same to me. But could he really pull the trigger? I was flooded with distress as I imagined us face to face, although for some reason, Alex wasn't the one I visualized with the gun.

The waves began to flatten when the wind abated, causing the sailboat to pitch less, though seawater frequently sprayed across the bow. As I lay back along the bench, the last drifts of cloud dissipated to reveal a clear sky. The coast seemed far off, low and black on the horizon, pocked by a few lights.

Alex cleared his throat. "I was just wondering…well…if Mom left anything for me. You know, in case I ever returned."

His sudden interest surprised me. "Yes, she did. After her stroke, when she couldn't write any longer, she dictated a letter, though it wasn't easy to understand her because of her impaired speech."

"Where is it? The letter?"

"In the safe deposit box at my bank."

He nodded. I thought he would ask me what the letter contained, but he was silent, as if the knowledge of such a letter was enough. Or perhaps the matter was too important to him, and he couldn't reveal his vulnerability.

I didn't know whether to say more or let him ruminate. His attention was so far away that a luff in the sail failed to attract his notice. The moment was precarious, a point of decision. We were now at sufficient distance, in deep enough ocean, for him to dispatch Marnie or me. I scanned the sea. We were alone.

"Greece is amazing in early September," Alex said.

"I haven't been there."

He looked at me. "It is. Particularly the islands. The wind blows—the Greeks call it the *meltemi*. The sightseers go home at the end of the month, or at least most of them. The Aegean gets rough, but I like it that way."

I decided to keep the flow of his conversation going. "Which island do you like best?"

Alex pondered this. "I don't know. Depends on what you're looking for."

"Which one do you think I'd like best?"

He smiled. "That's simple. Mykonos."

"The one with the windmills and pelicans? Why?"

"Lots of gay people on Mykonos. You can sit by the harbor and catch the parade. More gay guys than women, but still. Great food and nightlife. The architecture is pretty astounding. In the Little Venice section, the sea is just beneath a row of tavernas and restaurants. A great place to view cruise ships, drink coffee and Metaxa, and listen to music. You would like Mykonos."

"Sounds like it. Good shopping?"

"Yes."

"Sounds like Marnie's kind of place too."

He shot me a hard look. "Yeah. Marnie would like it." The way he said it, I knew Marnie was never destined to see its shores, never destined to set foot on land.

*

We stood well out of the channel when Alex brought the bow to bear directly into the wind, and I eased the mainsail down the mast. It seemed we were miles from anywhere, on some unknown, watery sphere. Though the late-night air was calmer, it was also colder, as if the chill of outer space had somehow enveloped our small, floating world.

The task of furling the sail was proving difficult for me to do alone on the unstable slick deck. Alex noticed this and yelled for Marnie. She pushed open the hatch, frowned, zipped her red parka, and climbed the ladder with difficulty.

"Can you help Alex with the sail?" Irritation tightened my brother's voice.

"Aye, aye, Captain." Sarcasm and inebriation mixed.

As much as I needed another set of hands, I wasn't pleased to have hers. She put one unsteady foot in front of the other, grabbing hold of anything she could, for as long as she could. When she was abreast of me, I demonstrated how to fold the flapping sail. Eventually, she got the hang of it, though the reek of beer on her breath made the shared task unpleasant. I secured flat ties to the boom and didn't bother to replace the cover since I doubted we would be in this location long. My brother ventured to the bow locker and dropped the anchor. A deep spot from the amount of line that went overboard.

When they returned to the cockpit, Alex sat next to Marnie, leaving a sizable space between them. She closed the gap and laced her arm through his. I lowered myself on top of the main cabin and tried to listen to their dialogue. Most of it was inaudible.

"We're going to be here for a while…a few hours," my brother said.

"When…" The rest of the sentence was lost.

She encircled his neck and kissed him. Although he bent to receive the kiss, he stiffened when her lips touched his, either because the kiss came from Marnie or because I was witnessing it. She was oblivious and pressed her body closer and whispered something. He disengaged her arms and mentioned my name.

"…right now?" she asked.

"No." My brother beckoned for me to come to him. When I did, he placed his hand on my shoulder. "Sorry, but I have to tie you up. I need some sleep. Let's go below."

"I'll take her down," Marnie offered.

"No, I'll do it," he told Marnie. "We're in there." Alex pointed to the stern cabin. "I'll be with you in a minute."

Marnie gave my brother a guarded look. Was she thinking of the gun in her knapsack and how she could retrieve it from the main cabin without raising Alex's suspicions? Finally, she shrugged and opened the aft hatch while I descended the ladder into the galley with Alex following. As he and I entered, we saw five crushed beer cans—the sixth was lying on the bottom of the sea. Three empty mini bottles of vodka were in the trash.

"Great," he muttered.

I considered trying to grab the revolver from Alex's pocket or fighting him, but enraging my brother would jeopardize the emotional gains we'd made, which might prove beneficial, and an attack was physically futile without a weapon, so I let Alex tape my hands and lead me into the bow compartment. I chose the left bunk and started to stretch out, but Alex quickly sat beside me. Because his back was to the light in the galley, I couldn't see his expression well.

"Sis, I…" He shook his head and sighed. A second later, he kissed me on the forehead, at first only lightly and then again with feeling. He framed my face with his hands, drew me close, and held me for a long time.

Fear rose like a dark plume. Would my brother attempt a sexual assault again? I tried to guess his intentions, yet he made no forward moves, and his embrace seemed more brotherly than sexual, more loving than predatory. And, in a strange way, in these dire circumstances, I let myself take comfort from the closeness, knowing we might never experience it again. We stayed together until he caressed my cheek and rose to his feet.

"Leave your hood on," he said.

"Why?"

"Just do it. Please."

I didn't understand why this was important to him, but I nodded.

He sighed and stepped into the main cabin. After locking the louvered door behind him, I heard Alex opening the refrigerator, rustling plastic, and popping the top on a can. Although I was somewhat hungry, I was glad he hadn't offered me anything to eat. My stomach was too unsteady, agitated by anxiety.

Eventually, the galley lamp was switched off and the hatch to the cockpit shut, thrusting the fore cabin into darkness. The air had become chilly as night progressed, so I was grateful for the parka, though I was perplexed by Alex's strange directive about the hood. I rested on the narrow bed, my head on a thin pillow, and unsuccessfully tried to analyze his rationale. As I did, the oppressive blackness in the cabin brought on a bout of claustrophobia. I gritted my teeth and tried to ease my panic and the powerful urge to crash through the thin louvered door. I thought of Marnie's bag a few feet away on the other side of my prison. Could I kick the door open and remove the gun before Alex investigated the commotion? With my hands bound, my actions would be slow, and in the small, contained space, I would be the proverbial sitting duck. He could shoot me easily, but would my brother do that? Was Alex really capable of harming me? Had his last kiss been a signal, a promise, or a farewell?

When I pictured my twin sharing the aft cabin with Marnie, I felt sicker. I knew I couldn't stand to be intimate with her. Could he? With all the alcohol Marnie had consumed, she might have passed out, but if she hadn't, Marnie could try a seduction. Would this provoke Alex to murder her if he hadn't already planned to do so? Would he strangle Marnie or smother her after she fell asleep?

I listened to the slip of the anchor line through its chock as the boat rocked—under different circumstances, a restful sound—and thought about my brother. If he'd arrived on my doorstep before I met Marnie, how would I have reacted? Would I have wholeheartedly welcomed Alex, grateful to have one family member alive? Or would I have been afraid of him, even if I was unaware that he killed my father? Another powerful emotion hovered in my consciousness, but in my exhausted state, I couldn't pinpoint the feeling precisely. All I knew was how complex and conflicted Alex was, with a history of harboring incestuous feelings.

But another Alex also existed: my twin, who longed for a time when he felt loved, a time when we were together.

When my brother made the final, ultimate decision tonight or tomorrow, this was the Alex I hoped would determine my fate.

Chapter Twenty-Five

THOUGH IT hardly mattered in the darkness, I kept my eyes closed. Soon, I drifted to sleep, until a dream about my father jolted me awake. He had been standing a distance away, one hand entreating me, his eyes desperate with fear; a wrenching, lonely image. I didn't know what the dream meant, but I'd had it many times before, over many years. Each time when I woke, I was crushed with its visceral reality, as if my father had once looked at me this way, begging to be rescued from danger.

I sat up, trying to shake the terror, but the terror from the dream transferred into my current circumstances. I wished I could be on deck to breathe the clean sea air or at least to be in the galley with its windows. As much as I wanted to be released from this confinement, however, what would my freedom mean? Would I have to watch Alex kill Marnie, if it hadn't happened already?

I recalled a scene from nursery school, before our parents' divorce, when Alex and I were sitting in the sandbox with two boys. The teacher had tried to persuade me to play with the dolls like the other girls, but I refused, saying I preferred to be with my brother. The four of us had little plastic shovels and were digging roads for toy cars and trucks. For some reason, one of the boys became annoyed with Alex and threw a shovelful of sand in his eyes. Instead of crying or cleaning the grit off of his face, Alex froze and stared at the perpetrator with glittering hatred. There was a moment of still silence, and then my brother lunged for the boy's throat, pulling him out of the sandbox effortlessly like a large teddy bear. With amazing speed and strength, my brother began to bang the boy's head rhythmically on the linoleum floor. The teacher rushed over to pull Alex away, but not before the boy was hurt and bleeding. A second teacher grabbed Alex by the wrist and dragged him into the bathroom to quiet my brother's rage, though his fury had already transformed into an eerie serenity, as if nothing had happened. When he was brought into the room again, Alex's face was clean of sand, his cheeks flushed from being scrubbed. He neither smiled nor frowned.

Thinking about that childhood incident, which was one of the first of its kind but not the last, I knew Alex would be capable of anything.

A while later, I heard movement on deck. Someone opened the hatch, came down the ladder, switched on the light, used the head, and walked to my door. The lock was turned and there stood Alex. For a second, I had the urge to hug him, as if he were my rescuer, but his expression was ominous. Following him into the galley, I noticed he'd drawn the white curtains over the four small windows.

"What time is it?" I whispered.

"A few minutes before six. Want something to eat? I forgot to ask last night."

"Yeah, thanks."

Was this my final meal? There was a reason for him to be up this early, after only several hours of sleep. Would he wait much longer to do his killing? Or had he already begun?

"Is Marnie still asleep?"

"Yeah." Alex reached into his pocket, removed the matt knife, and cut the duct tape on my hands.

"Good," I replied, meaning she was still alive.

My brother reversed the blade on the knife, crammed it and the tape in his parka, and passed me a sandwich and a bottle of water.

"How's the weather?" I asked, as if it really mattered.

"Cool and hazy right now, but it'll warm up and become a beautiful day." He said this in a dull voice.

I glanced at Alex and was afraid all over again. His eyes were as cloudy and unfathomable as the murky water beneath the boat. I forced myself to finish the sandwich, though I had trouble swallowing. I didn't ask about his plans. I was too scared.

Alex allowed me to use the head, then gave me a backward

glance before climbing the ladder. He settled on the bench, with only his knees and feet visible through the open hatch. I quickly moved closer to Marnie's knapsack, but as I was about to reach inside, my brother called for me to come on deck. I hesitated and then did as he asked, perhaps missing my only chance to take her gun.

I sat across from him. The air was invigorating after the hours inside the cabin. A white mist hovered around us, but it was swiftly evaporating. The sea was gray, needing the blue of the sky to improve its color, yet a rosy glow on the horizon heralded sunrise. Although we were anchored miles from both shores and a safe distance from the channel, three cargo ships could be seen heading into the Atlantic. Charter boats would appear in a few hours, but they would stay to our west. Some terns and glaucous gulls wheeled above before flying closer to shore where the fishing was better.

"A nice spot," my brother mused.

"Yes, very peaceful."

He cast an eye my way and didn't reply because Marnie opened the aft berth hatch. She arrived on deck in slightly better shape than the previous night. I was both relieved to see her and worried about her presence.

"Good morning. We're up a little early, aren't we?" she grumbled, rubbing her red eyes redder.

My brother said "good morning" but nothing else. I remained silent.

"Did you bring any coffee?" she asked Alex.

"No."

"Shit!" She flopped beside him.

As if her touch was repulsive, he pulled away and crossed his arms.

Marnie observed him, her eyebrow raised, and then surveyed the ocean in all directions, flicking her foot up and down. "Well, Alex, are we going to sit here all day?"

"We'll sit here as long as I want." His mouth tightened.

"Oh, my, Captain. Whatever you say." She laughed without

humor.

I froze, frightened at her tone.

Marnie's leg kept bouncing. Finally, she stopped and placed both sneakers on the deck. In a flirtatious purr, she said, "Hey, Alex, nice time last night…"

He turned to glower at me, as if I had uttered the comment, and then closed his eyes.

His lack of response didn't please Marnie, yet she seemed impervious to Alex's growing temper. She could be a bulldozer in certain moods, and one of those moods was on her now.

"What's the matter, sweetie? Don't want your sister to know what we did last night?"

Alex's eyes flew open. He shot her with a dark blue glare that should have been ample warning, but in her obtuse state, she didn't notice. "No, not particularly."

Marnie wouldn't be deterred. "Oh, come on. Who cares? It's not like she's going to tell anyone." This amused her. She grinned at me in a hung-over, deranged fashion. "I thought we were just going to sleep, but oh, no, not your brother. As soon as we got down there on the bed, he turned into a wild man."

I stared at her with distaste and saw Alex do the same. I was sure he wanted to hoist the sail and leave, if for no other reason than to escape Marnie's noxious conversation, but apparently we weren't going anywhere yet. He lifted his feet onto the bench, fidgeted with his shoelaces, and adjusted his socks.

Instead of being sensitive to Alex's volatile state, Marnie pushed his sneakers off the bench and forced herself into the curve of his shoulder. Brushing back a lock from his forehead, she ran her fingers through his dark hair with a proprietary gesture.

He shoved her hand. "Marnie, stop it. Leave me alone."

My brother had uttered the wrong words, the ones that would incite her the most. Her nostrils flared, and a sinister grin twisted her lips. At that moment, I realized one or both of them could be stoking their anger and might pull out a gun and set to the morning's grim work. But would it be Alex or Marnie?

"You didn't want to leave me alone a while ago," she reminded him with an ugly edge in her voice. "In fact, you practically raped me or maybe you forgot?"

He frowned and fixed his eyes on the horizon.

"He just couldn't get enough," she told me, a hint of narcissistic pride in her voice. "In fact, I'm still sore this morning." She moved apart from him, yawned, and stretched. "But hey, your sister knows how you are." This was said with malignant coyness.

"What do you mean?" he cut in.

Marnie smiled as if she had bested him. "Oh, I think you know exactly what I mean, Alex. Don't you?" She paused and then delivered the thrust, in the slow drawl she used to lethal effect. "I think you have always, always lusted after your sister."

Alex didn't look at either of us, as if he could staunch the flow of Marnie's words if he didn't make eye contact. "That's enough."

I tried to imagine the scene last night, if what Marnie was saying had indeed happened. I wondered if Alex had been so aggressive because he was displacing his frustrated feelings for me on to Marnie, or perhaps he was disgusted with her, and he needed to degrade Marnie by stripping away her personality, thus reducing her to an object, one that could be crushed or killed.

"Of course, I lusted after your sister too, in the beginning," Marnie said. "She was pretty good in the old sack. But you know all about that." She let the acid seep in. "So, Alex, when did it all start? How old were you when you realized you had to have her? Or did she come after you? Some night when you were all comfy in your little twin beds?" She glanced at me, claiming a mean victory.

"Marnie, you're out of line." Alex set his jaw hard.

She treated him to a catty expression. "I should be jealous, I suppose, but I came along so much later."

"Shut up, Marnie," I cautioned her.

Instead, she laughed, freely and easily, as if we were on a pleasure cruise, enjoying ourselves. "Oh, my! A nerve is hit! We have the truth."

My brother clenched his fists below the green cuffs of his parka. Everything seemed to be building to a crescendo.

"Well, I'll leave you to continue your sibling romance." Marnie stood. "I think I'll find something to eat." Holding on to the grab rail by the hatch, she descended into the cabin. A few minutes later, the toilet flushed, water ran in the sink, and then some noises could be heard. From somewhere in the rear of the cabin, she called up to him, "Alex? Sweetie? When does our flight leave tonight?"

His face flushed. Slowly, he came to his feet, unzipped his parka, and placed his hand in its pocket. The pressure in my ears increased, dulling my hearing. My body felt heavy, as if gravity had doubled.

"I don't think you're going anywhere, Marnie," Alex said in a quiet voice.

From out of the shadows below, Marnie emerged, a gun in her right hand.

"Alex!" I cried, but as I turned to look at him, I saw that he had removed the .38 and was pointing its silver barrel toward the cabin. The next seconds seemed like minutes. Marnie saw the revolver in Alex's hand. Without hesitation, she fired. The bullet pierced the center of his chest. He squeezed the trigger at nearly the same instant, blowing a hole in her head. As if she had been punched, Marnie fell backward and crashed onto the galley table. Alex staggered a few steps and collapsed on the bench across from me.

The sounds of gunfire reverberated across the waves, rolling endlessly. My ears hurt from the concussion, like an aural membrane had been shattered. I clapped my hands to my ears and shut my eyes. My chest tightened and I couldn't catch my breath. The sea air turned airless, blanched of oxygen. Suddenly, I was no longer at sea on a boat. I was somewhere else, somewhere I'd been long ago. It was hot, with shimmering waves blurring the yellow-gold landscape. Frightened, I opened my eyes. An enormous red flower of blood bloomed across Alex's blue-and-white pinstriped shirt. He stared at me in astonishment, sprawled against the wall of the cockpit, and lowered the gun, placing it beside him.

"She's a good shot," he said.

I couldn't move. Panic screamed through my being. My hands fell into my lap, useless.

"Sis…I…" A lopsided smile fetched up against the pain.

In a daze, I whispered, "The gun…"

A trickle of red appeared at the corner of his mouth. My brother coughed, spraying blood across his chin. "Did you know about it?"

I was unable to answer. He seemed to take this reaction as a "yes."

"It doesn't matter," Alex replied. "What was I going to do? I couldn't kill you." With great effort, he took a breath. "You know that, don't you? One tarp…one body." A grimace contorted his face. "The money and the coins are in my bag. The diamonds are here." He indicated his breast pocket. "Take them, Alex." His eyes swept past me and up the line of the mast, veering to include the sky, which was propelling itself into full morning blue. Then he looked at me again, as if my face was what he had been searching for. "Make this look like what it was…" He choked as more blood seeped from his lips.

I watched in horror as my brother struggled to clear his lungs.

"You were the only one. You know that?" His eyes flashed like the sun on the tops of the waves.

"We were always together, Alex," I murmured. Tears fell from my eyes and slid down my face and neck. As if sleepwalking, I stood and kneeled in front of him.

His hand rose to touch my cheek; his fingers were cold. "I never would have hurt you. Never. I was going to return the boat, leave you in Marnie's car…so I could get away. I had a ticket, just for me, for tonight. I figured…" He wheezed. "…figured you could sort things out. That the police would know I had killed Marnie. You're smart. You would have been okay. I needed the money…I needed to see you…to understand why…" A liquid gurgling replaced his voice. "To forgive you." He tried to inhale, his face stretched tight from the effort. Slowly, his head began to rock, pulsing with some inner beat that was ebbing away.

"I love you," I whispered, although the words sounded like they were uttered by someone else.

He stopped breathing. I waited for his lungs to fill, but they didn't. His head dropped backward against the fiberglass. His eyes were fixed, open, aimed straight at the sun.

In shock, I returned to the opposite bench and stared over his shoulder at the ocean. I didn't need to check Marnie. I was certain she had died from the massive head wound.

*

Of the hour after my brother's death, I remembered little. When a distant ship's horn nudged me into consciousness, or at least a semblance of that state, I glanced at Alex and felt numb. My brother was dead, I told myself over and over, trying to impress the truth on my disbelieving mind. Then I stood and peered into the galley and saw red—my old parka, blown open, and blood. For a moment, I couldn't perceive who was lying on the table, mouth agape, arms spread and immobile. The name "Marnie" finally came to me. In the center of Marnie's forehead was a cavernous hole full of blood and brain matter.

Chapter Twenty-Six

I SAT on the bench again, unable to fully comprehend what had happened. Images of the scarlet blood on my brother's shirt kept assailing me, a visual after-effect with tremendous power, as if I had lived through his death before. The gunshots echoed, careening within my head so that it seemed like the bullets had just been fired or else were trapped in the distant past, fated to reverberate forever. I felt wounded and bloodied, dead like my twin brother.

"'I forgive you,'" he had whispered.

I accepted the rightness of this without understanding the reason. I wished I had forgiven him in return and grieved that I hadn't. I stared at the shifting waters and thought about how much my brother loved me and I loved him, feelings that were complicated, subterranean, and resistant to extermination despite his treacherous sexual desires. His loss left me bewildered and incomplete, ripped and fragile.

As the sun climbed higher, I became more aware of my surroundings and realized I was on a boat with two dead bodies. If anyone discovered me, how could I explain that I was innocent? My brother had intended to return the boat and leave me tied in the car, set up as the victim. Now, it wasn't obvious that I was the victim. The police might easily make incorrect assumptions unless I steered them toward the right conclusions. How could I do this?

Avoiding the blood, I walked to the carryall that lay on the deck several feet away from Alex. In the open side pocket, I noticed latex gloves. Grabbing them with my fingers, I put them on before unzipping the main compartment. I pulled out a towel, spread it on the bench across from Alex, and dumped several thick packets of bills sealed in Ziploc bags on top—three containing $24,500 from the sale of my Jeep and another with several thousand dollars from my checking account. A double-bagged pouch with four

Krugerrands, several sets of coins in flat cases, and their bills of sale and affidavits of authenticity were also inside, which I added to the pile with a single Aer Lingus plane ticket, his cell phone, and a tube of sunscreen. I removed my driver's license, social security card, brokerage checkbook, a box of Zero bullets for the Smith & Wesson, a case holding the Rolex Mariner watch, another pair of latex gloves, and left a new roll of duct tape. No other passports or papers for Marnie or a second ticket were in the carryall, thus cementing the fact that Alex had never intended to leave with her.

After considering how my narrative would unfold, I returned the bullets, checkbook, watch, cell phone, and ticket into the bag. I concluded that Alex's strategy was to kill Marnie, dump her body overboard, clean her presence and mine from the boat, sail to the marina, and leave me in her Solara while he fled in his rental car, leaving no connection to him on the O'Day unless I told the police he had shot Marnie onboard. If this was his plan, was my brother trading my life for my silence, or did he believe he would be flying over the Atlantic before he could be tracked? The alternative might be to abandon me in his rental car, which was probably leased under an alias as had been the sailboat, drive the Solara to complete its sale, and take public transportation to the airport. Of course, I was assuming Alex had been honest about keeping me alive. Maybe I would have been tossed in the ocean with Marnie, the boat scrubbed of our fingerprints and sailed home to its slip, and the Solara sold, so it would appear Alex—or rather his alternative self—was missing, and Marnie and I had disappeared after she had committed financial larceny and possible assault.

To prove Alex's theft of my identity, I inserted my license into his bag and kept the cash, my social security card, gloves, sunscreen, coins, and their certificates on the towel. Although the thought of touching him made my pulse quicken and my hands perspire in the gloves, I reached into his parka pocket and withdrew the half-roll of tape and matt knife, placing both on the pile. The diamonds were in his breast pocket, but I was afraid of looking at his chest. After steeling my nerve, I edged aside the open jacket and withdrew his passport, which was glued together with blood. I wanted to keep it because it contained the only photo of Alex as an adult, but I returned it and kept the manila envelope full of diamonds. It, too, was smeared with red, but I twisted open the packet's metal clamp, sprinkled the gemstones into one of the plastic bags, tossed the envelope overboard, and rolled the bag and everything else into the towel. Alex's wallet was in his pants' pocket, but I didn't dare turn my brother's body. I then slathered sunscreen on my face because I couldn't be sunburned if I'd never left the house, which is what I planned on telling the police.

On wobbly legs, I climbed down the ladder. Marnie's right arm dangled over the table, and the Beretta lay where she had dropped it on the floor. The gun was covered in blood dripping from above. The pool was small enough to skirt, without leaving tracks, so I was able to stand close to my former lover. Her face was almost unrecognizable except for her perfectly shaped lips, which I'd kissed so many times.

I retreated around the table to where her red knapsack lay. Its flap was open, and inside were some personal items and two more miniature bottles of vodka. In the front pouch was a pair of yellow rubber gloves from our laundry room, gloves we had both used. Had she brought these to clean any trace of her from the boat? In the bottom of the pouch was a pack of fifty-dollar bills, an envelope with $17,500 from the home equity loan, her cell phone, and the plastic bag containing my mother's jewelry and my Seiko wristwatch. I took what was mine—the jewelry, watch, and money—and left the rest, laying the gloves on top of the knapsack, as a hint to the police about her intentions.

I fitted myself into the corner seat of the galley and wondered what I should do now that I'd recovered everything of value. After rolling down the left glove, I put on my watch, which Marnie had stolen due to spite rather than its value, and noted it was 9:35 a.m., although time seemed like an abstract concept. Part of me ached to lift the bodies over the side and sail away into the endlessness of the sea, wind blowing the gunshots out of my head, the sun erasing the visions of a bloody shirt. The other side answered that I couldn't. Everything needed to remain exactly in place, the guns left where they had fallen, so the police would believe my version of events. After weighing the alternatives, I resolved to move the sailboat after dark unless another boat ventured too close.

I kept my parka and hood on to prevent leaving hair samples, although my red slicker Marnie brought on the boat might contain a few strands, as could my cap that Alex had been wearing. It was ironic how both had accidentally provided a rationale as to why my hair was present, if the police found any traces, or had Alex deliberately insisted I zip the parka and tighten the hood for the same reason he had packed gloves? To eradicate evidence—hair and fingerprints—so I wouldn't be implicated in Marnie's murder?

The fingerprints were a big problem. Mine weren't on file, but the police would take a set to differentiate my prints from Marnie and Alex's. I grabbed a hand towel by the sink and a bottle of Fantastic, which the two of them had brought from the house, most likely for the identical purpose. The bow cabin would probably contain no prints because my hands had been taped together, but I cleaned the side I'd been on. Only Marnie and my brother had touched the louvered door or its lock—fine for their fingerprints to be there.

As I worked, I thought about the gun and the latex gloves in Marnie's knapsack. They supported the idea that she planned to shoot my brother or force him—and me—to jump over the side and then delete any signs she'd been present. This meant Marnie would need to sail to the harbor—a tall order for a landlubber—but she might have managed it under power. I recalled her curiosity about the channel markers and realized her question hadn't been an idle one. Once at the marina, she could finish her cleaning, leave the boat—hopefully with no one noticing her—and drive her car to the house. There, Marnie could fashion a story about Alex kidnapping and robbing me, all the while insisting she was an innocent victim. Except she would need to explain all the credit card purchases. More likely, Marnie would have sold the Solara for cash and fled.

My mind spun, trying to sort the convoluted possibilities, but the emotional duplicity distressed me the most. I sat on the seat opposite the table, fighting tears, and recalled happier times playing with my brother before our parents' divorce. Making sandcastles on the beach, swinging on the Jungle Gym set in the backyard, dressing in identical pirate costumes for Halloween. As small children, we had been close, but after he moved to Europe and especially when Alex reached puberty, I became increasingly wary of spending time alone with him.

I sighed, disturbed by these later memories of my twin and also by recollections of cooking elaborate dinners with Marnie, gardening and dancing together, laughing, and making love. She had been an adept and convincing lover, a woman who had cleverly constructed a persona that matched my ideals. How gullible I'd been!

Disgusted with myself, I rose, shoved the Fantastic and the hand towel in my parka pockets, and climbed topside, where I scoured the exterior starboard bow and mid sections: the hardware, grab rails, mast, boom, and shrouds. I straightened my aching back and duplicated my efforts on the port side of the boat. Returning to the cockpit, I cleaned the winches, cleats, and hatch cover. I hadn't touched the wheel or the bench where my brother's body lay.

When my tasks were completed, I replaced the worn gloves with Alex's second pair, returned to the galley, and ate the last sandwich and drank a Coke. Afterward, I dealt with the sink and refrigerator and then inserted the remains of my sandwich wraps, soda cans, water bottle, discarded gloves, and used duct tape into a garbage bag, which I threw on deck, leaving Marnie's beer cans, the chicken bones, and their plastic utensils and paper plates in the trash bin. Next, I examined the floor to be sure I hadn't stepped in the blood, but no footprints were visible. However, a forensic examiner might find traces of my sneakers, which scared me until I remembered Marnie's shoes were the same as mine and new. Hopefully, the treads were identical, without any idiosyncrasies in the patterns. Before the police found me, I would throw away my pair of Nikes.

Above, in the cockpit, I slumped on the bench across from my brother and wondered how I would return to shore. Though I wasn't sure of my exact location, Sandy Hook was at least an hour away. I found the autopilot manual among the charts and read through the directions several times before my brain processed the information. I decided to weigh anchor about 6:15 p.m.

Unsure what to do in the interim, I remained sitting, arms crossed, sweating in the latex gloves and parka, and returned to thoughts of my brother. Over the years, I'd never resolved my ambivalence about who he was and how I felt about him, and his death didn't clarify my confusion. Over recent days, some poignant memories had been resurrected along with shame and fear—emotions that had originated during our childhood.

We had never spoken about Alex's perverse attraction, which I now understood was interwoven with his genuine love. Did he view me as his bright side, the twin who could make him whole? Yet, in many ways, Alex also completed me, and, as during our past, I had entered into our unique space, filling the absences present since our separation. Now that he was dead, it seemed impossible to discern which emotions were his and which were mine, as if I had absorbed him, with our personalities entwined. No one, no matter how close, would ever replicate this assimilation.

A vast emptiness overwhelmed me as I stared at the expressionless ocean and moved unconsciously in rhythm with the boat. I should pick up the gun and discharge a bullet into my brain, hastening the end to this estrangement from my family. I thought about my mother and father. Did they exist on some spectral plane, waiting for us to be together? Had they mended their differences and called for Alex, their lost child, to come to them? Suddenly, I wanted to be there too, beyond this boat, this floating morgue.

But I didn't move. I didn't reach for the gun, which seemed to glint with supernatural power. Instead, I sat there helpless, inert, half gone with Alex, with my mother and father, as if I were fading in harsh sunlight like a poorly fixed photograph. I don't know how long I lingered in this daze or where I traveled in my head. I'm not a mystical or religious person, but it felt as though I soared past the confines of Earth. Tears welled up and began to fall. I closed my eyes and was swamped with images of Alex and his bloody chest. After I opened my eyes again, I couldn't shake the disquieting sensation that I was slipping into another self, reprising a situation that was eerily familiar.

As the clouds migrated eastward, the blue sky slowly diminished into a peach sunset sliced with thin purple clouds.

*

The coolness of evening soothed my feverish thoughts. Beginning the preparation for my escape, I used the head and then sprayed Fantastic on the toilet and its handle, the sink's hardware, and the ladder's rails, even if the lack of prints on the railings would look suspicious because everyone needed to climb in and out of the cabin. Once this was accomplished, I studied the marine chart, carried it topside, and placed it in the box by the hatch so I could refer to it without going below. Then, though I disliked throwing anything overboard, I flung the garbage bag and the sunscreen into the ocean, hauled up the main anchor, started the ignition, and set the autopilot on a heading toward shore.

Standing on the leeward side, where the wind would blow any hairs into the water, I stripped off my jacket and shirt. With care, I inserted the plastic bags of cash and coins into my bra and duct-taped them there and across the flat of my breastbone. A plastic bag with the diamonds and smaller rolls of money was placed in the front pocket of my cargo pants, its flap zipped closed, and my thigh girded with duct tape. The bag containing my social security card, the certificates of authenticity, and my mother's jewelry was stuck in the other pocket. Replacing my shirt, I added tape to bind it to my body, in case the inside tape holding the bags became loose. I donned my jacket, tightened the hood, and dried the sweat from my face with the towel before throwing the towel overboard.

I avoided looking at my brother, but my glance was often drawn to him as he lay stiff and pale on the bench, the wind ruffling his shirt collar and locks of his hair that fell below the confines of his cap. I imagined he was having an evening's rest and everything was fine.

*

The black strip of coast loomed off the bow, though visibility was diminishing due to the approach of rain. I turned on the light above the hatch door and consulted the chart once again. Fighting anxiety about the treacherous shoals running along the Hook, I steered out of the channel and sailed parallel to the land. When the Twin Lights were directly ahead, I edged in closer, raised the swing keel to decrease the boat's draft, and replaced the chart in the box. After removing my parka, I rolled it tightly except for the arms, which I tied around my waist. Then I circled the jacket with tape before throwing the tape over the side.

The sea was relatively still. I could see the distant beach, but as I stood on deck, the clouds slowly choked the last glimmers of sunlight, merging the land and sea into an undifferentiated mass. I didn't like to think of the stories I'd heard about ravenous bluefish biting swimmers, or worse yet, about the sharks that cruised the coast. One thing was certain: I didn't want a metallic sparkle to catch the eye of one of those omnivorous predators. Reaching into my pants, I pulled out a plastic bag and placed my watch inside, returning the bag to my pocket.

After slowing the sailboat to an idle, I debated whether to leave the lights on in order to prevent a collision with another boat but decided that if time of death was accurately established as during the morning, night lights would be suspicious, so I switched them off. There was enough gas to take the boat out to sea, far enough to preclude the possibility that someone had tried to swim ashore.

I sliced off the lower legs of my cargo pants with the matt knife and pitched the cloth and knife over the railing. Turning toward my brother, I studied his face in the pale light. He looked so young, almost angelic. Though his life force had departed, I knew my good brother, the one I loved, would always be with me.

I swung the boat so it faced east, reset the autopilot, and pushed the throttle forward at a slow speed. Then I jumped over the starboard side into the black water.

Chapter Twenty-Seven

THE OCEAN WAS surprisingly cold. After peeling off the latex gloves, I began a slow crawl toward shore, trying not to worry about the distance, which now seemed vast. Immediately, the duct tape became uncomfortable as it bound the free movement of my muscles and skin. The coins and cash against my chest also grew burdensome, giving me the sensation that I had to fight to stay afloat. I urged myself to swim steadily, stopping only to catch my breath and to alternate from a crawl to a sidestroke or breaststroke.

How far would the sailboat travel before it ran out of gas? I hoped it wouldn't be struck by an ocean-going vessel—not that it would cause much damage to a tanker or large ship—but if the O'Day sank, the evidence on board would be lost. Evidence necessary to support my story, which I was in the process of refining.

When the outline of a Sandy Hook kiosk appeared, I prayed it was the one near the park entrance and that no rangers were making rounds. It was after sunset, though the water was eroding my sense of time. Suddenly, something touched my foot, and I lurched in fright. A floating branch. I threw it away and waited to catch my breath and steady my nerves. Letting the waves carry me forward, I drifted. Part of me wanted to let go and sink. I felt so alone, chilled, and weary, but I continued on through the black water, kicking weakly, sometimes not at all.

As with pre-sleep thoughts, my mind circled like a roller coaster, around and around, rotating over the options I might have chosen to prevent Alex's death, even though, in actuality, I was helpless after I'd decided to return to the house and take the gun from the bedroom. My brother's determination to make me penniless, to exact revenge for some terrible grievance he held against me, were so powerful that I doubted he would have relented no matter what I had done. Did this plan originally include my death? There would have been no other reason to enter into the house purchase otherwise, unless this had been solely Marnie's idea. Or should I trust his last words, that he hadn't intended to kill me? I held this belief close and hoped it was the truth.

I turned once to see the sailboat, already a great distance away, its outline fast being concealed by the gathering mist, a mist that would obscure me when I reached the beach. As the swells became more pronounced, I checked the tape and plodded along, aided by the ocean. In the forming area of the waves, I caught a breaker halfway into shore. A second one deposited me on the sand, in the retreating white froth. I lay there, water coursing around me, and thought I would never get up until one large wave spewed sea over my head. I sat, coughing, my hands disappearing into the withdrawing sand. With a huge effort, I stood and walked to the crest of the dune, hoping the incoming tide would erase my footprints nearest the ocean. Then I collapsed.

*

I rested until rain began falling. I came to my feet and, with trembling fingers, unraveled the tape from my thighs, jacket, blouse, and chest and made a pile of the plastic bags, which were thankfully intact. I restored my blouse, slipped my arms in the parka's clammy sleeves, raised the hood, and filled all the pockets with bags. Then I dug a deep hole in the sand to bury the used tape.

Being in the rest area was risky because rangers checked it regularly, but walking through the dunes, which were thickly covered with poison ivy, wasn't an attractive alternative. After climbing up to the kiosk, I used the foot shower to rinse off and then pushed my legs to a trot, crossing the blacktop parking lot and the main road into the park. Just as I was stepping on the far curb, headlights pierced the dark night from the north. I tottered unsteadily down the path to Plum Island and hid, peeking to see a white car with green stripes careen into the parking area and loop back toward the station house. When the ranger was out of sight, I climbed to the street and proceeded toward the exit, jogging up the incline of the overpass and slowing my pace as I reached the bridge.

There, a chilly wind blasted me, and rain needled my face.

I cursed, rushed over the bridge, averting my face from the bridge keeper in his booth, and hurried down the ramp into town, where I kept to the back streets, wary of meeting a passing patrol car. Finally, the road ascended and narrowed, rising steeply to my father's driveway.

By a hydrangea bush, I found the spare set of house keys. After opening the door next to the garage, I removed my shoes, dried my feet with a beach towel, went into the kitchen and stared blindly through the window, overcome with deep and unutterable exhaustion. How could I return to the house Marnie and I had bought, call the police, and answer their questions? All I wanted to do was vanish within the shelter of my father's home, to surrender to the oblivion of sleep, hoping I'd wake with no memory of what happened.

I poured a glass of cold water and drank it, ate some stale crackers. Then I emptied my pockets and carried everything of value to a wall safe except for forty dollars and my social security card. I stripped off my parka and sodden clothes and placed them and my Nike shoes in a brown grocery bag. Stepping into the bathroom, I was terrified to look in the mirror, but I did. My eyes were scarlet, and my left cheek and body were painted with blue and purple bruises. The wound on my chin still hadn't healed.

A hot shower helped. I scoured my skin with soap and shampooed repeatedly to remove any residue of sea salt. My hair would appear cleaner than it should, but if I let it dry uncombed, it would look appropriately tousled and unkempt. From the bedroom closet, I selected fresh clothes, a pair of running shoes, an old trench coat, and placed my Seiko watch on my wrist: 8:40 p.m. Time to go. I grabbed the keys to my father's old Audi and went into the garage, raised the car's hood, and attached the battery connections. I had taken the Audi for a drive a month ago and prayed it would work now. After one nervous sputter, it started. I checked that my travel umbrella was in the back seat, in case I needed it, and exited the house.

The weather had improved slightly. On the way to the

Parkway, I stopped in a strip mall and lobbed the bag of clothes and shoes into a trash container. Once on the highway, fatigue proved adversarial. I raised the volume on the radio and rolled down the windows so the night air would keep me alert. Forty minutes later, I drove into a commuter parking area two miles from the house. I took the Audi's key, the two house keys and those for my father's place, and locked the car. I began running, grateful the rain had stopped, and I wouldn't need to explain a wet coat or umbrella.

On the front door was tacked a sodden letter. Using my jacket sleeve pulled over my hand, I lifted the corner to read a date. The notice had been left by the police a few days before. I ignored it, slipped off my shoes, and went inside without turning on any lights. I hid the keys to the Audi and my father's house as well as the two twenty-dollar bills in a pair of white pants, hung my clothes in the closet, and replaced the social security card in my open wallet in the bedroom. Naked except for my underwear, I walked into the kitchen, looped the house keys on the hook, and entered the laundry room, where I changed into the bloody clothes I'd worn during the fight.

Next, I returned to the living room and stared at the bloodstained carpet, trying to banish the ghosts of Alex and myself rolling on the floor. The high-backed chair stood in the middle of the room, apart from the cluster of furniture. It was surrounded by ropes and tape, evidence of my confinement. I thought for a moment and moved the chair and some of the bindings beside the dining table. After searching the kitchen, I found a cheese spreader, whose blade lacked a sharp edge, and cut sections of the rope and tape with the spreader—not an easy task. And then, as my brother had done, I tied bowline knots to re-section the laundry line sliced by the carving knife. After rubbing my wrists and forearms with the rope to chafe my skin, I dropped the cheese spreader on the floor and groaned. Blood was on my clothes. None was on my face. The scab didn't appear recent, so I ran to the bathroom, used my fingernail to prick the wound on my chin, and blotted the blood with a hand towel. I hoped the police would conclude the cut had been freshly opened when I cleaned my face prior to calling them.

To deter close inspection, I added two large Band-Aids. To support my story about not knowing the time during my captivity, I placed my watch in the back of my jewelry box.

I waited until my breathing was even. At 10:36 p.m., I switched on the lights and telephoned the police.

*

The police arrived promptly. The uniformed officer entered first, a tall, heavyset man named Fantana, and then a plainclothes officer walked in, a stocky woman with short-cropped gray hair and wearing a blue pants suit. She introduced herself as Detective Denise Griscoe. I showed them into the living room.

Detective Griscoe studied my bruised face and bandaged chin. "You didn't say you were hurt when you called. Only that a theft occurred. Should we summon an ambulance?"

"I'm sorry. I was just so upset on the phone. Yes, I'm sore and have a bad headache, but you need to catch my brother and Marnie. They can't be allowed to get away."

"Are you sure you don't need a doctor?" Fantana asked.

"Not right now, but could I please sit down?"

"Yes, of course," Griscoe said as she and Fantana slipped on blue latex gloves, explaining this was a precaution at a crime scene. "We'll take a look in here and be right with you."

I went into the kitchen and sat at the table while they examined the room and commented to each other about the blood on the beige carpet. Once the two officers joined me, I reassured them the blood in the living room was mostly my twin brother's and began recounting the outline of my narrative and the basic details of the robbery, beginning on August 6, the night I'd been chloroformed, and providing Marnie and my brother's full names and birthdates. Fantana and Detective Griscoe wrote notes on metal clipboards, glancing at me with incredulity whenever I mentioned the more improbable events.

"When did they leave?" Griscoe asked.

"I'm not sure. Sometime very early this morning." I hoped no one had seen the two cars exit the driveway or witnessed our arrival at the marina on Thursday. "They ate dinner around nine last night—I'm guessing because they took my watch, and I couldn't see the clock in the kitchen when I was sitting near the windows. Marnie had a headache and went to bed early. When my brother took me to the bathroom, on the way back, I grabbed a paring knife that had been left on a plate of appetizers. I lunged at him and grazed his shoulder and hand."

As I described the fight with Alex in the living room, tears filled my eyes. I wasn't sure whether they came from sorrow, confusion, or fatigue, but I stood and walked to the counter for tissues, grateful for a brief chance to order my thoughts.

After returning to the table, I pointed to my chin. "Alex hit me several times and knocked me out."

"And you just got loose a little while ago?" The policewoman sounded skeptical.

I nodded, worried about the fictitious timeline I'd devised, which was close to implausible. "When I woke, it was sometime in the morning because light was coming through the skylights. I was in the chair again, with laundry line tied around my chest and knotted in back. My wrists were bound with duct tape—only my fingers were free. I sat there for hours, terrified they would come back and kill me. Alex had a gun. A .38 Smith & Wesson." I wiped more tears away and focused on my trembling hands.

Griscoe recorded the information about the revolver. "What happened next?"

I inhaled a deep breath. "I kept trying to stretch the duct tape and the ropes but had no success. There was nothing useful I could reach, either, though it occurred to me something might be on the dining room table or in the cabinet. I had no idea how to cross the room until I came up with the idea of lifting the chair and carrying it on my back. I could only move a few inches at a time and then had to lower the chair and drop down again because my muscles ached. When I was about halfway, my leg started cramping, and I had to stop. My head also really hurt and I became dizzy—"

"Perhaps you have a concussion?" Griscoe suggested. "I would be more comfortable if you were medically evaluated."

"We can do that, but I really want to finish telling you what happened so you can begin searching."

The detective agreed. "All right. Well, first, do you know where they went?"

"I think they planned to leave the country tonight. My brother has a fake passport and identification papers, using one of several aliases. He told Marnie he was buying a forged Irish passport for her, in the name of Megan O'Connell, but I never saw him show it to her. When she demanded to see it, they had an argument."

"What about the destination?"

"I overheard something about Shannon. Alex told Marnie he had ordered a car there, and they would take a few days to drive to Dublin before traveling to Europe."

"What about the make and model of their cars?" Fantana asked.

"Marnie has a 1997 Toyota Solara convertible. Red with a black top. They were talking about selling it in Perth Amboy, but I have no idea if they did."

Fantana wrote down this information. "Do you know her license plate number?"

I recalled only the last three digits.

"And your brother's car?"

"I glimpsed it once from the bathroom window. A black sedan. Maybe a Honda or a Toyota. With New York plates. Alex said it was a rental."

"Can you give us a physical description of both of them? We'll get photos in a few minutes."

I told them height, weight, hair and eye color, about my brother's chest scar, and repeated the location of his two knife wounds.

Griscoe turned to her partner. "Will you place an APB out on Ms. Hardwick and Mr. Wyce? And request crime scene guys and a photographer to come here?"

After Fantana left, the detective asked, "So, Ms. Wyatt, let's go back to when you were in the living room. Can you continue with what happened?"

"Well, when I was sitting in the chair, I must have fallen asleep again—I hadn't slept more than a few hours each night for over a week." I shut my eyes, hoping the lies would knit together into a believable tale when increasingly my real recollection was blending into the fabricated one. "I'm sorry. I'm just so tired." I opened my eyes and fought to concentrate. "After I finally maneuvered the chair to the cabinet, it was growing dark." I picked up the cheese spreader from the floor and laid it on the table in front of Griscoe. "I found this and used it to saw through the tape. It took forever because the blade's dull and because I couldn't get a good angle. The circulation in my hands also kept being cut off. The rope was easier to slice, but it was looped under my arms, with two layers of line."

I shook my head, weariness overtaking me, and waited until I heard Fantana returning. Once he was seated, I resumed my narrative. "When I finally got free, I rushed into the bathroom, desperate to use the toilet. After I did, I washed the blood from my face and hands, added the bandages, and felt faint—I hadn't had anything to eat or drink for over a day. As I stepped into the hall by the bedroom, I passed out. When I woke, I ate some lunchmeat and drank some orange juice. Then I called you."

Griscoe reiterated my account to Fantana. They stared at the blunt cheese spreader and exchanged doubtful looks.

"That's quite a story," Griscoe said.

For a second, I panicked, thinking she meant I'd made up what happened. I kept my composure and didn't reply.

"So, for the record, was this a physical or a sexual assault by Mr. Wyce?" Fantana asked.

I didn't want to explain Alex's incestuous feelings. "Physical. To prevent my escape."

"I see." The policewoman eased against her chair. "Fantana, will you make a tour of the house to be sure no one is inside and check if you see anything odd?"

He agreed and walked through the door to the laundry room. Griscoe faced me. "Do you have photos of Marnie and your brother?"

I led her into the bedroom and selected a framed picture of

Marnie lying on the deck chaise, surrounded by boxes of yellow and purple pansies. She seemed so relaxed and so in love as she smiled for the camera, for me. As I gave it to Griscoe, I couldn't help but think it was evidence of how convincing Marnie had been, that if Griscoe had been treated to a look like this, she, too, would have succumbed.

I rifled through my desk and found a scrapbook from the trip to Zimbabwe, one my mother had assembled using prints made from film I'd shot. I'd only looked at the pictures a few times over the last fourteen years and not recently because memories of the visit were too painful. As I flipped open the cover, the first photograph was of my brother, handsome in a navy blazer and pink dress shirt, his eyes sparkling, his smile bright and easy. I stared at the picture in shock. Who was he here? Was he the loving brother, the charming young man of nineteen? Or was this a façade? Had he been flirting with me as I snapped the shutter? It hadn't crossed my mind at the time, but after wine and dinner, and after my father had retired to bed, I realized too late that Alex's childhood sexual curiosity had ripened into adult lust. Though there were huge gaps in my memory after that, I remembered staring at the dark ceiling of a thatched hut, begging and pleading with Alex to stop. I recalled the searing pain of violation, but I didn't know how he brought me to the hut or where it was in relation to the main camp.

In the late morning, when the police came to report that my father was dead, the commissioner found me on my bed in my room, wearing shorts and a khaki shirt rather than my evening clothes. Red blood was dried on my legs and underwear, my arms and thighs were bruised, and my breasts and neck had been bitten. I had a terrific headache, probably from a swollen lump by my ear, and told the police I didn't know how and when I had returned to my room or who had attacked me.

Griscoe had been viewing the scrapbook and reached for the photograph of Alex. Tears began again as I experienced anew the futility of understanding my damaged twin, or for that matter, myself. I went into the bathroom to splash cold water on my eyes.

The detective peered in as I held a towel to my face, sobbing.

"Are you all right? Is there anything I can do?" she asked, her eyes filled with concern.

I shook my head and neatly folded the towel, as if I could control everything that had become a tangled mess with this single mechanical act. In the small, tiled room, I felt like I was still in the water; deep, dark water that had the power to make me sink and drown.

Griscoe noticed the second towel, the bloody one, and instructed me not to touch it. I nodded and then became light-headed. To keep from toppling over, I grabbed the counter.

"Whoa…come on. Let's get you seated." Griscoe clutched my elbow until I stopped weaving, then helped me through the hall and foyer.

She was acting as if I were only half there—perhaps I was. Exhaustion was decelerating everything. My world had turned into a kaleidoscope that was falling into each new pattern with infinitesimal slowness and disturbing brightness.

On shaky legs, I walked to the kitchen table and collapsed on a chair. Head in hands, I waited for the spinning to stop. "I'm sorry, but this is such a shock. I was positive they would shoot me before they left…or that they were going to return, and I'd hear the garage door open and…"

"I understand," she said in an even voice. "Relax for a moment. Our team should be here soon, and then we can get you to the ER—unless you need to go right now?"

I tried to quiet my ragged breathing and racing heart. "Not yet."

Fantana returned from his search with evidence bags containing the bloody towel and Alex's linen shirt, which I confirmed was what he wore during our fight. Fantana reported that no one was in the house. Griscoe asked him to take the photos to the station and have the airports notified. "Especially those with carriers flying to Ireland today and tomorrow."

"Before I go, do any of you have cell phones?" he asked me.

I started to say Alex had his on the boat and stopped. "They owned phones." I recited Marnie's number. "I use house and office landlines. Marnie's computer is in her study. In there."

I pointed to the room, and Fantana nodded. Then there was a brisk knock on the front door, and he left to open it. A forensic team, a female photographer, and three uniformed officers entered.

Griscoe stood, gave them directions, and requested the photographer to take pictures of my bruises, cut chin with the bandages removed, the ligature marks on my wrists and arms, and my bloody clothes. We went into the bedroom to do this in privacy, and afterward, I was allowed to replace the Band-Aids on my chin and to change into a blue, button-down shirt and white pants, the ones with the keys and money hidden in the pocket. I set my dirty clothes on the hamper and packed a bag with toiletries, pajamas, socks, underwear, and a book while Griscoe followed every move I made. When I reached for my wallet on the armoire, the detective prevented me. She opened it with her gloved fingers.

"They left your credit cards. And your library, insurance, and social security cards. No driver's license. Let's keep everything here except for the insurance card and social security ID, which we'll need for the hospital."

Griscoe compiled a list of items I was wearing and what I'd placed in my suitcase. I grabbed my trench coat, and the detective handed the house keys to an officer so he could lock the front door when the police were finished.

"Now, should I call an ambulance? "she asked.

"Can you drive me instead?" I was suddenly anxious about going to the hospital in case the doctors would realize my wounds weren't fresh or my concussion wasn't serious, thereby contradicting some of my time sequences and explanations.

The detective agreed and escorted me to a black Ford. Rain was falling, and the red and blue flashing lights on the police cars were reflecting on the slick driveway. Men and women were hurrying to unload gear and bring it into the house.

I sat on the back seat of Griscoe's car. She handed me a bottle of water from a cooler beside me and took her place behind the wheel.

"Probably best not to tell me anything else. If you're cleared by the docs, we'll go to the station after the ER, and then you can make a formal statement. We'll also make arrangements for a motel—unless you have someone to stay with? You won't be allowed in the house for several days or longer."

I couldn't suggest my father's house because of what I'd stashed in the safe. "A motel is fine."

Chapter Twenty-Eight

THE EMERGENCY ROOM PHYSICIAN decided I was suffering from a moderate concussion but didn't require admission, though he warned me to call him or my doctor if the headache persisted or new symptoms developed. Afterward, I went to the police station with Detective Griscoe. There, I was fingerprinted, and hair and DNA samples were taken. The detective met with Fantana, and together they ushered me into the interrogation room and offered lukewarm coffee and stale doughnuts. We ate and drank for a few minutes, yawning frequently due to the late hour, until Griscoe announced it was time to begin recording.

"You reported earlier that the primary motive was robbery. How much did Mr. Alexander Wyce and Ms. Marnie Hardwick steal?"

Fatigue made my brain freeze. I sighed, trying to organize the details in my mind, and then proceeded to list the theft of my Jeep, money taken from my brokerage and checking accounts, the fraudulent application of the home equity loan and stolen cash, and how Marnie had maxed out my credit cards to buy a ton of things, which I said were probably in her car. I asked Griscoe if I would be able to return everything for refunds if the merchandize was found; she thought this was likely. If the purchases remained missing, she said the companies would determine compensation based on their individual policies.

At this point, the money really didn't matter.

"We'll put a hold on her account and yours once the banks open," Griscoe promised. She explained that since Marnie had cashed only half of the loan, the rest of the money deposited in her account would be transferred to the lending bank if it hadn't been withdrawn yet.

Of course, the cash Marnie had withdrawn was in my safe, but

I didn't volunteer this.

The policewoman then asked about theft from my brokerage account.

"Although Alex might have spent more, I'm certain he bought about half a million dollars' worth of gold coins and diamonds."

"Wow! Pretty smart. Small, transportable, and easy to sell."

"My brother had underworld contacts and worked for shipping companies overseas. And the scrapbook I showed you earlier…it was from a hunting trip to Zimbabwe in 1985." I described my father's death at my brother's hand. "All these years I thought Alex was dead like my father. He stayed away because he was afraid he would be charged with murder."

"Then he had previously committed a homicide? And never was caught or charged?"

"Yes. When we were nineteen." I finished my coffee. "And there's one other thing I just remembered. Part of a conversation I overheard between Alex and Marnie. He said something about renting a sailboat, which made no sense to me, so when they drove away, I thought they were meeting with another dealer and would return. Now, I'm wondering if they went sailing."

"If they did, that's really calm and cool," Griscoe commented. "To go on a cruise before escaping the country and with the possibility you might get loose and call us."

"I know. The only explanation is that Alex was connecting with someone offshore to buy more coins or diamonds. Or perhaps that's what he told Marnie to make her come with him." I stared at Griscoe. "I could be wrong, but from his perspective, it isn't logical to take Marnie to Europe. I think he was intending on disposing of her instead. Maybe in deep water. There was something about the way Alex was behaving, an expression I noticed once when her back was turned, that made me think Marnie was in danger. I tried to warn her, but she didn't believe me."

"Do you know where the boat might be?"

"No, but I doubt he'd travel far." I considered for a moment. "We spent some time sailing in Sandy Hook Bay when we were kids."

Griscoe nodded and asked Fantana to organize a search for the bay area and nearby rivers and ocean, with a relay of information to the Coast Guard and police marine units. After he left the room, she turned to me.

"This complicates the situation if there's a possible homicide. The fact that your brother admitted to killing your father increases the likelihood that he'll repeat his violent behavior."

I dropped my eyes, afraid I would start crying again.

She poured us more coffee and made some notes. When she finished, the detective veered to another subject. "We're aware that you phoned an attorney to revise your will. He called us because you had canceled those revisions, and he thought you were in jeopardy, most likely from the original beneficiary, Marnie Hardwick. Officer Fantana came to your house to see if you were okay." She paused, examining my face closely. "Could you tell me more about this?"

I related how I'd learned of Marnie's intentions, her reading of my email about altering my will, and how my brother forced me to telephone Jim Reilly to nullify the new document so the one favoring Marnie would stand. "By telling Mr. Reilly that he should revoke the will he had in his possession, when he knew I had taken it with me, and conveying other incorrect details, I was able to signal I was in trouble. When the police came to the door, I was gagged and tied."

Griscoe shook her head. "You mean the plan was to kill you and inherit your half of the house?"

"Yes. They wanted my down payment of $85,000."

"That's brazen. Patient, too, since it's not always easy to sell a house, especially if one of the owners is missing or has died under suspicious circumstances."

"The real estate plot might have been Marnie's idea, not my brother's. Or maybe he planned to impersonate me. He already did that successfully with two dealers. Then he could take his time marketing the place."

"He impersonated you?"

"Yes. Alex looked very convincing."

Griscoe added this information to her notebook. Then she looked at her watch. "Okay, I think that's all we need for now. You must be really beat—I know I am." She handed me a pad of white paper and a pen. "We'll pick up again later, but after you get some sleep, would you please write a detailed statement for our records?"

I agreed to do so, though I dreaded the possibility that my timelines might not match the ones I'd told her.

*

When Griscoe and I arrived at the Coach & Carriage, it was almost dawn. The motel manager had been called ahead, but he was grumbling about the hour as he escorted us to a room and started the air conditioner, which recycled the ancient smell of cigarettes.

After he left, the detective asked if I would be all right alone.

"I'll be fine. Just don't forget me."

"I won't forget you," she promised. "I'll see you later." She wrote her cell number on the back of her card. "You can use the room phone. And you have a voucher for meals at the motel's diner but please stay on the premises until you hear from us."

"Thanks for all your help."

Her eyes twinkled. "My pleasure."

I switched on the battered television that clung precariously to a bracket in the corner of the room and fell into a dreamless sleep.

*

I was disoriented when I woke at 2:45 p.m. Opening the blinds, I saw that it was still raining heavily, which was useful because the sailboat's deck would be washed even cleaner, though it was disturbing to imagine my brother's body exposed to the weather. I had also left the hatch open, so hopefully the shoeprints and blood on the galley floor had been smeared, and any fingerprints I'd missed were degraded. I didn't know if the cloth sails or the flat boom ties could be analyzed, whether the technology used by the local police was sufficiently sophisticated, but perhaps the wet material wouldn't yield any traces of my presence.

Upset by visions of the boat, I concentrated on the room. The walls were hung with a collection of cheap bullfighting scenes, thick daubs of gold and black and red paint standing in relief against the mechanical reproduction. The gray carpet was threadbare and stained, especially near the entrance. The lilac air freshener was cloying. The shower dripped.

With nothing much to do, I worked on my statement, taking care to replicate what I'd already reported to Griscoe and Fantana. I ripped up numerous pages and flushed them down the toilet because the erasures might reveal mistakes that could deviate from my recorded version. The finished summation was eleven pages long. After reviewing it four times, I signed the bottom and printed my name and the date.

At five-thirty, Detective Griscoe knocked on the door. I opened it to find her holding a dripping black umbrella and wearing a blue nylon jacket that rustled when she entered.

"Good afternoon, Ms. Wyatt."

"Call me Alex, okay?" I sat on the edge of the bed. "Any news?"

"No, not really. We had a false alarm—a red Solara parked near the docks in Oceanport. The local cops scared its owner when they pulled him from a tavern, off of his favorite bar stool. Probably the guy figured he was being arrested for a DWI before he even got in his car." She chuckled at the thought. "We also checked the passenger manifests for all international flights to Ireland yesterday and today. There was a no-show. Male. For last night."

"Really? Under what name?"

The detective gave me a sidelong glance. "Yours."

"What?"

"Yes. Alex Wyatt."

I covered my mouth with my hand. "I can't believe he did that."

"Guess your brother has an odd sense of humor." Griscoe studied me. "One thing we're sure of, if that was his flight, no one fitting Ms. Hardwick's description was on it. We sent her photograph for review by the airline personnel. All the female passengers were accounted for."

"Then he didn't fly to Ireland, and Marnie didn't either."

"Right. Maybe he booked the flight to confuse us and they're meeting elsewhere, though I don't buy that idea." The detective checked her notes. "Also, this morning, Fantana contacted the managers at your bank and the guy at Ms. Hardwick's branch and successfully froze all the accounts. We were able to confirm that the second half of the home equity hasn't been withdrawn."

"That's a relief."

"Yeah, all good." Griscoe came to her feet. "However, until they're caught, I'm sorry to say you're still in jeopardy and will need to remain here."

I didn't like staying in the motel, but I had no choice.

*

After Griscoe left, I walked to the diner, which featured a silver and white façade from the 1950s. The food was awful. An open-faced roast beef platter with two slices of white bread underneath the meat and a huge mound of mashed potatoes drowned in thick brown gravy. A thin, faintly red tomato sliver and a leaf of iceberg lettuce were intended to provide color.

I returned to my room and laid on the bed to read. At nine o'clock, Denise Griscoe called.

"Just wanted to give you an update. We located their cars but not them. The agent for a rental sailboat, a 32-foot O'Day, reported it overdue for return, and when shown your brother's photo, he identified him as the renter, though Mr. Wyce had posed as a female—as you. An air and sea search are underway."

I didn't say anything. I could hear Griscoe flipping pages of paper.

"They found a suitcase in Mr. Wyce's car. No diamonds, money, or coins inside, just his fake passports and IDs. In Ms. Hardwick's vehicle was a suitcase and a bag packed with the purchases you described, including a woman's gold Rolex watch. We'll document the items so you can contact the companies and ask for extensions on their return policies."

"That would be a big help."

"I'll keep you posted. Perhaps we can do breakfast at eight-thirty?"

I agreed to this, wondering why Griscoe wanted to dine on a Sunday morning. Was she attracted to me? I hoped not. I didn't need more complications, especially with the police.

*

Detective Griscoe was on time. I gave her my written statement, and we chatted about nothing in particular as we walked to the diner. After sitting in a booth, the waitress arrived with coffee and took our orders.

"The Coast Guard located the boat." She described where it was found and from which marina it had sailed. "I'm waiting for more information."

We made more small talk until the waitress landed huge platters in front of us. The sight of the food made me feel sick. The detective flooded her pancakes with maple syrup and tucked in, while I toyed with my mushroom omelet, certain that a dozen eggs had been used. As Griscoe was halfway through her meal, her cell phone rang. She excused herself and stepped outside.

When she sat in the booth again, she looked serious. "The sailboat is being towed to port because it ran out of gas."

"And my brother and Marnie?"

"They were on board."

"Thank goodness! Do the police have them in custody?"

"Not exactly." The policewoman sighed, looked through the window, and then at me. "I'm sorry to tell you that both your brother and Ms. Hardwick are dead."

"Oh, no!" I whispered, thudding against the red padded seat. It was my turn to stare through the window.

Griscoe was silent, letting me deal with the shock. Finally, she continued. "It appears as if the two had an argument, or maybe you were right about your brother's intentions…that he rented the sailboat in order to kill Ms. Hardwick and dispose of her body."

Visions of Alex's bloody shirt bombarded me. Tears started in my eyes.

Griscoe pinched napkins from the table dispenser and handed them to me. I wiped my face and fought the urge to run out of the diner. Even though Griscoe was saying what I already knew, for some crazy reason it felt like I was hearing about my brother's death for the first time.

"I hoped he would leave the country…" I began, my voice thick with emotion. "He was a disturbed man, but he was also the last of my family."

The detective sipped some coffee and waited for me to stop crying.

"What happened?" I asked at last.

Griscoe glanced at her notes. "Well, as far as we've learned, it seems that Ms. Hardwick was killed with a .38 Smith & Wesson."

"That's the gun I told you about."

"Yes, your brother had the .38, but Ms. Hardwick also had a Beretta. Preliminary reports indicate they shot each other. We'll know more after the forensic team files a report."

I looked at her. "Where was Alex shot?"

"In the chest. We believe Ms. Hardwick was coming up the ladder from the cabin or standing in the galley next to the open hatch. It's likely she shot him first, then he fired at her, since Ms. Hardwick died almost immediately from a head wound."

"And my brother?"

"The coroner thinks he died within a few minutes. From asphyxiation. Mr. Wyce was on deck when the boat was found."

"From asphyxiation?"

"Blood in his lungs," she said quietly.

I stared at her, lost. It didn't take an effort to produce more tears. They were genuine. Griscoe was silent as another surge of grief overcame me.

"I'm sorry…I just can't imagine all of this. First, I learn Alex has been alive all these years and now that he's dead."

Griscoe handed me more napkins, listening, as I talked about my brother. After I ran out of words, she cleared her throat.

"I shouldn't speculate, especially to someone who's involved—a victim of a crime—but this whole situation is strange. We don't know what the provocation was, but it's damned odd to rent a boat just before an international flight. I'm sure your brother had a reason. The ocean is a great place to hide a body. Even so, why did Ms. Hardwick agree to go sailing, particularly if she was suspicious of him? Maybe she brought the Beretta as protection."

"So, you believe Alex meant to kill her?"

"Seems that way." Griscoe shrugged. "And maybe the explanation for her willingness to accompany him is a simple one. That she planned to double-cross Mr. Wyce. Grab the money and valuables, murder him, and make a run for it."

"Really?" I wiped my eyes again and rested my head on my hand. "I have no idea what either of them planned to do—with each other or with me. It was my hope that my brother would take what he'd stolen and leave. Maybe agree to meet Marnie somewhere and then not show up. I wish he had. No one would have died."

"Like I said, we're not positive why they shot each other, only that they did." She took up her fork and stabbed a chunk of pancake. "One thing's weird. Nothing of value was on the boat except for a man's Rolex watch, some twenties in Ms. Hardwick's purse, and two hundred dollars in his wallet. The money, coins, and diamonds weren't there or in either car."

I blew my nose, leaned against the window, but my sorrow didn't prevent Griscoe from her speculations.

"If I had that kind of loot, I wouldn't let it out of my sight. He had his plane ticket, a phony passport and driver's license, the Rolex, and a disposable cell phone, which might provide some additional information regarding his contacts. Also, we have your driver's license and brokerage checks, which will be returned tomorrow." After parading a bite of sausage through the maple syrup, Griscoe swallowed and laid down the knife, resting her arm alongside the plate. "Your brother probably had some safe spot he was using where the missing items are stashed. Maybe he stayed there during the months they were hatching their scheme. Any ideas about the location?"

I shook my head.

"Well, this is now an official homicide investigation. Your prints and hair and DNA samples are being compared with what was found on the sailboat. The forensic team and the photographer have finished at the house, but even so, you won't be allowed home for a while. We can bring some things from the house if you make a list."

"That would be nice of you."

"No problem. And Fantana will contact your broker tomorrow morning. The banks will also maintain surveillance for suspicious activity in case any additional checks are presented for payment. With the deaths of the perpetrators, that's unlikely to happen. I'm sure you'll be able to access your finances very shortly. Don't worry. We'll get you back on track as soon as we can."

*

I relaxed my Luddite ways and purchased a cell phone to call Cope, who was shocked when I gave her a synopsis of the events, and to continue my communication with Denise Griscoe. Being confined in the motel was a trial, but the detective brought more books to read, some of my clothes, and my driver's license. She reported that all of my computer files and e-mails had been screened, and the home and office landlines checked for incoming and outgoing numbers. The police provided a list of Marnie's catalogue purchases so I could contact each company. My broker was extremely apologetic and explained the firm had a fraud division that would assist in recovering the coins and diamonds. He also informed me that because I was a preferred, long-term customer and the checks had been used in a crime in which I was blameless, the company would consider a partial reimbursement. I didn't tell him that I had the coins and diamonds purchased with the money. I should have, but I didn't.

Though my bank account contained less than a hundred dollars, my portfolio was still healthy with bonds, mutual funds, and some cash, and I was soon allowed to use its charge card. Visa, MasterCard, and American Express mailed new cards immediately.

From Alex's cell phone, the police located the coin dealer, who recognized Alex's photograph. The man was concerned the Krugerrands and other coins were lost, explaining that one coin, an Eagle, was very valuable. The payments for the diamonds were eventually traced to a disreputable money lender in Jersey City. There the trail ended. The police speculated again that Alex had a safe house and the outstanding stolen items were there.

I was brought to identify my brother's body and Marnie's. Griscoe came along, apparently supportive, perhaps a bit doubtful underneath, or so it sometimes seemed. When the coroner's assistant peeled back the cover to reveal Alex's face, ghoulishly picked apart by seagulls and burned by the sun, I almost fainted. It took a few minutes to recover in a room set aside for friends and family who had to undergo these grisly viewings. I then returned to identify Marnie. Her red hair was shockingly bright compared to the bleached white of her skin. A large gauze pad covered the bullet hole in her forehead.

I rented a car so I could get around, and two weeks later, when I believed no one would follow me, I returned it, took a bus to the commuter parking lot, and drove the Audi to my father's place. There, I inspected the coins and diamonds and confirmed that my name—Alex Wyatt—was on the bills of sales and the certificates of authenticity. My brother had done this to match the brokerage checks and had presumably created a passport in this name in order to prove ownership at the airports or when he sold the items. By coincidence, this would benefit me when I attempted to sell them. The audacity and complexity of my twin's plot was astonishing. It was sad that Alex hadn't turned his brilliant mind to legitimate endeavors.

The police never researched my background or learned about my second house. The picture I painted of my captivity was accepted with reluctance bred of caution, though there was a small flap when the police found a few strands of my hair in the boat's cabin. As I hoped, they decided the hair had been transported on my red parka or baseball cap, a theory I supported, saying that Marnie was wearing my red parka when she left, and Alex had probably taken my cap from a hook in the laundry room.

Chapter Twenty-Nine

I MET WITH GRISCOE on several occasions. One morning, over coffee, she mentioned again how illogical it was for Alex to rent the boat, especially when there were easier ways to hide a dead body, if that had been his goal. She was also still unsettled about the missing cash, diamonds, and coins, as well as Marnie's willingness to go sailing with him.

"There were no signs Ms. Hardwick had been bound or forced onto the boat, so Mr. Wyce must have offered a persuasive excuse, or it suited her purposes to go, as we discussed." Griscoe sighed. "Just bothers the heck out of me that she had a thousand dollars from your checking account and half of the home equity loan—or so you told me—and was willing to risk dying in order to get more. And that none of this money was with her or in her car."

I nodded. "Alex might have pressured her to give him the cash, which he hid somewhere. If Marnie assumed the money was still in his possession, perhaps she went on the boat to get it plus the rest of the stuff."

"So, he ditched everything before they drove to the boat. Or did he stop at his apartment on the way? They took separate cars, so I guess that's possible, but what a lot of conniving." She blew out a breath of frustration. "I shouldn't share this detail, but we found tread marks from Ms. Hardwick's shoes on the passenger side of his car and a few strands of her hair on both front seats."

"You did? Well, Marnie knew him for several months and might have been in his car."

"A possible explanation." Griscoe ran a finger slowly around the rim of her coffee mug. "We're still researching the period after they met and trying to find where he was living. Not easy because he used cash or fake credit cards. One other interesting fact. Ms. Hardwick had a juvenile record for petty theft, shoplifting, and some adult misdemeanors."

"I didn't know that." Although I was unaware of this news, I wasn't surprised.

"The woman was a slippery character, a real chameleon." Detective Griscoe patted her mouth with a napkin and sighed. "This case is so darn maddening. The perps' behavior was weird, and the crime scene on the boat was a mess. Although fiberglass is a lousy surface to retain prints when it's pounded with heavy rain, the strange thing was that there were few fingerprints in the galley and the head and none on the ladder rails, yet Ms. Hardwick had died inside and certainly your brother had been in and out of the cabin. I doubt they flew from the cockpit to the galley and vice versa or wore gloves before they shot each other. We've concluded that Ms. Hardwick believed the cash and valuables were onboard and was preparing to steal everything from your brother after killing him. And cleaned the interior in anticipation of committing his murder. But then did she plan to sail to the harbor wearing the latex gloves we found near her body?" Griscoe scratched her head. "Why not shoot him, throw his body overboard, and then take time to remove her prints, using the head and galley at her leisure? And, besides, the forensic guys aren't sure the rain completely erased the exterior prints. It's more likely Ms. Hardwick did this, but when was she able to do it while Mr. Wyce was alive and could observe her?"

Denise Griscoe scrutinized me closely. I sipped some coffee to disguise my reaction and silently swore at myself because I hadn't considered this line of logic.

"I see what you mean. The lack of prints outside doesn't make a lot of sense."

"No, it doesn't." She paused. "Also, there were knives and a pair of scissors locked in the boat's safe. Why?"

"Perhaps a previous renter brought children on the boat."

"Yeah, except the key was in Mr. Wyce's pocket."

I arranged a bewildered expression on my face. Then Griscoe pursued an angle of inquiry I dreaded.

"You know what also keeps me up at night?" She answered

her own question. "Why did they leave you in the house? They could have brought you with them and tossed you in the ocean. Then you would be missing, which would stall our investigation and give them time to escape. Leaving you here alive was potentially dangerous because you could testify against them."

"I've been wondering the same thing—why they didn't kill me. Marnie and Alex said they would return and do that. I was sure they would," I said. "Maybe my brother couldn't murder me face to face and thought he would be safe before I was found...alive or dead. And, as horrible as Marnie was, she may have felt the same way."

"Hmm. I don't know. Bringing you on the boat and killing you seems like a solution Ms. Hardwick and Mr. Wyce could agree upon. If they each planned to shoot the other and take the loot, it would suit both of their purposes to do that. Going sailing would then make more sense."

Had Griscoe jumped to the next reasonable explanation? That I had been on the O'Day?

The detective swallowed the last of her coffee, stood, and walked to the cashier.

*

Eventually, the police permitted me to return to the house. Marnie's will was read, and I inherited her part of the house as well as her estate, which, after her debts were paid and the Solara was sold, amounted to $26,000. I listed the house without using a realtor and found a cash buyer, clearing more than our original purchase price, the increase due to our landscaping. The second half of the home equity loan had already been transferred to the bank from Marnie's checking account, and the first half was deducted from the house sale and remitted to the lender, although that same amount was in my safe. After closing expenses, including the cost of replacing the living room carpet, I made a small profit. With the future reimbursement from my brokerage firm, my net for the nightmare would be in substantially positive territory.

My finances were secure, though I felt miserable about my deceitfulness, which had been necessary to avoid blame for the deaths of Alex and Marnie. Some of these deceptions were outright illegal and some might be morally justifiable under the circumstances, but my behavior weighed heavily on my conscience. I felt guilty as hell and knew my trespass into criminality would gnaw at me until I did something to resurrect my integrity. Perhaps, when all was quiet, I'd sell the Krugerrands, coins, and diamonds in Europe and return the money to the brokerage firm, who was in the process of compensating me for Marnie's fraudulent sale of my stocks and withdrawal of cash. I could repay them anonymously, though I had no idea how to do this without leaving a trail. The last thing I wanted was for the police to reexamine my involvement in Alex and Marnie's crimes.

In addition to these regrets, I suffered from the effects of the tangled enmeshment with my brother and with Marnie. Although they were both gone and I was alive, I wasn't optimistic about my future. How could I trust someone after Marnie? How could I believe in my judgment and begin a new relationship? And, above all else, I grieved for Alex despite the horrible things he'd done. I had found my other half, my twin, and now he was dead.

*

On the day the movers arrived, a heavy rectangular box covered in brown paper came via UPS. The original address listed the township instead of the town and the wrong zip code. Both errors had been corrected, but the mistakes had delayed delivery. A name I didn't recognize was above a street I'd never heard of in New York City, nor was the handwriting familiar. Although curious to open it, I didn't have time. I asked one of the men to store the package in the van.

Late that afternoon, after the movers left, I stood in the basement of my father's house, staring at the delivered parcel, which now rested on a stack of boxes. I picked it up but hesitated to unwrap it. Though I couldn't explain why, I found the package disturbing, as if ominous vibes emanated from it, but at the same time, the box evoked a kind of magnetic quality that I was unable to resist. I pulled off the tape and ripped the brown paper. Inside was a wooden crate with a plastic sleeve attached to the top. Within this was a letter. I brought it close to the window and stopped breathing. The note was from my brother.

Dear Alex,

This is all I have to remember you by—what you left behind so many years ago. That morning, I saw you. Why you did it has haunted me ever since. Was it because of our night together, or what I did to Father?

You may never forgive me, but I forgive you.

Love, Alex

P.S. A friend of mine—using a fake name and address—agreed to send the package if he didn't hear from me in two months. If you received this, you will probably know why I couldn't call him.

The meager light in the basement dimmed as my vision flooded with darkness. What did Alex mean? And what was inside? I desperately wanted to drop the box and run upstairs out of the house, to light and safety, but I stood there, his message seeping around me like a noxious fog, the same message of forgiveness he'd whispered as he died.

Finally, I carried the crate to the workbench and pried up the front wood panel with a screwdriver and hammer. As I stared at my fingers hovering over the box, they seemed like the shaking hands of a stranger. Sweat broke on my temples, and I suddenly felt feverishly hot, like lava was oozing in my veins, blistering through my fragile skin. The urge to flee was still powerful, but I was immobile with panic. Then, as if unloosed from an ancient tether, a memory pierced my consciousness and coupled with the recurring image of my father pleading for help, an image that had plagued my dreams for years. Now, in an instant, the picture clarified. I saw Alex lifting a rock to strike my father, my father pitching forward into tall, golden grass, my brother catching sight of me and smiling, proud of his killing. A second later came the deafening reverberations, sounds that went round and round between my ears, pulverizing my brain.

I lifted the .270 Winchester rifle from the box and examined its dusty walnut stock, long steel barrel, black scope, and cracked leather strap. Instinctively, my finger curled around the trigger, just as I'd been taught with this gun many years before. My gun. A bolt-action rifle for shooting lions and leopards and cape buffaloes and brothers who rape and, yes, who murder fathers.

I stood there in a trance, terrified to see the flickering images from a fourteen-year-old movie behind my eyes. Unable to touch the Winchester a second longer, I leaned it against the workbench, and as I did, I saw something else in the crate, something more fearsome than the rifle. A white shirt with a broad, dark brown stain. Alex's bloody shirt.

I froze as the oxygen was sucked from my lungs. My legs buckled and I fell; my skull struck the concrete floor.

*

I woke in darkness, lying in thick, warm liquid. I knew what the liquid was. Panic set in and skyrocketed my pulse into a fast beat. My mouth was dry, so I swallowed hard, and then I moved. Pain shuddered through my head, which ached with a fierceness I'd never experienced before. Was I dying? Would anyone find me?

No one knew where I was. It didn't matter that I owned a beautiful house, a safe full of diamonds and coins. I was forsaken. I was lost.

From beyond the basement walls, the wind chimes jingled according to their pitch, metal voices that rose and lifted me from the dark room onto the strong shoulders of buoyant waves. I closed my eyes and surrendered, drifting under a yellow sun, and imagined my hot blood blending into the cool water. Soon, all I could hear was the murmur of the ocean's heart as my own heart quieted its frenzied pace. In the distance, through white clouds pierced by brilliant sunlight, the tall mast of a sailboat became visible. My brother stood on the deck, his arms outstretched. He called my name.

But I didn't follow Alex, although I yearned to do so. Overcome with sorrow, I watched him slowly disappear, his face receding past the horizon until only blue sky remained.

Time passed. I traveled through sleep until my eyes opened and beheld the shadowy basement room, with its cinderblock walls, packing boxes, and tan ceiling panels. Lying there, my head throbbing, I decided that I couldn't give up.

After taking a deep breath, I rolled onto my side and planted one hand on the bloody floor, raised to my knees, and staggered to my feet, clutching the workbench for support. Vertigo assailed me, and I struggled to remain standing, telling myself that if I didn't, if I collapsed, I would die here alone, without making amends, without absolving my guilt.

"You are like your brother, but you are *not* your brother," I whispered, turning toward the stairs.

I would sell my bonds, stop the reimbursement from my brokerage firm, and refund any money already transferred to my account, telling my financial advisor it wasn't fair to ask for remuneration when the company wasn't at fault. Then, I'd fly to Antwerp, the diamond capital of Europe, and sell the stones and coins. From there, I'd travel to Mykonos, like Alex suggested, and paint large, joyful canvases bursting with sunlight. Dance, sing, drink wine, and forget. And maybe, if fortunate, find a lovely woman and give love a second chance.

ACKNOWLEDGMENTS

My sincerest thanks to R. Lee Fitzsimmons, publisher of Desert Palm Press, for accepting *Doublecrossed* and thereby beginning a new and valued connection. It has been a pleasure to work with Lee, and I look forward to collaboration on future projects. My editor, Kaycee Hawn, offered excellent advice and did a fine editorial review of the novel. Thank you to both!

Without the support of my wonderful friends and readers, the task of writing would be daunting. I wish to extend warm thanks to Karla Linn Merrifield and Carol Oberle, both of whom have been consistent advocates, as have Beverly Jean Harris, Julie and Tom Stewart, Jane Rundell, Lauren Lepow, Sandy Thatcher, Shari Friedman, Mark Conover, Michael Ungs, Cynthia Bonner, and Mary McCue. The talented Angela Previte provided the cover photograph—a perfect image. PhotoShop wizard Vicki DeVico assisted in the technical interpretation of my cover design, utilizing her usual brilliant skill.

Note: "The Peach" is reproduced from *Snow, Shadows, a Stranger* by Laury A. Egan (FootHills Publishing, 2009).

Photo by Vicki DeVico

About Laury A. Egan

Laury A. Egan is the author of *Jenny Kidd, The Outcast Oracle, Fog and Other Stories, Fabulous! An Opera Buffa, A Bittersweet Tale, The Ungodly Hour, The Swimmer, Turnabout,* and *Wave in D Minor*. Four poetry volumes were published in limited edition: *Snow, Shadows, a Stranger; Beneath the Lion's Paw; The Sea & Beyond; and Presence & Absence*. She lives on the northern coast of New Jersey.

Website: www.lauryaegan.com

Note to Readers:

Thank you for reading a book from Desert Palm Press. We appreciate you as a reader and want to ensure you enjoy the reading process. We would like you to consider posting a review on your preferred media sites and/or your blog or website.

For more information on upcoming releases, author interviews, contest, giveaways and more, please sign up for our newsletter and visit us as at Desert Palm Press: www.desertpalmpress.com and "Like" us on Facebook: Desert Palm Press.

Bright Blessings

Made in the USA
Middletown, DE
15 September 2022